Nick Middleton was born in London in 1960. He has a doctorate in geography and as a geographer he has travelled in more than forty countries. He teaches at Oxford University on a part-time basis and has worked as a consultant to the World Conservation Union and the United Nations Environment Programme. His travel and environmental articles have appeared in a number of magazines and news-papers, including the *Independent* and *The Times*, and he has written several books on geographical topics.

By the same author
The Last Disco in Outer Mongolia

Kalashnikovs and Zombie Cucumbers

Travels in Mozambique

NICK MIDDLETON

PHŒNIX

A Phoenix paperback
First published in Great Britain by Sinclair Stevenson in 1994
This paperback edition published in 1995 by Phoenix,
a division of Orion Books Ltd,
Orion House, 5 Upper St Martin's Lane, London WC2H 9EA

Copyright © 1994 by Nick Middleton

A CIP catalogue record for this book is available
from the British Library.

ISBN: 1 85799 247 4

Printed and bound in Great Britain by
The Guernsey Press Co. Ltd, Guernsey, C.I.

CONTENTS

ACKNOWLEDGEMENTS

In Maputo, I would like to thank Adrian Fozzard, Milù Salomao and Noel Cooke; in England, Mark Carwardine, Lorraine Desai, Rita Middleton and Doreen Montgomery. I also want to acknowledge all the Mozambicans who helped me along the way; their good nature was a source of inspiration throughout.

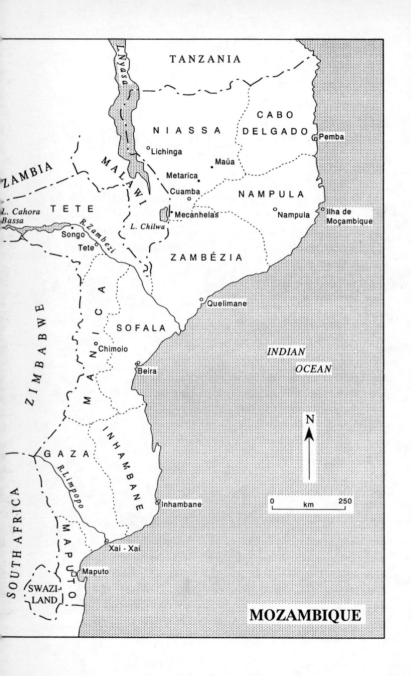

PREFACE

John Scott Banda grabbed another mango from the row on the dashboard in front of him and expertly ejected it from the cab window with a backward flick of the wrist before answering. The small boy who had gestured to him from the roadside dived into the long grass to retrieve the green fruit.

'For these people it is good,' Mr Banda said with a smile full of white teeth and one eye on the road, 'for they have had too much suffering. But for me, the end of the war is bad.'

The Malawian truck driver changed up a gear and the seventeen-metre *Wheels of Africa* lorry thundered down a slight incline in the tarmac road which led to the border. J. S. Banda pointed towards a twisted pile of charred metal which had once been a lorry like his, its trailer lying flat without wheels, and a neat row of bullet holes across the door of its burnt-out cab showing how a soldier of the Resistência Nacional Moçambicana, or Renamo, had successfully halted the vehicle's progress.

'Three months before, this was a very dangerous road,' he shouted above the roar of the engine, 'only possible to drive in armed convoys because of Renamo ambushes. For this reason we were paid big money.' The round trip, across Mozambique's north-western Province of Tete from Harare in Zimbabwe to Blantyre in southern Malawi, earned J. S. Banda and his fellow truck-drivers 1000 Zimbabwe dollars apiece. He had been driving this route for five years, but now that Mozambique's war was over, the fee had been cut by half.

1

'Were you ever attacked?' I asked him.

'Plenty times,' he replied, 'but I always drive near the back of the convoy because usually Renamo attack at the front. Not always, but usually.'

But being shot at was not really a big deal, J. S. Banda told me. All he did was grab the handbrake, jump out of the cab and run away, often closely followed by the government troops whose job it supposedly was to fight off the Renamo attacks.

'Those Renamo guys really knew about fighting,' he said with another smile, 'but you want to know the real danger?' I nodded.

'Mines,' he said.

There had been only two occasions when he had considered throwing in this perilous route, he explained. Both had involved land mines in the road. Once he had been driving in a convoy behind a bus full of people and the bus had 'stepped on one of those mines', as Mr Banda put it. Thirteen people had been killed. There were bodies all over the highway and unidentifiable pieces of flesh plastered across his windscreen. A second time he remembered swerving to avoid a pot-hole, a favourite location for a mine, but the lorry behind him had not swerved and had been blown up. J. S. Banda took his hands off the large steering wheel and threw his arms into the air. 'Bang. Finish', he said.

'These times I thought maybe no more, but then when you get to Harare and you see that thousand dollars in your hand, you say "OK, maybe one more time." '

It was noon on a hot and humid day at the end of January. Large circles, discoloured by sweat, had formed beneath J. S. Banda's armpits on his red and blue T-shirt, reaching down as far as Madonna's pouting head and Bruce Springsteen's lowslung guitar. It was mid-summer and 34 degrees Centigrade. The empty lorry was making good progress through the parched savannah grasslands towards the border with Zimbabwe at Nyamapanda, where our paths would part – me to continue to Harare and a flight home to London, J. S.

Banda to refuel and drive on down to the Indian Ocean port of Beira where he would load a cargo of maize bound for Mozambican refugees in Malawi.

It had been a long and gruelling guerrilla war, fought largely in the countryside, sporadically and without a front. It had begun in 1976, the year after Mozambique's independence from Portugal, itself the result of an eleven-year armed struggle by the Frente de Libertação de Moçambique, or Frelimo, as it is usually known. But almost as soon as Frelimo had taken control of an independent Mozambique, they were faced with a new struggle, against Renamo, a group without any ideological aims, simply bent on death and destruction.

J. S. Banda and his fellow truck-drivers were among the few who dared venture along Mozambique's highways during the war years. Most lines of conventional transport, roads and railways, had either been destroyed or were for ever prone to ambush, and for more than a decade the Frelimo government controlled the main towns and cities like islands in a sea of uncertainty, their only safe mode of transport by air.

The war had all but destroyed Mozambique's social fabric and economy. Of an estimated population of just over sixteen million, four and a half million people had been displaced from their homes in the countryside, flocking to the more secure towns and cities, and another one and a half million had taken refuge in neighbouring countries. At least a quarter of a million children had been orphaned, abandoned or lost contact with their families, and up to a million people had perished, both directly and indirectly, as a result of the war. The catalogue of destruction made equally depressing reading: more than 2500 primary schools destroyed and over 800 rural health posts, as well as countless homes and villages.

At the same time the newly free Mozambican people had suffered natural calamities. There had been drought in the north in 1976, and massive flooding in the south in 1977 which left hundreds of thousands homeless and devastated the fertile Limpopo Valley. During the early 1980s a pro-

3

longed drought sparked a famine in which 100,000 perished, and southern Africa's worst drought in memory in the early 1990s helped to reduce nearly two million people to reliance on emergency hand-outs from foreign donors which had to negotiate difficult pathways through the war-torn country.

In 1991, the World Bank estimated that no less than sixty per cent of Mozambicans lived in absolute poverty.

After crossing the wide, grey flatness of the River Mazoe, a tributary of the great Zambezi, J. S. Banda's truck was gradually climbing towards the distant granite mountains that marked the border with Zimbabwe. We sped past huge baobab trees and small boys tending herds of goats. Occasionally, we would pass the wreckage of other ambushed vehicles beside the road or the roofless shell of a brick house, with bullet holes spattered across its peeling whitewashed walls.

War is a bad enough situation to live through at any time, but the nature of Mozambique's conflict had an especially sickening quality. Renamo was established by the Rhodesian security forces in the mid-1970s to hit back at the newly independent Frelimo government for their stand against Rhodesia's Unilateral Declaration of Independence and for harbouring guerrillas fighting the liberation war in Rhodesia. When in 1980 Rhodesia became Zimbabwe, control of Renamo was moved lock, stock and barrel to Phalaborwa in South Africa's Transvaal, and Renamo activities were stepped up. South African interest in controlling an anti-Frelimo operation in Mozambique stemmed from the fact that the African National Congress had a base there. That Frelimo had adopted a Marxist-Leninist approach to running their country also allowed foreign right-wing groups, in the USA particularly, to support Renamo's actions on ideological grounds, as 'freedom fighters' struggling for democracy in a totalitarian state. The same reasons allowed Western governments to turn a blind eye to what was going on in Mozambique.

Whatever the rights and wrongs of these viewpoints, one

thing is clear: in practice Renamo became one of the most arbitrarily violent military organisations to have fought anywhere and at any time in Africa or anywhere else. Renamo's founder, Ken Flower, former head of Rhodesia's security forces, admitted forlornly that he had created 'a monster beyond control'. Renamo's victims were usually ordinary Mozambicans; a senior US State Department official, speaking in 1988, said Renamo were perpetuating 'one of the most brutal holocausts against ordinary human beings since World War Two'. Using the desensitising jargon of modern warfare, words like 'destabilisation' and 'low-intensity conflict' were often used to describe the war in Mozambique, words which cut little ice with the victims of Renamo's horrific methods for dispatching innocent citizens whose crime was to be in the wrong place at the wrong time. The war has left an entire generation of people traumatised and terrorised.

This was the background to the country when I first arrived in Mozambique in early 1992. I found myself doing a short job in Namibia and decided to take a week off to visit an old friend named Alex who was working in Maputo, Mozambique's capital city. I was so taken with the city during that week that I decided to return and see more of this country which was reckoned to be the poorest in the world. As a geographer, I had worked in several black African countries, and I was well aware that there is a great deal more to Africa than the standard clichés usually served up in Europe: Africa is the continent of debt and corruption, familiar stamping ground for the horsemen of the apocalypse – war, famine, pestilence and drought; Africa is the cradle of mankind, explored and exploited, an elephants' graveyard and the epicentre of the world population explosion; it is the notorious dark continent ravaged by poverty, AIDS and crazy dictators.

Of course there is more than a grain of truth in all these perspectives, and if any one country encapsulated all these distortions Mozambique had to be the best bet. I was interested in a poor country trying to make its way in a world dominated by the West and curious to see how people had coped with 500 years of colonialism, 28 years of war, 18 years of communism and a visit from the Pope. Three months later I was back there, this time to take a good look at the place. Towards the end of this second visit, a monumental event in the country's history occurred: a prolonged series of talks in Rome between the Frelimo government and Renamo resulted in the signing of a Peace Accord on 4 October 1992.

The streets of Maputo were quiet and deserted that Sunday morning as everyone huddled around radio sets to listen to the live Radio Mozambique broadcast of the signing ceremony at the Italian Foreign Ministry. After the speeches had droned on for an hour, I walked the streets in search of spontaneous celebrations. The city was becalmed. I sat in Independence Square looking down the wide avenue leading to the port and two policemen moved me on.

'It is a big day for Mozambique, Senhor, but you can't sit here,' they told me.

The following day was declared a national holiday and crowds thronged the road to the airport to meet returning President Chissano, 'bringer of peace'. That evening a special broadcast of the day's events at the airport was shown on local television, an event in itself, since no programmes are usually shown on Mondays. Again silence reigned on the streets of the capital, as Mozambicans gazed at the smiling faces which meant an end to so many years of war.

Yet, in the days following the Rome Accord, caution tempered the air of optimism. A piece of paper had been signed by the leaders of the opposing forces, it was true. But the curved signature of Frelimo President Chissano next to the stilted and almost childlike scrawl of Renamo President Dhlakama at the bottom of a treaty was one thing, the question of how the fighters in the bush would respond was another. 'Vamos a ver' was a phrase that lingered on the lips of many Mozambicans in those early days of peace: 'Let's wait and see'.

I returned again, in January 1993, to see for myself whether the signatures on a piece of paper had made a real difference to the lives of Mozambicans. To my astonishment, just three months after the Accord had been signed it was possible to travel most roads without fear of attack. The apprehension that guerrillas would turn to freelance banditry had largely failed to materialise, most of the countryside was safe, and refugees and displaced people had begun to return to their places of origin to pick up the pieces of their lives which, for some, had been disrupted for ten years or more.

So it was that I was able to hitch a ride with J. S. Banda on the final leg of my trip through Mozambique. We pulled up behind a long line of trucks parked waiting to clear the border post in the early afternoon heat. I bade my farewell to the Malawian as he drank gulps of liquid from a white plastic water bottle, and walked the short distance to the dilapidated customs building. An official entered my name and details in an enormous ledger and stamped my passport. At the barrier I showed the stamp to a bored policeman wearing odd socks, and strolled down the line of trucks waiting to pass through no man's land and enter Zimbabwe. Large black clouds had gathered on the horizon. It looked like rain.

1

CEMENT CITY

Maputo is an enigma. As the capital city of a country at war, I expected it to be a dangerous and unpredictable place. Far from it, it was one of the friendliest, most easy-going and least threatening cities I have visited.

This was not my initial impression, however. I first arrived on a night flight from Johannesburg, where the doyens of Jan Smuts airport had placed an appropriate symbol of my turbulent destination. On the wall beside the X-ray machines was a display of authentic life-sized terrorist weaponry, including a limpet mine and an assortment of hand grenades. The purpose of the exhibit was far from clear; I assumed that most self-respecting hijackers would be familiar with the tools of their trade, and that the airport security personnel would also be *au fait* with the objects of their scrutiny. Stupidly, I asked a boorish-looking uniformed Afrikaner standing nearby what it was all about.

'Have you any of these items in your baggage?' he asked witheringly.

'Well, no,' I said.

'Then be on your way, sir.'

It was a short hop to Maputo, and as the plane descended through some straggling grey clouds the light from an almost full moon made a river winding to the sea glisten like quicksilver. Below me, Maputo looked strangely dim for a capital city, and rather sinister bathed in the moonlight. When the aircraft came to a rest on the tarmac, and the doors were opened, a heavy, humid, musky smell pervaded the cabin – the smell of Africa.

8

Floodlights were trained on a red carpet rolled out from the gangway. Someone whispered that the president of São Tomé and Principe (former Portuguese Islands off West Africa) was on board and we would have to wait for him to disembark. A fleet of black Mercedes-Benzes with police outriders whisked the VIP away and we were allowed off. Inside the terminal building I was thrown by the illuminated sign above the baggage carousel. It did not indicate our flight number from South Africa, but advertised the Miami Fashion House.

Alex stood at the exit sweating profusely in the throng of black faces. We jumped into a car he had borrowed and careered into town. Street lights did not appear to be popular accessories and the place had a medieval air, with hurricane lamps and open braziers flicking shadows across the makeshift stands of street vendors. Smells of dust, rotting garbage and cooling tarmac were delicately blended on the torrid air, and I could just discern the outline of a huge bullring which Alex pointed out from the moving vehicle. It hadn't been used for years.

'The Mozambicans don't kill bulls any more,' he said, 'they kill each other instead.'

It took about ten minutes standing in the pitch black outside his house for Alex to unlock the front door. I counted seven different padlocks, metal bars and bolts.

In its heyday, before the exit of the Portuguese colonists, Lourenço Marques as Maputo was then called, was a playground for the beautiful people of southern Africa. The beautiful white people that is. Its wide tree-lined avenues and grandiose colonial architecture provided the ideal setting to enjoy the subtropical climate, the limitless supplies of seafood and the long white sandy beaches lapped by an Indian Ocean warmed to perfection by the Mozambique Current. And when the beautiful people tired of lotus-eating and prawns beneath the coconut palms they could take an air trip across the bay to marvel at the herds of elephants roaming the Maputo Plains.

The city sits on the west side of a bay some twenty-six

9

miles long by twenty-two miles broad which was first visited by the Portuguese in 1502, when Antonio do Campo, captain of one of Vasco da Gama's ships, happened upon it en route to India. The city's first name came from a Portuguese trader named Lourenço Marques, who explored the area in 1544, and in that year a fortress was built, on the opposite bank of the River Espirito Santo to where the city stands today. For a hundred years or more the port was a regular stopping-off point for ships trading in ivory and slaves. The frequency of calls fell away as the Portuguese temporarily lost out to Arab rulers farther up the coast, and in 1721 the Dutch tried to establish a settlement on the shores of the bay. Their tenure was short lived, and the settlement was abandoned after suffering heavy casualties from fever.

In 1771, it was the turn of the Austrians to try to settle on one of southern Africa's finest natural harbours. A private trading company set up shop on the bay, only to be expelled by the Portuguese ten years later. The 1780s saw the establishment of a military settlement at Lourenço Marques, with a Portuguese governor appointed for the first time, and the construction of a fort on the left bank of the Espirito Santo, from which the present city was developed. The city superseded the Island of Mozambique as the capital of Portuguese East Africa in 1907, as Mozambique's centre of gravity moved south, with the completion of a railway line to Pretoria at the end of the nineteenth century and the increasing movement of Mozambican labour to the South African mines.

As the ties with South Africa strengthened, Lourenço Marques thrived and developed into the Beirut of Africa, a holiday playground for the Transvaal and beyond. But not for Mozambicans. The Portuguese exercised a very strict policy of urban segregation in the capital and other towns and cities. This meant that Europeans lived in the modern apartment buildings or private houses in what became known generically as 'cement city', while the vast majority of Mozambicans lived in the surrounding 'reed city' shanty towns, named after the flimsy materials used in their construction. Until the 1960s, vigorously enforced laws and social conventions prevented Africans from entering white restaurants, theatres and bathrooms, or indeed from being in the cement city at all after dark without explicit permission.

So it is only since independence in 1975 that Maputo has been a city for Mozambicans to enjoy, but the relaxed carefree atmosphere that made the place so attractive to whites before them has remained. The basic fabric of Maputo's cement city has also remained of course. But there appears to be a distinctly temporary disposition among most of the resident Mozambicans, almost as if they are squatting in a place which, although now theirs, was never really intended for them. This feeling has been exacerbated by the war, which has seen hundreds of thousands of displaced people, or *deslocados*, arrive to set up home in any available vacant building plot or disused ruin.

The once fine Portuguese style of architecture is now mostly derelict and decrepit. The buildings need a coat of paint and many require major structural work. Jacaranda, frangipani, acacia and flame trees still line the streets of cement city, but virtually every concourse has swathes of broken paving stones, dead cars and piles of rotting refuse. A squashed cockroach or a dead rat usually adorns the pavement, and unexpected holes offer the unwary direct access to the city's sewers. But this description is relative. Maputo seems rundown and derelict on arrival from Europe, but compared to most other Mozambican towns and cities it is in prime condition.

Although surrounded by war, Maputo was little affected by the conflict. Every road and rail line out of town was prone to ambush, and Renamo soldiers regularly crept into outer suburbs to steal, often kidnapping people to carry their booty. At one time Renamo had planted anti-personnel mines on the beach to discourage anyone fool enough to go paddling in a war zone, and some years before the fighting had come close to the city, with tracer fire lighting the night sky across the bay and gunfire audible when the wind blew from

11

the east. But fighting never reached the streets of cement city. For most of the war, Maputo was like an island of relative tranquillity, cut off from the realities of a country being torn apart.

After dark, the inadequate street lighting, occasionally rendered ineffectual by power cuts, gave the cement city a dimpsy feeling which in many other cities would be threatening, certainly to someone brought up on the well-lit streets of Europe. But not so in Maputo. You were much more likely to be accosted by smiles and greetings than with a knife or a gun. There were occasional stories of muggings, particularly in the smarter streets of Avenida Mao Tse Tung and Avenida Julius Nyerere, where many of the embassies were located, and the residents of cement city took the threat of robbery seriously, employing guards and innumerable padlocks and iron bars across doors and windows. But Maputo was still a safe place for a city in the midst of a country at war.

The mentality of not quite belonging in cement city may have had something to do with the poor condition of the city's fabric, but more important was the fact that at independence Mozambique was a desperately poor country, unequipped to run itself. Repainting buildings which were infinitely more robust than the shacks of reed city came low on the new city council's list of priorities. Soon after independence, all rented property was nationalised, and the dwellings of cement city were turned over to Mozambicans at minimal rents. But the admirable aims of a government committed to ideals of equality had reached ridiculous extremes in the early 1990s when the government housing department did not receive enough money from six months' rent of an apartment to paint one room or buy a new padlock for its front door.

There were some exceptions to the general air of faded grandeur, in certain areas the buildings were well kept and freshly painted. There was a certain irony in the fact that two of the best kept streets were named after Mao Tse Tung and Kim Il Sung, with regularly swept roadways, neatly trimmed lawns, towering radio antennae and satellite dishes, and 'beware of the dog' signs affixed to the gates of drives where smart new cars were parked. These were the homes and offices of foreign aid workers.

Mozambique is known as the 'aid capital of the world' to that roving band of international bureaucrats who runs the aid game. It is the most aid-dependent country on earth. Foreign aid, or official development assistance as it is known in the jargon, accounted for no less than 77.5 per cent of the country's Gross Domestic Product in 1990. Needless to say, with all this foreign money and help coming into Mozambique, there was a need for an army of foreign workers to administer it. And they had to live somewhere.

The old friend who had been my original reason for visiting Mozambique had joined the ranks of this army. Alex had been in the country for a year or so, initially in the offices of the United Nations Development Programme (UNDP), where the mind-numbing routine of paperwork had driven him to seek an alternative position. When I arrived in Maputo, he was working for the government, helping to draw up the Plan for National Reconstruction which was to be implemented when the war eventually finished. His offices were located in a converted apartment block on Avenida Julius Nyerere. They overlooked the former Greek businessmen's club, which now served as a wedding palace and marriage-counselling centre, and a small Italian restaurant, inappropriately called El Greco's, where a coded system of ordering had been developed in which salami always appeared looking suspiciously like ravioli.

Alex and I had been at university together ten years before. He had roughly chiselled features and frizzy hair that was never combed but probably would not have looked any different if it had. He was large, loud and restless, radiating energy thanks to an over-active thyroid which never let him rest. When channelled towards work this gave him an awesome capacity for getting things done, often working all day, forgetting to eat. If he read a book for pleasure, he would as often as not sit down and finish it in one sitting. I remember the chaos he caused on one occasion on the staircase where he lived at college when he took a copy of *War and Peace* to read in the bath one morning and did not emerge until he had finished it late that night. His restlessness and size also gave him the ability to cause chaos and potential destruction, though blissfully unintentional, a characteristic which made some of our mutual acquaintances in England nervous in his company.

Although we had been good friends at college, after he left to go to Durham to write a doctorate, which involved spending an extended period in North Africa, I didn't hear a word from him. Then one day we met again by chance. Both of us could now call ourselves 'Doctor' but neither was content to continue full-time in research or education or find a real job. We set up together as freelance writers, earning a living writing reports and books for anyone who would employ us. During those days the isolated existence of typing away in our rooms, he in London, and me in Oxford, was relieved by meetings to discuss various projects. We would always drink too much and I would always feel terrible the next morning. But Alex, apparently unaffected by anything as mundane as a hangover, would be up at seven, working or pulling all the books off my bookshelf to satiate his restlessness.

Alex talks to anyone and everyone, and this gift often led to some interesting jobs, for me as well as for him. The greatest tribute to his outgoing nature came after he got stuck in a lift in Vienna with a big fat Cameroonian gentleman who worked for the United Nations. The result was my first contract in the bewildering world of international aid in Vienna, compiling an atlas of the African iron and steel industry, a topic I knew virtually nothing about.

After a couple of years Alex got bored with working alone and living in England where it was always cold and miserable and the people reserved and unfriendly. So he joined the ranks of the international civil service and was posted to southern Africa. He was in his element in Mozambique. He was doing something he felt was worthwhile and since Mozambicans are friendly and fun-loving people he was never short of things to do in the evenings. He lived in a former Portuguese 1930s house in Avenida Salvador Allende, where the maid grew mandioca and marijuana in the front garden. It was just around the corner from the Central Hospital, outside which a continual stream of people with one leg missing hobbled on crutches past the rows of girls selling fruit and cigarettes on the pavement.

There is not really a shortage of places to live for expatriates in Maputo, but since expats cannot buy property they have to rent, and it is a sellers' market. Some of the rentals paid by foreigners for properties in the capital would not have been cheap in Manhattan or central London. Number 739 Salvador Allende, at $600 a month, was cheaper than most for a three-bedroom house, and was owned by a Mozambican woman who lived in England with her son. Alex had seen a cardboard 'For Rent' notice on the railings one day and had arranged to look at the place. Used syringes and needles littered the parquet floors and human excrement lay in piles in the corners of the rooms. Upstairs, a dozen decaying mattresses were strewn about the bare rooms. His low rent reflected the fact that he had cleaned the place up and made it habitable. Done up and dusted, the polished wooden floors, high ceilings and streamlined curves of the staircase were very smart. But the place still had the air of a student house, with few pictures on the walls and few cupboards or drawers to store clothes in the bedrooms. Alex lived like a nomad who could pack a bag and move on tomorrow if necessary.

Being close to the Central Hospital meant that water was seldom a problem, a luxury in Maputo, but the antiquated shower in the bathroom never produced more than a drip from one end of the huge Brazilian head protruding from the wall and a gentle trickle from the other. But after a few trips out of the capital which involved staying in places where you were lucky to get a bucket of fetid liquid, both to wash in and to flush the toilet, the facilities at Salvador Allende seemed opulent.

My room, at the front of the house, contained a large mattress with vicious springs capable of inflicting fairly serious flesh wounds, and a small chest of drawers – nothing else. The only other aspect of note was the fact that the empty room acted as a very efficient sound box; cars shooting down the long street at night sounded as if they were in a stock-car race taking place at the foot of my bed. On the odd occasion when the household was woken in the early hours of the morning by gun battles in the street outside, I believed for a few agonising, somnolent seconds that the automatic weapons were being fired in my room.

Not long after my arrival in Maputo, another English friend of Alex's appeared. Noel was a forester whom Alex had met while working in Swaziland. Noel's contract in Swaziland had ended and he had returned to Britain, but jobs for foresters in the United Kingdom were few and far between, so he had packed his bags and come to Mozambique in the hope of finding work. It was ironic, as Alex pointed out, that he should turn up in a country with ninety per cent unemployment to look for a job which, for an expatriate, would pay at least ten times the average national wage.

Noel was in his late thirties and had the appearance of a distinguished Shakespearean actor with a prominent and furrowed brow and curling locks. He had the makings of a wayward avuncular figure who would keep a new generation of awe-struck siblings entertained for hours with his stories of endeavours in Africa.

Noel and I spent our first few weeks in Mozambique getting to grips with Portuguese, which was not too difficult for me since I spoke some Spanish. But Noel had a distinct lack of aptitude for languages, and struggled for long hours with the basics of Portuguese grammar. He approached his task with good humour and a dogged determination, writing everything down on sheaves of paper which were always to hand, and reciting words back in his very English accent. We whiled away our time exploring the city between regular visits to a tailor where Noel was having a jacket made. The small premises were situated on the wide Avenida 25 de Setembro, opposite a watch-seller which was patrolled every day by the same gentleman of the military who carried his Uzi sub-machine gun dangled over his shoulder from a long piece of sisal string. The exhausting linguistic procedures involved in explaining the intricacies of pockets, darts and button holes required frequent visits to cafés for the consumption of coffee and doughnuts. One day, on leaving the tailor, set in a row of similar tailoring establishments, I noted that they were all run by the same family: the Alfaiates. Noel paused with a frown on his face, rustled his papers and then called me an arsehole.

' "Alfaiate" means tailor,' he said, pointing to a grotty page, and I felt appropriately stupid as we adjourned to the café. Noel was picking up the lingo faster than I was.

We explored a city full of odd contrasts, where pictures of Donald Duck shared the walls of junior schools with political slogans urging children to study, produce and fight, and where a Save the Children Fund vehicle was usually parked outside the Central Hospital next to a large bin regularly plundered by small boys who did not seem ever to make it to school. Each day, the same pair of young men sat by their piles of pillows for sale on the corner of the road opposite the British Embassy, an elegant colonial building dwarfed by concrete apartment blocks, like a Wren church in the City of London. While the fabric of these concrete façades quietly crumbled, an army of gardeners was always hard at work in the nearby Botanical Gardens, cultivating an oasis of sub-tropical tranquillity for people to sit in the shade reading books and newspapers. At the main gate of the gardens, a golden statue of Samora Machel, the country's first president, stood opposite the Gil Vicente cinema, one name from their

Portuguese past with which Mozambique could identify. Vicente's sixteenth-century humanist dramas targeted the corrupt clergy and the superficial glory of empire. Machel's waving statue was overlooked by a three-storey house made entirely of metal and reputed to be the first prefabricated building of its kind. It was designed as a DIY dwelling by Alexandre Gustave Eiffel, of tower fame.

Mozambique is notorious among international shipping agents as a place of no return for cargo containers, and each evening we would wander up the road to buy cold beer or soft drinks from one container which would never see the high seas again since it had been cut open at one side to serve as a bar. Alex would arrive home from work with a comment like, 'the place is falling to bits.'

'Well, it's already fallen to bits,' Noel would say.

'And no one seems to know how to put it back together again,' I chipped in. We would talk the situation over before Alex lay on the sofa to devour a novel and scratch his feet, while Noel wrestled with his irregular verbs, and I wrote up my notes before the evening degenerated into long sessions of gin rummy.

One weekend we got it together enough to buy tickets on a small plane to Xai-Xai, a twenty-minute hop up the coast to Gaza province. Five of us arrived at the airport early on Saturday morning to find that Sabinair, the air charter company, had sold twelve tickets for the nine-seater plane. Showing a healthy disregard for aviation regulations, the Sabinair representative told us all to jump in and hope that the pilot wouldn't notice. Noel was in his seat and I was just climbing through the small door when the pilot arrived. He saw the situation immediately, and was in no mood for compromise.

'Who told you to get on to my plane, hey?' he asked Noel in aggressive South African English. Noel disembarked, feeling like a naughty schoolboy, and the pilot threw a wobbly at the Sabinair representative, then stomped off leaving the Sabinair man to coax three passengers off the aircraft. Alex, Noel and I stood quietly on the tarmac with Alex's girlfriend Betinha and her friend Milu, hoping that we would not be the ones thrown off. After half an hour's wrangling, the disappointed three passengers were led away. We arrived at Xai-Xai an hour late, the pilot cursing loudly throughout the journey.

We spent a relaxing weekend in a derelict beach house belonging to Milu's family. Her father, who was president of Xai-Xai city council, drove us the fifteen kilometres out of town in his pick-up full of mattresses, via his new maize-grinding mill which was under construction. The beach house sat in a line of similarly unreconstructed beach houses and two old hotels in a grove of pine trees on a small cove. Nearby, a hotel which was still functioning provided fish and squid and had ashtrays shaped like crabs. There was also a night club for evening entertainment, where rich Mozambicans turned up in their smart new cars. It opened at midnight and didn't close until daybreak. On a previous visit, Alex had met a Dutch aid worker who had spent the entire night drinking at the club before stumbling out at four in the morning to drive home. But the inebriated Dutchman went to sleep slumped at the wheel with his foot out of the door, and his head on the horn which sounded until the battery went flat. He was back at the bar drinking at lunch time the next day.

We walked up the path parallel to the beach late one afternoon. A constant stream of people, mostly women and some small children, passed us with huge bundles of fire-wood on their heads. A group of small kids had made a comprehensive mini-house of sticks and stones by the path-way. Alex asked what was for dinner and one of the little girls looked up from sweeping the entrance to announce proudly: 'Meat.'

'What meat?' Alex asked.

'Chicken,' the little girl replied triumphantly.

'And to drink?'

'Whisky.'

The path seemed to go nowhere, and as the light began to

fail we remembered that this was an active Renamo area and we were a bit off the beaten track. There was no one around, but we would have been sitting targets should any stray guerrillas have come across us, so we walked back on the beach, a beautiful, seemingly endless stretch of golden sands that continued northward more or less without a break for at least another 300 kilometres. We played taunting the waves and running away without getting wet where the breakers came right up to the reef. The sun setting through the sea haze gave the beach and buildings a soft, velvety atmosphere. When we came to leave, there were very few vehicles around due to a fuel shortage in Xai-Xai. A South African entrepreneur beach bum gave us a lift to the dirt airstrip and told us of his plans to refurbish one of the disused hotels for South African tourists once the war was over. Close to the airstrip, a suspension bridge over the River Limpopo looked sad and helpless; it had lost its main section over the river in 1989 because no one had remembered to keep the suspension wires at the right tension.

Our journey back to Maputo was in a five-seater. The pilot arrived. He was lean and gangling and bounced towards us on his Nike pumps with the sort of broad smile on his face which made him look like a lunatic on parole from an asylum. He had a glint in his eye, because he wanted to carry six people, the sixth being a very fat woman. We refused. The potential horror stories of an overloaded plane, retailed by the South African on the outward flight, still rang loudly in our ears. The pilot shrugged and leaped into his seat, turned the radio to maximum volume and asked whether we wanted to fly high or low. When we said low he swept down the Limpopo at 1000 feet, banking sharply with the curves, following it to the coast. The river looked grey-green and greasy all right, but not particularly great since it hadn't rained in this part of southern Africa for a year or more.

We flew over endless miles of yellow sands, backed by dunes and lagoons, with not a human footprint in sight. The pilot was flying like a madman let loose in a fairground dodgem car, and we were all enjoying ourselves immensely until Alex spotted a large warning sign in front of the pilot. It suggested that low-level flying was not advisable, for health reasons: should an engine stall, an immediate loss of 500 feet in altitude could be expected, and at least another 500 feet would be necessary to recover and climb out of the fall. It didn't take a degree in mathematics to work out that by then we would have been a crumpled mess on the ground. Alex shouted to the pilot over the music; might it not be advisable to gain just a little more height? The pilot grinned manically and took no notice; he was enjoying himself. It also crossed my mind that flying at this altitude would make us a suitable target for Renamo personnel in need of target practice, but I'm sure this thought would not have bothered our pilot either.

The flightpath into Maputo airport took us past the gleaming white Polana Hotel on the cliff top, with the gridiron pattern of cement city laid out in orderly fashion behind. We swung into the bay and glanced up the wide black ribbon of Avenida Samora Machel leading to Independence Square before passing over tiny ships tied up beside Meccano cranes at the port and an arterial mass of lines splayed out from the railway yard. The neat geometry of cement city gave way to the trigonometrical nightmare of reed city; we descended over crowds of ants swarming in the open market of Xipamanine before crossing a wide highway, with parallel storm drains, to land at Mavalane International Airport.

2

THE STRUGGLE CONTINUES

Soon after my arrival, I went with Alex to this large market in the north-west of Maputo, in a suburb called Xipamanine. We strolled down Salvador Allende to pick up a *chapa*, a minibus which plies a set route, and with thirty other passengers we squeezed into the yellow Peugeot wagon designed for fifteen. Stickers of the Pope, commemorating his 1988 visit to Mozambique, shared the interior with Rambo, Arnold Schwarzenegger in Terminator pose and wrestling celebrity Hulk Hogan. Angolan pop music throbbed through the packed vehicle as we sped along the city streets picking up and putting down passengers at every corner.

Xipamanine was a suburb built in 1921 as a sort of half-way house between reed city and cement city. It was purpose-built for *assimilados*: Africans and mulattos whom the state considered had mastered the Portuguese culture and language and earned privileges not extended to the majority of natives. These privileges included access to better jobs, exemption from forced labour and protection under civil law, so *assimilados* could therefore register their property. These properties were in Xipamanine, and in a second special community built at Munhuanna twenty years later. Xipamanine was the more fashionable of the two, where only the most affluent *assimilados* could afford to live since rents were higher than the monthly salary of middle-range civil servants. Although residents were promised free water, a garden, a market and regular bus services into cement city, it turned out that the water was charged for, the gardens never materialised and the bus fares were so exorbitant that most residents had to walk to work.

But Xipamanine was still an idyllic location relative to the reed city, which was deemed by the authorities to be simply a temporary settlement of migrants and thus not in need of basic necessities such as water, sanitation, paved roads and street lighting.

When we arrived at the open-air market we were met by a sea of people, bubbling with activity. The surrounding buildings looked as if they hadn't been touched since they were put up in the 1920s. Splodges of green and black mould had overtaken the brick and cement façades and begun to eat them away. There were no other white faces to be seen, since Xipamanine was outside the city's security zone and thus forbidden territory for diplomats and foreign aid workers. This was due to the regularity with which Renamo personnel visited the market to shop in their own cute little way, at gunpoint and without money, or not when they started.

The market had more than 5000 traders and was divided into sections according to the product on sale. There was a fruit and vegetable area, a zone for home-made furniture and mattresses, and stalls of sparkling clean hardware. The kitchen equipment stalls offered an assortment of stoves fashioned out of recycled metal, roughly hewn wooden spoons, pottery and wooden bowls. Canned food, dried food and large brown slabs of soap were piled high beneath a roofed section of the market. Most of the edibles had been smuggled from South Africa or Swaziland, Alex told me, or 'specially imported' according to a large smiling man with brown teeth sitting behind one of the stalls. Past the displays of tools laid out on brown matting was an area where a brisk trade in live animals was going on. Chickens and ducks hung upside down from the handlebars of bicycles propped against a towering mango tree, or were ensnared in elongated egg-shaped cages made of sticks. A man wearing a torn blue T-shirt, who sold goats, told us that he purchased good animals from outside town and brought them in to sell at more than twice the price paid. He made 60,000 meticais (the local currency), about £12 sterling, on each animal – well worth the danger of being robbed by Renamo on the way to and from Xipamanine.

Alex pointed out an area of bare ground where you could buy electrical items when available. Availability depended upon the suppliers, who were erratic, but on a good day you could buy cheap computers, hi-fi systems, videos and a range of professional-looking cameras with lens attachments. The occasional electrical area operated like a lost-and-found bureau, Alex explained. Whenever an expatriate's house was robbed, he could make his way to Xipamanine and buy back most of his possessions, usually at reasonable prices.

Some months after my departure, Alex had occasion to visit the Xipamanine electrical store on his own account. His house at Salvador Allende was cleaned out and he went straight to Xipamanine to look for his portable computer. Sure enough, an exactly similar model to the one he had just lost was for sale, but, after checking its files to make sure it was his, Alex accused the vendor of robbery. He marched him to the nearest police station to press charges.

The Mozambican criminal justice system operates on a reverse bail principle, and Alex had to part with $200 before the police would lock up the culprit. A day or so later, the man's accomplice arrived to get him released. The price he was quoted was 40,000 meticais, and the accomplice paid the fine in kind, with Alex's large cassette player. Later the same day, a policeman was seen at Xipamanine touting a cassette player and making a quick sale at the handsome price of 200,000 meticais. The accused robber, dissatisfied with Alex's unreasonable law-abiding response to his procurement methods, and piqued by the local constabulary's adroit commercial skills, came after Alex with a gun. Alex no longer lives in Salvador Allende; he moved out pretty fast.

A maze of narrow pathways led through the mass of humanity sitting in the dust on rugs or sacking. A line of women broke off from their animated chatting to call to us as we passed, offering sea salt, which was piled in heaps before them. Farther on, flour, rice and tea were being measured by the cupful from bulky sacks. The clothes section merged into the firewood department which led to a string of women sitting behind small piles of evil-smelling fish covered in flies. All around, small boys were milling about offering boxes of matches or cigarettes, or plastic bags tied to sticks and held aloft like banners. I examined a box of matches that an eight-year-old was keen to sell me. They were Pala Pala brand, made in Mozambique, with a picture profile of the horned animal on the front of the yellow box and a map of Mozambique on the reverse side. Three cities were marked and labelled on the map which had been printed with a plate dating back to colonial times. Moçambique, the former island capital on the north coast, was marked, Tete in the north-west, and in the extreme south the city of Lourenço Marques. I pointed the mistake out to the boy, who looked at me with a puzzled expression. 'These are good matches,' he said defensively, and took the box from my hand, opened it with a push of his finger and removed a stick which he struck on the striker. He smiled triumphantly as it burst into a large flame. I bought two boxes.

Close to the firewood area, where a frenzy of men were loading and unloading piles of cut trees on to and off huge pushcarts, our attention was caught by a wild banging and crashing from a line of metal tables surrounded by a throng of people. Some sort of gambling was in progress as we approached the tables, each encircled by an excited group of punters. The bangs came from old tin cans being smashed on to the metal table-tops. Bets were being placed with red 1000 meticais notes on a series of numbers painted on one side of each table. Once the stakes were in place on the nearest table, the man in charge, dressed in a brightly coloured Hawaiian shirt and wrap-around reflective sunglasses reminiscent of a Tonton Macoute, collected the money and counted it out with a flurry in front of the onlookers. He took a single bill which he popped into a tin can as his cut then shook another can above his head before slamming it upside-down on the worn metal surface. He whisked the can away to reveal a die, and the backer of the winning number grabbed his wad of notes with a shriek of delight. The Tonton Macoute shouted to us to join in and we lost about 10,000 meticais before making our exit, a young woman following to tell us how stupid we had been to gamble away good money like that.

I stopped to buy a bootleg cassette of Mozambican pop music from a man sitting behind a cardboard box with six tapes on top. He was not terribly interested in making the sale because he was engrossed in cutting callouses off the soles of his feet with a rusty nail and a Stanley knife.

We came to an area of herbalists and witchdoctor suppliers, which had the most interesting selection of articles laid out on the ground. Piles of amber-coloured resin lay next to an assortment of freshly dug long roots, with clumps of clayey soil still clinging to them for authenticity. The root was very good for improving sexual performance, a customer explained with a smile as he carefully picked over the elongate tubers. A number of different tree barks lay among innocuous-looking lengths of wooden stick, a large chunk of elephant hide and a pot full of porcupine quills, which are used by witchdoctors to prick the skin and administer medicines.

I asked the shopkeeper what the neat piles of animal skulls, claws and hands were for. 'All for different things,' he said, as if it was a stupid question, which it probably was. I pointed to a set of birds' skulls.

'Those are vulture heads. They make you go into a trance and see other places,' he explained matter of factly.

'How do I use it?' I asked.

'You must take it to a *curandeiro*,' (a witchdoctor), he said. He gestured towards a set of small monkeys' hands which grasped the air beside the vultures' skulls, as if these might be of more interest to me. 'Monkey hand is a good luck charm for goalkeepers,' he said.

The selection of potent materials continued with animal horns and hooves, small leather drums, dried lizards, dried starfish, and bags of shells. Strapped to the leg of a table was a long stick from which hung strings of dried puffer fish which make an effective potion to stop people stealing, the storekeeper explained. On the table was the *curandeiro* haberdashery department, which consisted of piles of animal skins and hides: monkey, leopard, pangolin and crocodile. Beside these were long belts made from strips of plastic sacking studded with hundreds of small cowrie shells, and dangling from the front of the table were a line of round fez-type hats made of the same cowrie-studded material. These were articles no self-respecting witchdoctor would be seen without.

One of the fruits of the progressive society which Frelimo had chosen to pursue since independence was a commitment to modern, 'scientific' medical practice. The traditional curative forms of medicine and their magical counterparts had been shunned by the state, both because they were incompatible with a modern society and because their practitioners represented traditional authorities in society which threatened the power of Frelimo. This course of action had obviously failed in the medical and magical fields, as the Xipamanine market stalls indicated, and had also alienated Frelimo from many members of Mozambican society, who saw their traditional lifestyle threatened by a government which had failed on many of their revolutionary promises.

The image of Frelimo as a beleaguered revolutionary government committed to their people but forced from their path by Western governments who did not want a successful socialist regime in Africa is only partly correct. Since independence Frelimo have made some serious mistakes of their own which have contributed to making them unpopular in their own country. But then the scale of Frelimo's task in running

Mozambique is difficult to comprehend. The country which won its freedom after a bitter eleven-year struggle had been the target of wanton exploitation, rape and pillage for an incredible five centuries. When the Portuguese finally exited the country in droves, many sabotaging anything they could not carry with them, they left an ill-educated, unhealthy, poverty-stricken people who had ideas on how to organise themselves but were simply not equipped for the twentieth-century task of putting to right the wrongs of 500 years.

Academics who research such things trace the underdevelopment of the area known today as Mozambique over the centuries, identifying three periods of what they are pleased to call the 'primitive accumulation by merchant capital'. These periods are divided according to the dominating commodity. The sixteenth and seventeenth centuries were concerned with gold, the eighteenth with ivory and the period from the 1780s to 1870 with slaves.

When the Portuguese navigator Vasco da Gama turned up on the northern Mozambican coast, landing at Quelimane and the Island of Mozambique in 1498, en route to being the first European to travel by sea to India, he found a series of thriving Arab coastal city-states comparable in wealth and culture to the most advanced in Europe and Asia. The Portuguese aim was discovering the sea route to the Indies and the Far East, but they needed staging posts in Mozambique and kept the Arabs in line without much effort. Once established on the south-east African coast, they found another reason for hanging around. They got gold fever.

In 1505, the Portuguese built a fort at Sofala, just south of today's Beira, a port which has a history of trade in gold and ivory with the East stretching back beyond Christian times. Some believed Sofala to be the Old Testament city of Ophir, source of King Solomon's cargoes of riches. The Portuguese soon realised that much of the gold came from the empire of Monomotapa, which at its zenith covered roughly the area of present-day central Mozambique and north-eastern Zimbabwe. The sixteenth century saw several Portuguese expeditions into the interior to 'meet the natives', an attempt to conquer them and eventually the acceptance of a tidy commercial arrangement. The extent of Portuguese infiltration into the interior of Mozambique was limited. Indeed, although the claim is that their Mozambican colony dates back to the beginning of the sixteenth century, it was not until the end of the nineteenth century that Portugal took control of the whole country. Until then, all they had really done was sit on the coast for 400 years and suck the interior dry by controlling the flow of resources.

By the end of the seventeenth century the gold had begun to dry up and ivory took over as the main commodity emanating from the interior. And while the eighteenth was the ivory century, it also saw the beginnings of the slave trade: having appropriated the desirable commodities, the Portuguese thought they might as well take the people as well. To be fair, it was not just the Portuguese who were in on the act; the Arabs had been keen purchasers of human cargoes for a long time. By the mid-1700s slaves were being shipped to the Indian Ocean islands of Ile de France and Bourbon to work on the sugar plantations. In total, it is likely that more than a million Mozambicans were forcibly removed from their homelands and sold during the course of the nineteenth century.

The result of the Portuguese tendency to sit back and milk the interior without really controlling it, buying their slaves from powerful potentates inland, nearly backfired when the so-called 'scramble for Africa' took place in the 1880s. Portugal nearly lost the whole colony. At the Berlin Conference of 1884–5, where the fate of Africa was decided among the colonial powers, one of the options tabled for Portuguese East Africa was to carve it into three, the north going to German Tanganyika, the central areas to Britain, linking into Nyasaland and Rhodesia, and the remaining southern area to South Africa. In the end it was decided to leave the colony nominally in Portuguese hands, on condition that regions with economic potential be leased to foreign companies to exploit what natural and human resources were left.

So the centre and north of Mozambique were sublet to non-Portuguese chartered companies. The Niassa Company was issued with a twenty-five-year lease over Cabo Delgado and Niassa, while the central provinces of Sofala and Manica were taken over by the Mozambique Company. A patchwork of smaller companies governed the remaining northern provinces of Tete, Zambézia and Nampula. To all intents and purposes, these companies ruled their own sovereign territories, setting up customs posts and issuing their own currencies, which in most cases were pounds sterling. But although the new chartered companies had carte blanche to do what they wanted in their territories, there was one serious snag to be overcome. These provinces were only nominally Portugal's to auction off; in practice they belonged to the powerful slave-raiding states which Portugal had unwittingly created. Simply taking over these pre-existing power structures proved incompatible with the *raison d'etre* of the new companies, who were there to make money out of plantations worked by a system of forced labour known as *chibalo*. At the same time the companies introduced new taxes and monopolised the marketing of agricultural produce. These unpopular measures led to regular revolts and uprisings. 'Pacification' of their new acquisitions was a task which kept the companies occupied until the end of the century.

Meanwhile, the southern third of the country remained in Portuguese hands, where they had pacification problems of their own, and it was not until 1895 that they defeated the last king of Gaza province, Gungunhana, who they exiled to the Azores. Twenty-two years later, the warriors of the Gaza state were fighting on Portugal's side, helping to suppress the Barue rebellion, the last great effort at independence before the rise of Frelimo.

The period from the 1880s to 1930 was particularly important because it was when the operation of Mozambique's economy became entirely geared to its neighbours. Portugal, without the necessary manpower and money to exploit the colony, had only one option for maintaining control: to rent out Mozambican labour, land and other resources to foreigners; in other words, play the role of the shopkeeper. Hence Mozambique was put up for sale. In addition to the leasing of the northern two-thirds of the country to the chartered companies, there were two other central aspects to this special promotion: Mozambican labour was hired out to the neighbouring states, particularly to South Africa; and railways were built from the coastal ports to service the needs of South Africa and Rhodesia.

In terms of Mozambique's national development, which was not of course on the agenda, the sell-off had serious ramifications, which are still felt today. Whole provinces were deprived of male labour and virtually all the traffic of the railways and ports was for transit.

This pattern remains. South Africa is still an important employer of migrant labour and source of foreign exchange for the Mozambican government; the transport infrastructure is still geared to serving its neighbours, and although the chartered companies have long ceased to exist, they have contemporary counterparts. Lonrho, for example, is heavily involved in Mozambique, and in the words of its chief executive in Maputo, 'runs the economy of Cabo Delgado'.

The 1930s saw the dawn of a new Portuguese approach to Mozambique. The dictator Salazar was in power in Lisbon, and he made strenuous efforts to limit the economic control of the colony by non-Portuguese and to turn Mozambique into a direct source of profit for Portugal. Forced crop cultivation and forced labour were intensified to produce inputs into Portugal's new industries. Contract labour was put on the statute books in 1930, and all able-bodied African men from the age of fifteen, with the exception of *assimilados*, were expected to work for six months a year on agricultural plantations. They were paid a wage, but after deduction of taxes this did not amount to much. The deal was not terribly popular among Mozambicans, so labourers were often kept

31

in chains. The penalty for running away was a beating and imprisonment.

The imposed labour obligations led to a new phase of migration, to the farms and mines of Rhodesia and South Africa, where conditions were better. By 1960 an estimated 500,000 males had escaped to neighbouring countries. The new exodus of men led to a fresh dent in the demographic make-up of the countryside. Men were traditionally responsible for clearing fields and harvesting crops, so there was a marked decline in food production, exacerbated by the forced cultivation of cotton and rice as cash crops for the Portuguese. Women were not only left holding the babies, but had to produce their quotas of cotton and rice and what food they could to feed their families. Usually it was not enough. Throughout the 1940s and 1950s famines were common. A confidential government report in 1959 acknowledged that the majority of the population was underfed and warned that cotton producers should have sufficient food to enable them to work. Women were paid for the rice and cotton they had to grow, but the state prices were so low that it was never sufficient to buy the food they did not have time to produce themselves. Those who did not die in the famines suffered from a variety of nutritional diseases – kwashiorkor, rickets, scurvy, beriberi and pellagra.

Forced labour and cultivation were abolished in the early 1960s, after Portugal was severely shaken by an uprising in Angola in February 1961. Production of cotton and rice crashed, as peasants went back to growing things they could eat. But the abolition did not come before an incident which sparked the rise of the independence struggle and Frelimo's eventual victory. On 16 June 1960, at Mueda in the far northern province of Cabo Delgado, an officially sanctioned meeting of villagers organised by a peasant cotton cooperative gathered to air their grievances about taxes to the Portuguese administrator. Midway through the proceedings, at a sign from the administrator, the peaceful crowd was fired on by Portuguese troops, killing an estimated 600 people.

A year later the Mozambique African National Union was formed, drawing its support from the kinsmen of the massacred Maconde tribesmen. At about the same time, two other independence movements were established among exiled Mozambicans in Rhodesia and Nyasaland, and in June 1962 the three groups united to form Frelimo. After training in Algeria, the Frelimo guerillas began their armed struggle in 1964.

Portugal fought the insurgency threat, with a great deal of help from NATO allies. Once again Mozambique was thrown open to non-Portuguese investors in a desperate effort to pay for an expensive war. But when a bloodless military coup in 1974 led to the restoration of democracy in Portugal, the game was up. Mozambique gained its independence in 1975.

So after 500 years of being pushed around, exploited and beaten into submission, Mozambicans finally became responsible for their own affairs. But the country which Frelimo was to govern had only been a single entity since the last of the company charters lapsed in 1941. Not only had it been sucked dry of every conceivable commodity, including its people, but it had inherited an economic structure geared to anything but the country itself. The task of putting Mozambique to rights was monumental.

Samora Machel, the country's first Mozambican president, put it quite candidly in 1975:

The truth is that we understand fully what we do not want: oppression, exploitation, humiliation. But as to what we do want and how to get it, our ideas are necessarily vague. They are born of practice, corrected by practice. . . . We undoubtedly will run into setbacks. But it is from these setbacks that we will learn.

And let's face it, when I visited the country in 1992, they had been at it for only eighteen years, so it was early days. One of Frelimo's revolutionary slogans, used during the fight against the Portuguese, will apply for some time to come: 'A Luta Continua', 'The Struggle Continues'.

3

THE COLONIAL THEMEPARK

The small crowd went wild when the woman slipped the clasp and removed her bra. There was ecstatic cheering and clapping, banging on the tables, and wolf-whistling that must have had all the taxis within a half-mile radius speeding towards the nightclub. I had been embarrassed when the unexpected striptease show came on, but looking around the largely Mozambican audience, I saw that more than half the spectators were women and they seemed to be enjoying the spectacle as much as anyone. In fact, most of the people standing on tables and chairs for a better view were women cheering more vociferously than the men.

All eyes were fixed on the exotic young half-Chinese half-mulatto woman parading in front of us on the small dance floor, her black hair flowing down to her slender waist. For a full half-hour the young woman fondled her chair, removed her dress, slip, bra and several pairs of knickers, each time to a round of enthusiastic applause. At strategic times she snaked her way through the tightly packed tables to remove a man's shirt and play with it, to crown another with a pair of her knickers, or to sit on someone's shoulders. She stopped short of removing her last pair of fluorescent orange and black tiger-stripe briefs, and slinked off the small stage as the DJ faded in The Beatles singing *Hey Jude*. It was a rather truncated end to a slick display of eroticism.

A group of us were in ZoZo's night club, tucked away in a corner of the Feira Popular in downtown Maputo. A year before, everyone at the club witnessing such an event would have been arrested. This was ZoZo's way of celebrating the end of Marxism–Leninism. The crowd's fascination was as much in seeing something previously forbidden as in any carnal desires.

The Feira Popular is an open-air complex of fair stalls – a shooting gallery, dodgems and other rides – restaurants, bars, cafés and ZoZo's night club. A large corrugated zinc roof covered an otherwise open shed full of table football games, two small pool tables with their green baize ripped, and a dozen or so computer games permanently manned by small Mozambican boys addicted to the computer generated explosions, bangs and crashes. Bored soldiers, semi-automatic weapons capable of firing real ammunition dangling from their shoulders, wandered the sandy compound. It was a regular haunt for Mozambicans with money to spend, aid expatriates and visiting ships' crews looking for a girl and a good time. Mozambicans like to dance and ZoZo's was always full. Some of the open-air bars also turned into impromptu dancing joints, where tables were on a routine itinerary worked by grubby kids selling roasted peanuts from plastic bowls late into the night, and young women were willing to chat over a beer at the tables occupied by roughneck Filipino sailors.

The striptease show was an appropriate end to an evening of diverse entertainment. We had grabbed a quick bite to eat at the Continental, a bar-cum-café on the Avenida 25 de Setembro whose blue neon strip lights had given up the ghost but for a flashing ' – tal'. As we waited for our order to arrive a young boy carrying a large cardboard box appeared and asked politely if we wanted to watch television. None of us was sure what he was on about.

'What do you mean, Senhor?' Alex asked the lad.

'Do you want to watch?' the boy insisted.

'OK, let's see what's on TV,' Alex said.

The boy placed his box on a seat and asked for a match. We gave him a box of matches and he crouched down to light a candle inside the cardboard TV set which was open at his end. A cut-out screen with a piece of white paper taped over it faced us. He replaced the matchbox on our table and ducked back into the set.

'Ready?' the boy asked from inside the box.

'Ready.'

'This is Orlando's TV,' his voice said, and he announced a Kung Fu movie. Two cut-out fighters, one carrying a club, the other in action pose, battled in silhouette, complete with a sound track of baiting and grunting from the boy. Still inside the box, Orlando asked whether we wanted to see the sex show on the other side. Alex bent forward and switched channels. An authentic looking couple appeared on the screen copulating furiously to muted giggles from inside the box.

'More Kung Fu?' Orlando asked. I switched the channels again and the street fighter dispatched another aggressor. Orlando obviously enjoyed the Kung Fu best.

'How many channels do you have?' I asked.

'One more,' he replied.

We turned over again and saw a superb longboat being paddled by half a dozen oarsmen in perfect synchronisation. They were going up the Zambezi, Orlando explained.

'The end,' he announced, and we all clapped. We were still clapping when our food arrived and Orlando made a rapid exit clutching his licence fee.

After the usual adjustment to the bill – the waiters always claimed to be poor at addition, but they invariably made the total too much – we dashed across the road to the Scala cinema. None of us particularly wanted to see *Rambo*, especially after Orlando's marvellous performance, but we were bored and it was something to do. The huge art deco building was pretty empty, but the sparse audience was full of enthusiasm, notably during the violent bits, which generated gales of laughter. The print of the movie was ancient, juddery and scratched, but the Portuguese sub-titles were almost as entertaining as the action. They were operated manually, from a roll projected on to the bottom of the screen, and the words had been typed on a manual typewriter. The operator seldom kept up with the spoken dialogue, and each time a pause in speech came along there was a furious winding to catch up with the action.

An ugly episode was in the making as we entered the compound of the Feira Popular. A group of Russian gorillas whom we had seen earlier drinking beer in large quantities at the Continental were flexing their tattoos outside a small bar. Aggressive guttural Russian was flying through the humid night air and knuckles were being exercised. One of the Russians pushed his way past us into the street and rushed to a parked car. He opened the boot and pulled out a long metal baton which he hid up the back of his jacket to move back into the fair past the armed guard. He brandished his weapon threateningly, but didn't seem sure who should be introduced to his iron bar. Some of his semi-inebriated countrymen were being held back from one another when a couple of armed Mozambican soldiers suggested they might like to leave. The pickled Russians spilled out on to the street, still shouting at each other, and two rolled up their sleeves to fight in the middle of the highway. At that moment a military patrol arrived and the Russians climbed into their vehicles and roared away, leaving some of their tyre rubber on the tarmac. It was the only violent incident I ever saw at a night spot. The nocturnal cocktail of alcohol and sexual jousting which leads to explosive aggression in so many countries did not seem to apply in Mozambique.

No Mozambicans I spoke to had kind words to say about the Russians. They were often summed up as a bunch of racists who had fished all Mozambique's prawns and taken all their food. The only thing the Russians had given in return was weaponry for Mozambicans to fight and kill each other. Mozambique had been famous for her prawns, which were reputedly as large as you could imagine. They were still available in Maputo restaurants, but their size was not a patch on the old days. A fisherman lamented their loss to me one day on the beach at Catembe, a group of fishermen's lowdowns and defunct beach houses – immediate village

Africa, a startling contrast to the fledgling Manhattan of Maputo, the cement city across the bay.

The long stretch of fine white sand was alive with teams of people pulling on ropes as if they were trying to haul the sea itself on to land, not just nets. A small boat with outboard motor left a line on the beach and chugged out several hundred metres to drop the net which was then tugged to shore by the teams of men, women and boys. Many of the haulers wore a bandolier across one shoulder which was attached to the main rope by a short string and hooking device so that the pulling could be done with the whole body. Each individual, when he had pulled his segment far up the beach, unhooked himself and rejoined the effort at the sea's edge. And so on for an hour or two, exhausting toil beneath the hot sun. Many of the bandoliers were made from the plastic sacking which arrives in the country containing grain, and is put to many different uses in Mozambique, as well as being made into hats, bags and clothing. One guy was wearing a huge khaki vest which enveloped him to below his knees. It was the sort of outfit which would sell for £500 if it had been designed by Calvin Klein.

I had arrived at Catembe on a rusty hulk which ploughed through jellyfish-infested, combat-green waters shimmering in the early morning sun with multi-coloured oil stains. Maputo port was full of trawlers, container ships and tankers, with half a dozen others anchored in the bay. Looking over the side of the vessel, being careful not to lean too much on the handrail which had broken off from its vertical strut, I could see the boat's sheets of rusting metal like pieces of burnt bread and butter pudding, bubbled and curling and separating at the edges.

The polluted bay had been further damaged by a Greek tanker that had run aground and spilled its oil some months before. My fisherman said that this hadn't exactly helped him to make a living from the subtropical waters. For many weeks all they had caught were dead fish and lumps of oil. I asked whether there would be compensation for the disaster, and he looked at me as if I were simple. The Greek tanker captain had fled the country. 'First the Russians, then the Greeks,' he said with a shrug. It was remarkable that there were any prawns left at all.

The absence of giant prawns, the presence of the guns, and Russian jeeps repainted in bright colours which plied the streets of Maputo, were among the few reminders of an influence which waned rapidly with the end of Marxism–Leninism. The abruptness of the Russian pull-out had also left some casualties among the ranks of Soviet aid workers, technicians and advisers. All the Soviet citizens who were in Mozambique to work had been issued with return tickets on Aeroflot, but there was an unseemly rush when Aeroflot announced out of the blue that they would no longer be flying from Maputo to Moscow. Aeroflot tickets were not transferable to other airlines and the remaining two flights could not carry everyone out. Maputo was left with a residual population of Russians stranded in southern Africa. Few had been paid in hard currency, so purchasing another ticket was difficult. Even for those who could rustle up the cash to return home, that prospect was unnerving since the rapid political changes in the former USSR and elsewhere in the Eastern Bloc meant that they would be returning to a very different homeland. So they were left, abandoned in a country where they had once been powerful and were now not the foreign flavour of the month. Many stranded Eastern aid workers tried to bribe their way into jobs as UN Volunteers, because otherwise they had nothing.

Mozambicans too had suffered with the fall of the European communist regimes. More than 10,000 Mozambican workers had been sent home from East Germany. Many were skilled factory workers who could run a production line but there were no production lines back home. They were not only unemployed but without the savings they had been repatriating over the years, eaten away by rampant inflation. One of these men approached me one evening simply to tell me that he had worked for ten years in East Germany. He had been in a coal mine near Leipzig and then in a lens factory in Berlin. There was nothing for him to come back to in Mozambique.

Disaffected Mozambican migrant workers and stranded Eastern Bloc *cooperantes* were widely believed to be the sources of anonymous letters which occasionally did the rounds in Maputo like chain letters. These letters criticised the government in very frank terms, criticism which was a rarity since the media were more or less under the control of the government. One such letter I saw began: 'Dear ex-comrade and Senhor Major-General Joaquim Alberto Chissano and his Corrupt Government'. Among accusations of corruption, mismanagement and jobs for the boys, these letters also attacked Indians, mulattos and whites. Indians were described as blood-suckers, mulattos as dogs not fit to live in houses, and whites as profiteering from the country and dishonouring the daughters of Mozambique. One letter urged Mozambicans to kill aid workers on the streets, an incitement taken seriously enough by the British Embassy who advised British subjects not to walk on the streets of Maputo, a strategy which would have made everyday life rather difficult. Other letters said the Portuguese were now only fit to be slaves, after using Mozambicans as slaves for hundreds of years.

These letters were unrepresentative outbursts in a country which was remarkable for its lack of racist sentiments. It was true that the Indian community was not well thought of: Indians were traders and shopkeepers who kept very much to themselves and were disliked for being rich and successful. Many of the expensive cars on the streets of Maputo had an Indian behind the wheel, and some accused them of getting hard currency out of Mozambique in strange ways. Stuffing dead bodies sent home for burial was alleged to be a favourite method.

The Portuguese had long said that they were running a racially harmonious colony in Mozambique. While Mozambicans were in need of Portugal's civilizing mission, they were not discriminated against in any way, the Portuguese claimed. Portugal's sociologists had some odd ideas about ethnic serenity. As one Western writer on Mozambican affairs has put it, the myth of racial harmony in Portuguese Mozambique was rooted in the fact that the Portuguese male mated freely with coloured women. Given their long history of foreign domination, it is remarkable that Mozambicans are not more anti-white, but they simply aren't.

In search of answers to this puzzle and other aspects of foreign influence, I made an appointment to see the chief executive of the most powerful foreign company operating in Mozambique, Lonrho. I arrived at the third floor of number 1509 Avenida 25 de Setembro to present myself at a gate in the metal security bars which caged in the corridor containing Lonrho and its Mozambican subsidiaries.

Lonrho chief executive John Hewlett was a brisk, blond, tanned, 'suffer no fools gladly' type in his fifties. He strode in wearing an open-necked blue check shirt and said 'Hi'. I had the feeling that here was a man used to power: not arrogant, but someone who would talk straight from the hip. He had eyes which must have reduced many a board-room opponent to a shrivelled mess.

I sat in his aircon office with the usual photographs of company projects on the walls and said I wanted to talk to him about Lonrho activities in Mozambique. He replied: 'Well, we have an information sheet; if I give you that we won't have to talk, will we?' He called his secretary and asked her to bring the information. We made strained small talk for a few minutes until the secretary returned and said she could not find the information, so we talked after all.

In the early days of independence Frelimo overextended themselves in their nationalist fervour. They nationalised hairdressing salons, tearooms and funeral parlours, but soon realised that there were more important things for governments to do than cut people's hair, serve them tea and bury them. But not everything abandoned by the Portuguese at independence was nationalised. Although communism and national ownership were their guiding principles, Frelimo turned a blind eye to private companies which took control of some of the remaining enterprises. Frelimo could not run everything, so it was only pragmatic to allow the odd entrepreneur to do things privately. Enterprises not absorbed into government control were taken over by private companies or left to rot. Some are still rotting.

Lonrho's involvement in Mozambique predated independence, in the form of a pipeline which supplies oil to Zimbabwe from the port of Beira. During the years of Rhodesia's Unilateral Declaration of Independence (UDI) this pipeline was shut down, but was subsequently reopened and supplies a very high percentage of Zimbabwe's fuel needs. Other activities in Mozambique date from 1985. Lonrho had become heavily involved in agriculture, producing more than half of Mozambique's cotton among other things. They also ran an air charter company, a gold mine, a motor business franchise and the Hotel Cardoso in Maputo, an elegant colonial pile perched on the former cliff top with a panoramic view over the city and Maputo Bay.

Operating in Mozambique was an unorthodox business. Lonrho's agricultural plantations were protected by their own armed militia, costing a million dollars a year to run, according to Hewlett. Despite the private army, twice as much was lost in war damage each year. Agricultural produce had also been hit badly by declining international prices and the drought. 'The drought is a disaster,' Hewlett told me, his piercing eyes boring into me as if the drought were my fault. Some of the Lonrho irrigation schemes at Chokwe in Gaza province used high-tech 'centre-pivot' systems: huge long booms on wheels which trundle round and round to spray crops with water from the nearby Elefantes River. But the river had no water, so most of the booms had stopped trundling. More than one hundred workers had been laid off in consequence.

'We have achieved Africa's highest yields in some crops

such as cotton,' Hewlett said, drumming his fingers on his expensive desk, 'but three years ago, we sold cotton for $1700 a tonne, now it's $1100 a tonne. It's very difficult to make money in those circumstances.'

I asked him how things had changed during his time in Mozambique. They were definitely worse for the average Mozambican, he thought. During the communist years, everything was in short supply, but a ration card at least guaranteed people some basics, albeit after a long period queueing. But now, although there were a few more restaurants in Maputo and the shops had a wide range of goods, nobody but an élite few could afford to buy.

'The Indians are making a fortune here,' he said. They were the only ones who could get loans from the banks now that the money supply had been tightened under the World Bank's structural adjustment programme. With profits of 60–70 per cent on imported consumer goods, they were the only ones who could afford to pay the interest rates.

Even for the privileged few ('of which I'm lucky enough to be a member,' he added) things had got more expensive. 'When the dollar shops were operating, you could buy a bottle of whisky for four dollars, now consumer goods here are three or four times more expensive than in South Africa. You're looking at a country which is going to implode, it can only collapse. All structural adjustment has done is expose the country as being totally bankrupt, which we all knew before anyway.'

When I asked about the prospects for the October cease-fire he said he could not comment since he was closely involved in the negotiations. He looked at me, his eyes saying 'change the subject'. Lonrho had played a key brokering role between Renamo and Frelimo. Most of the journeys Renamo President Dhlakama made from his headquarters in Gorongosa were in Lonrho executive jets. I said that I thought that even if a cease-fire were signed in October, it would be a long time before peace returned to the entire country. He wasn't convinced, but said, 'It's like Europe in the Middle

Ages out there; war-lords, bandits and Robin Hoods. Whether they are Robin Hoods or not, you don't change that overnight.'

While Hewlett knew what was going to happen he was not about to say, but he commented that he couldn't understand why Renamo wanted to get involved in Mozambique politically, since it was a thankless task. It was impossible to make a go of the country: 'There's no way of getting it right. This country is going to be reliant on foreign aid for ever. It costs about a billion dollars a year to keep the place going and their export earnings are only $100 million. And with world commodity prices falling in virtually all of their exports they haven't got a chance.'

Things were getting worse; the place was going down the tubes; Mozambique would never be viable. He rattled off the phrases in machine-gun fashion. Foreign aid would continue to flow in because it was so strategically important – too many countries were reliant on Mozambique as a thoroughfare. He paused after each pronouncement and fixed me with those eyes, as if he were willing me into the shrivelling process. But I was quite enjoying it.

'Is there no hope at all?' I asked.

'They could make a success of it as a service state,' he said, 'with a few areas of development, the transport corridors, but it only needs very few people to run it. Let the rest of them go back to being subsistence farmers.'

At the same time Mozambique could revert to its former role as a playground for the beautiful people of southern Africa. 'They have definitely got something in the atmosphere here,' he said in an uncharacteristic digression from hard realities. 'The one great advantage of this country is that there is no racialism here, unlike any other African country I've been in.'

Why did he think that was so, I asked. He paused and said that some put it down to the fact that there were so many poor Portuguese here. Being white was never associated with being rich and privileged, he said. When Portuguese peasants had arrived at Xai-Xai in the mid-1950s to go to the new irrigation scheme at Chokwe, they walked all the way barefoot.

But the atmosphere of friendliness and safety had deteriorated. When Frelimo was Marxist–Leninist there were no robberies or crime. It was really a very pleasant place to live, so long as you didn't criticise Frelimo and saluted the flag when need be, or whatever other stupid things they made you do, he said.

Lonrho has been criticised for being a multinational and for its activities in Africa. It was of course the company that was accused of representing the 'unacceptable face of capitalism', and its chief executive, 'Tiny' Rowland, has long been a familiar figure at high-level meetings of African heads of state, often a more widely known face at such occasions than any single African leader. In Mozambique, he enjoyed close relationships with former President Samora Machel and his successor Joaquim Chissano, as well as Renamo President Afonso Dhlakama. Observations that ousted African leaders had left their capitals in Lonrho planes and were replaced by incoming leaders arriving in Lonrho executive jets, have been common currency among those who throw mud at the British-based multinational. According to the conspiracy theory, Lonrho were also in on the recolonisation act.

There may be some truth in these allegations, and if you are a signed-up advocate of world revolution and the overthrow of the capitalist system Lonrho's presence in Mozambique is a ripe target for attack. But the case was too often presented in simplistic terms, I thought as I took a seat at the Continental to write up my notes after the interview with the representative of the 'unacceptable face of capitalism'.

It is true of course that Lonrho is a profit-making company. 'I'm a capitalist,' John Hewlett had told me in no uncertain terms. But while it was probably fair to say that the Lonrhos of this world are a part of a system that exploits the poorer countries for the disproportionate benefit of the rich, another side to the equation is often swept under the ideological carpet.

Lonrho was widely regarded in Mozambique as a good employer. My mind wandered back to a conversation with Lonrho's financial director in the country, a pale-faced man with red hair whom I sat next to on a Linhas Aéreas de Moçambique flight. He had not been in Mozambique nearly as long as John Hewlett, but he was a lot more positive about the country's future. He kept telling me what nice people Mozambicans were and seemed genuinely committed to helping the country realise its potential. He told me that he employed Mozambican clerks who took five times longer to do a job than people he could easily bring in from South Africa. But you have to train them and help them, he told me.

'Mind you, it can be very frustrating at times,' he said, tugging at his red curls in mock anxiety, 'but it's also very rewarding since they are so eager to learn. They keep coming back to say, "sorry to bother you again, but is this right?" '

Even criticism of the low wages foreign companies pay their African employees is not necessarily a clear-cut issue. Oxfam had tried to redress the imbalance between their expatriate staff and local staff by upping Mozambicans' salaries. The policy, which was enacted with the best of intentions, had led to some unforeseen consequences. One of Oxfam's employees told me a cautionary tale concerning her guard in one of the northern provinces. Before the near eight-fold increase in his salary, to $125 a month, the guard had been diligent, trustworthy and dedicated. He had saved hard on his previous wage, built himself a new house, bought some land to cultivate and been a good husband. But trouble had begun after his wage hike. He splashed out on a new bicycle and radio, was often seen drinking to excess in the town's bars, and began to mess about with other women, sometimes even sleeping with them in the Oxfam worker's bed. Things came to a head when a large sum of money, which the woman had been saving to buy a tractor for one of the villages, disappeared from a chest underneath her bed. Although the guard never admitted that he had stolen the money, he was the only person with a key to her room, and he eventually offered to pay the money back.

When it comes to the profits made by foreign companies in Mozambique, these have to be weighed against the risks involved. There are numerous examples of countries suddenly turning around and nationalising assets, often without compensation, and in Mozambique there was the war to contend with.

The true meaning of the phrase 'risk capital' was brought home to me during another LAM flight, when I got into conversation with an young Irishman named Terry. His company, a six-man outfit based in Dublin, was in Mozambique to develop mineral sites in the north: a high quality graphite deposit not far from the coast in Cabo Delgado, and a coastal sand dune in Nampula full of titanium sands. The project was a logistical nightmare, Terry said in his relaxed Irish burr. Everything, from fuel to nuts and bolts, would have to be brought in from South Africa to build and run the mines. The cost would be enormous, a seven-figure sum. Security was one of the biggest headaches. Terry's company employed ex-Gurkhas for the job.

These were high-risk ventures, but with potentially very high returns. The graphite deposit could be worked for thirty years and the profits were not far off $1000 a tonne. So long as they could fend off attacks from Renamo, and the operation wasn't nationalised or squeezed out of existence if and when peace came and a new government was elected, Terry's company would do very nicely thank you. They would cover their costs after three years of operation and hoped to continue for at least ten years.

There is a graphic wall mural opposite the Ministry of Agriculture at one side of the first roundabout as you drive into town from Maputo's Mavalane airport. It portrays the anguished story of Mozambique's last 500 years of history, from slave trading to Portuguese colonialism, to the war of independence, with guerrillas brandishing kalashnikovs and a black baby dangling upside down from the fist of a white man who is cutting its throat, to today's independent country symbolised by a ripe maize cob and a loaf of fresh bread with an image of the new flag. It is a long curved wall, and in a moment of irony as we passed it one day Alex said that it ought to be extended into a circular structure to represent the downward spiral courtesy of the World Bank with their economic structural adjustment programme. Mozambique was going full circle, from Portuguese colonialism, to independence, to Marxism–Leninism and now back to a capitalist system in which the rich would get richer and the poor would inevitably get poorer.

A landmark in the dawn of the new age came in mid-1992 when Maputo's Polana Hotel was officially reopened. The hotel, built in 1922 by a Scotsman named Walter Reed, is to Maputo what Raffles is to Singapore, 'a national monument', as the new general manager described it to me. David Ankers, an overweight Portuguese-speaking South African, looked as if he could have had a career in the movies playing South American *bandido* bit parts if he hadn't chosen hotel management as a profession. He had a long drooping moustache and dishevelled black hair which needed a cut.

He told me that when he had arrived in May 1990 the Polana was a sad wreck, with no soap or hot water. Forty million rand later, the largest South African investment in post-independence Mozambique had brought back the hot water and the soap. But much of the character of the place had been lost during the refurbishment, lamented Mr Ankers's Mozambican secretary, a redhead. The parquet floors had all been ripped out to be replaced with polished marble and the atmosphere had become more efficient and much less friendly. But at US $150 a night (just less than Mozambique's minimum annual wage) the international bankers and South African business clientèle appeared to demand the 'you could be anywhere' atmosphere of an international hotel. The official reopening had taken place amid a blaze of publicity, with Mozambican President Chissano and South African President de Klerk in attendance. An insensitive press release issued by the hotel management to mark the occasion suggested that Karos Hotels of South Africa were expecting a return to pre-independence days, when the Polana stood on the Rua A. W. Bayly: 'South Africans will again be able to sip sundowners on the patio of the Polana overlooking the warm Indian Ocean with its palm-fringed shores', the statement read. 'LM prawns' and abundant fresh fish 'cooked in traditional Portuguese style' were offered as irresistible attractions. The 'LM' of the prawns referred to Lourenço Marques, as if seventeen years of independence had counted for nothing.

As Mr Ankers rightly said, Maputo is an island and the Polana is an island within Maputo. It is a five-star, credit-card, satellite TV world of grilled prawns and champagne cocktails, a little enclave of opulence custom-built inside the shell of an old building, with every brick and stone and slab of marble imported from South Africa. It is a million miles from the prostitutes who stand in twos and threes in their T-shirts and flip-flops on the street corners a hundred yards away.

Many of the Mozambicans who worked the streets were different from those I had come across in other poor countries. Here they had an innocence, they lacked the aggressive or devious edge so often present elsewhere. I couldn't decide whether this was simply a reflection of the good nature of the people or of the fact that street walking, trading and begging are recent phenomena. Their presence on the streets was an emblem of the new market economy and a result of the war in the countryside.

While I was sitting outside the Continental watching the traffic directors with their white gloves flick their wrists at the end of their ballerina-like waving with a flurry of fingers, a constant stream of street kids plied the pavements in search of trade and nourishment. A new tribe of children, most of them boys, almost always with broad grins on their faces, had emerged to sell stuff on the streets of Maputo: one had two bags of marbles, another a single French video cassette. Others touted two ironing boards (one under each arm), a short-sleeved shirt on a hanger, a box of Heart Juicy chewing gum, and endless supplies of cigarettes. It was Mozambique's version of shopping by television – the shops came to you.

The kids' ideas for presenting their wares were often creative. Some of the cigarette sellers had made their own cardboard presentation stands complete with a flapped hole in the top of an attached box behind for money to be posted. A boy selling pens had mounted them on a piece of cardboard. Very few were simply begging on the pavement, only the old. Even blind people were led around by a youngster, doing the rounds of the cafés. It was a stark contrast to people begging in the UK with a sign saying 'homeless and penniless'.

The Continental kids were also for ever hovering in search of sustenance. They would approach to ask to drink the glass of water that came with coffee, or the sachet of sugar you hadn't used, or to grab the empty soft drink can after you had left, break the can amidships and suck out the last few drops of sugary liquid. Any uneaten cake was a nourishing scrap, but they would always ask politely. How long, I wondered, before an outstretched hand became a grab-and-run hand? It never seemed to cross their minds.

I suppose these roving junior entrepreneurs may one day save enough to set up a more permanent stand, to accumulate savings and invest in their own futures, as an economist would put it. I asked one kid selling cigarettes what profit he made on each pack. He bought them for 2000 meticais and sold them for 3000 he told me. At the time 500 meticais would buy him a loaf of bread. But the sad aspect was that this ten-year-old was having to sell cigarettes at all. A whole generation of children were not in school because of a war fuelled by rich white men who no doubt held their family values in the highest esteem. Just because these kids had been living in a leftist society they had been denied everything which the Western protagonists held dear.

Some children worked a well-known alcohol quarter, a makeshift block of shacks and metal cages in a residential zone between Avenida 24 de Julho and Avenida Patrice Lumumba. All types of Western black-market beer and hard stuff were on sale, most brought in from Swaziland or South Africa, at large profits reputed to average $1000 a trip. The booze was sold in meticais and the meticais converted to dollars in illicit money-changing kiosks and shops all over the capital. One estimate suggested that fifty million dollars leaves the country each year this way. The operation is said to be run by Indian traders, but the visible faces are Mozambican. The alcohol quarter was buzzing twenty-four hours a day and a mad rush of kids crowded every expatriate vehicle which drew up to tout the wares of their stalls. Alcoholic offerings were brought to the car window for inspection, at night by candlelight. The smell of urine in this area was overpowering, and crushed cans were embedded in the tarmac like a surrealist attempt to decorate the place. Apparently the government had served notice to shut the quarter down some time before and all the stall-holders had thrown a big party on their last night. But no one had come to clear the place the following day so everyone stayed where they were.

At night, the open fires burning in the dim street and the surges of children towards potential customers gave the place a feeling of uncertainty. Expatriates seldom got out of their vehicles and kept their engines running while conducting their business. But on one occasion I ventured into the alcohol quarter's dimpsy warren of metal cages, fully expecting at least to be robbed and knifed, if I was lucky. It was like stepping back into the Middle Ages among the maze of poky iron-barred lock-ups. Candle power prevailed, with the odd kerosene lamp. Grilled chickens were spreadeagled over tiny charcoal braziers and white eyes looked at me out of the shadows. Yet everyone behind the bars and sitting propped in front of them was friendly and talkative. They did not see many white people in here, they told me. Some offered me drinks, others asked me to teach them some English.

Other kids were in the salvage business. Large mobile bins, presented by the Spanish government as part of an aid package, were on almost all the streets, and each was regularly rifled through by teams of kids or grown-ups looking for discarded goodies. One man collected dog-ends, and boys, discernible only by their little legs poking out of the top of the bins, salvaged food scraps, particularly in the expat areas, or bottles or old drinks cans. Many of these children were simply lost or orphans of war and far from home, and had not cottoned on to the ways of the street sellers. They were innocents abroad whose only way of surviving was to search the bins for nourishment. Sometimes they would pluck up the courage to ring a doorbell and ask for food. One little boy, who might have been five years old, rang at the door of Alex's house in Salvador Allende one day and nervously and self-consciously said that he was hungry. Alex's maid gave him a plate of soup and rice, and he sat on the doorstep, looking bewildered, pushing spoonfuls of food into his mouth. Some other kids materialised outside the gate, so he was asked inside to eat in the kitchen.

He returned a week or so later and sat in the kitchen with his hands in his lap. He smelt as if he hadn't washed for a month. He was full of 'please' and 'thank you' and started to wolf the spaghetti down so fast when we gave it to him that we had to tell him to slow down. He looked remorseful and apologised. As he sat nursing a cup of tea, and we filled a plastic bag with more spaghetti for him to take with him, we asked the lad where his parents were. He said he didn't know.

4

CAPE THIN

'Exatamente', my self-appointed guide said for the tenth time. He was beginning to annoy me. No matter what my comment on the exhibits in front of me his response was the same: 'exatamente'.

We were wandering though the towering house on Maputo's Avenida Eduardo Mondlane which was the Museum of the Revolution. Inevitably, I suppose, it resembled a shrine to the Mozambican revolutionary hero Eduardo Mondlane. Just inside the entrance door sits the shiny Volkswagen he used while he was in Dar es Salaam in Tanzania planning the armed struggle for independence, and pictures of him in various poses are everywhere on the walls of the three-storey museum.

I could not make out whether my guide was an official of the museum or someone who had wandered in off the streets to show me around. He could have been either. Alex had moved on ahead and left me victim to this man's aggravating approach to tour guiding.

'This is a photograph of Eduardo Mondlane,' he would say, snapping his fingers and pointing at a wall. 'And here is a photograph of Eduardo Mondlane again,' gesturing to a picture next to the first, 'and look,' he continued, introducing an element of surprise, 'over here is a picture of Eduardo Mondlane.' The man was accurate, but made his pronouncements in an uninterested way, as if he had guided too many parties of rubber-necked tourists who weren't listening to anything he said. He was on automatic pilot, he smelled faintly of alcohol and his eyes were glazed.

I pointed to a black-and-white photograph of Eduardo Mondlane standing on a low platform by a tree. The caption said he was addressing freedom fighters in Niassa province.

'This is a photograph of Eduardo Mondlane?' I asked. He didn't react to the sarcasm. The lids came down over his smoky eyes as if in a little prayer of thanks that this subnormal Englishman was getting the idea.

'Exatamente,' he breathed with some relief.

We moved into the next room, thankfully lacking in photographs of Eduardo Mondlane. 'Here we have a pen, a whistle, some boots,' my guide pointed out. I held my breath as I read the caption on the glass case in front of us. 'They belonged to Eduardo Mondlane,' the patient voice explained.

'This is a gun,' he was at the next case now, 'here are binoculars, for looking.' He held his open fists up to the glazed eyes to illustrate how to use a pair of binoculars.

We walked past more old photographs of Frelimo soldiers in the bush, and a display of large polystyrene letters and numbers on the wall spelling out Mozambique's 1950 illiteracy rate: 97.68 per cent. Further photographs showed 'bourgeois colonialists' on the beach at Lourenço Marques and a provincial governor looking relaxed in a sedan chair held by two worried black men with no shoes. A detailed plan of the attack on Chai in Cabo Delgado on 25 September 1964, the first battle in the war of independence, was on display below a photograph illustrating how the Portuguese dealt with captured Frelimo combatants. European soldiers were hanging Mozambicans from a mango tree and around each neck hung a scribbled sign which read: 'I was in Frelimo'.

In the next room, one complete wall was taken up by a painting in the style which I think is referred to as 'Soviet realism'. A waving, smiling Frelimo leader (Eduardo Mondlane) paraded down a cityscape dressed in army fatigues and forage cap. He was surrounded by beaming onlookers and soldiers in neatly pressed uniforms and gleaming black boots, with flowers in their gun barrels. It contrasted with the black-and-white photographs of the struggle in the countryside which showed many of the Frelimo men in tatty uniforms and an assortment of footwear. With the customary click of his fingers my guide told me the name of the central figure in the painting and then took me gently by the arm to show me another glass case full of domestic implements used in the zones liberated by Frelimo.

'This is a bowl, used for water. The water was for drinking,' he told me mechanically. Next to the bowl was an assortment of bottles, also for water, again for drinking. It was fascinating stuff.

In another room we saw Eduardo Mondlane's suit and military gear, together with his skipping rope, and books, diaries and copies of his letters and speeches. His passport and university degree certificates were also on display. Eduardo Mondlane had been the first Mozambican to become a PhD, at the Northwestern University, Evanston, Illinois in June 1960. He had worked for the United Nations before returning to Mozambique to join and then lead the struggle for an end to Portuguese rule. My guide gazed at the passport and the degree certificates and in an uncharacteristic deviation from his usual utterances said quietly, 'He was a great man,' which he meant. I felt like a shit for getting annoyed with him.

Two more floors were packed with similar exhibits. There were Portuguese instruments of punishment and torture, including the notorious *palmatoria* which looked like a huge long wooden spoon with a hole in the flat bowl. It was used to smash the hand of a recalcitrant, reducing it to a useless mess of lacerated and bleeding flesh. Everywhere old guns lay in glass cases and walls boomed out slogans such as 'Long live the Mozambican revolution' and 'Down with Portuguese colonialism and all its lackeys'. A sophisticated, if old, coloured plastic wall map could be switched on to illuminate in temporal sequence the course of the armed struggle, showing bases, conflicts and congresses.

Downstairs in the entrance hall, letters of thanks and congratulations from foreign dignitaries were laid out. There was a message from Sassou N'Guesso, president of the Congo, and another from Eric Honecker of East Germany. My guide's job done, he turned to me.

'Can you give me one thousand meticais?' he asked tonelessly. His eyes followed my hand down to my trouser pocket from which I took a wad of notes, pulled out a red one and handed it to him. He put his eyes on the bill and pointed to the smiling head and shoulders of a middle-aged gentleman with a very high forehead. 'Eduardo Mondlane,' he said simply, then turned on his heel and left the museum through the plate-glass doorway.

Africa needs heroes badly and Eduardo Mondlane has a rightful place among them. He was born in 1920 in the southern province of Gaza where his father and one of his uncles were chiefs. They both died resisting the Portuguese regime, his uncle after serving twenty-five years in prison. Eduardo Mondlane also lost one of his brothers, drafted to work in the gold mines of the Witwatersrand, who died from a lung disease common among those who worked underground. Mondlane was lucky, he got some education, first in a mission school and later in South Africa, briefly in Portugal and then in the USA. But having experienced at first hand the oppression of his fellow Mozambicans, he returned to work towards the day when they would be free from foreign rule. He was a charismatic leader and a major force in the armed struggle for liberation. But he didn't live to see a free Mozambique. He was 'assassinated by colonialism' as the inscription on the statue of him in Maputo says, by a parcel bomb that exploded in his face in his office in Dar es Salaam in February 1969. It was the combined work of the Portuguese secret police and internal Mozambican opposition. But though Mondlane was a great protagonist of unity, Frelimo was never built around a single personality, and his dream of a free country was turned into reality by his compatriots.

Alex and I walked out of the museum into a dull Sunday afternoon on the streets of free Mozambique. We wandered in search of a café, crossing the road to pass Maputo's military headquarters where sentries have been known to relieve the boredom of guard duty by arresting passers-by who dare to walk in front of their barracks. Places of high security like this were marked by notices telling you not to make any noise and not to stop, to keep moving, or face the consequences.

'They arrest you if you're lucky,' said Alex. 'A few months ago a woman working for the UN who had only just arrived in Maputo was driving to see someone and took a wrong turning, into the presidential compound. As she was turning the car around at the barrier they started shooting at her.' The woman lost an arm for her mistake.

When freedom finally came to Mozambique the country was an institutional vacuum. Most of the 200,000-odd Portuguese in the country had left after independence. Years of neglect of the African population left them with an acute shortage of people trained in basic skills, let alone advanced ones. At independence Mozambique had an incredible eighty-seven doctors for the entire country, and most of these were white and lived in Maputo. Of the 350 railway engineers left working in 1975, only one was black, and he was an agent of the Portuguese secret police. Mozambique was similarly deficient in virtually every other area of expertise necessary to run a modern country: administration, accountancy, shop-keeping, farming, teaching, law. As the graphic polystyrene letters on the wall of the museum had pointed out, in 1950 only 2.32 per cent of the population could read and write.

It is remarkable that Mozambicans were able to do anything at all with their new country under the circumstances, but they made notable progress. A mass literacy campaign was launched and a rural vaccination programme which reached into the most remote areas and was considered by the World Health Organization to be one of the most successful campaigns of its kind in Africa. Frelimo drew the entire Mozambican society into the effort towards reconstruction and development. But they were not just content to take over and Africanise the colonial way of running the country

– so often the fate of other African national movements. They wanted to turn society on its head, to transform a liberation struggle into a social revolution.

In the second half of the 1970s and the early 1980s Mozambique became a mecca for foreigners interested in socialist practice. As the realities of Eastern Europe had hit home to some, here was a socialist society which seemed to be working. And in black Africa to boot, the oppressed continent. Where better and more appropriate for true socialism to develop than in a continent which for so long had suffered the exploitative yoke of capitalism? Idealists flocked to Mozambique to offer their badly needed skills. The atmosphere was heady. Bob Dylan wrote a song about the place.

And then things began to go wrong. Slowly the idealists started to wake up, suffering from an ideological hangover. Somewhere along the way Frelimo lost themselves and lost touch with the people they were trying to help. Why this happened will become clearer in the course of time, but there are some pointers. It may have been the strain of trying to transform a centralised bureaucracy which they had barely enough people to run, let alone to understand and change it. Or perhaps it was the shock of entering cement city, after so many years in the metaphorical and literal wilderness, which made the leaders forget the way of life of the countryside where they had lived for so long and where their people continued to live. Part of the reason was the contradiction between Frelimo's popularly stated goals and the Eastern European model of socialism they were encouraged to adopt by their Soviet mentors, with its emphasis on centralised planning and state authority. And, as time moved on, the realisation of their dreams became increasingly difficult as the war of destabilisation took hold and access to their people in the countryside became more and more difficult.

An agreement was reached with the South African government by which both countries guaranteed to stop supporting groups in opposition to the other. The South Africans did not take much notice of the agreement, and by this time

59

Renamo had got a bit out of hand anyway. As the USSR started to go cold on the Mozambicans, they were forced to turn to the West for help. They joined the World Bank and the International Monetary Fund and this opened the floodgates to foreign aid from the West. Frelimo woke up one morning and decided they were not Marxist-Leninists any more and the scene was set for peace. A cynical view says that the Western powers had achieved their aim: destroying socialism in Mozambique by reducing the country to its knees and recolonising it with aid and aid workers.

Now Mozambicans had to start again on their reconstruction. But it was no easy mission, quite apart from the difficulties inherited at independence, which had changed little in the eighteen years to 1992. The shortage of trained people was still acute. Much of the groundwork to prepare for revitalising the country after the war was being done by people who had been educated only as far as secondary school, and the information they had to work on was incomplete and outdated.

'No one really knows how many *deslocados* there are or whether they'll return to their villages, assuming the villages are still there,' Alex explained.

So few government people had ventured outside the main towns and cities for so long that the situation in large parts of the countryside was almost completely unknown. Even basic aspects which would have remained unaltered by the war were often a mystery. Many of the maps and much information about things like rural water resources and the quality of soils had been taken by the Portuguese when they left. The job of Alex's department was to collect reconstruction plans from all the provinces and ministries and present them as a package to foreign donors for funding. 'But at a meeting in one province I asked the guy in charge of water resources where his plan was for providing water to returning *deslocados*. He asked me how could he say where to drill wells when he didn't know where the water was.'

From our position outside the café, I could see a line of

women and girls squatting behind a row of cardboard boxes on top of which South African cigarettes were for sale. I wanted to go over to the kerbside and ask them if, when and where they would return to when the fighting was over. They might have told me, if they had known. Whether they would answer to an official was a different matter, but to ask four or five million people the same questions was an impossible task anyway. The operation seemed to be an exercise in self-delusion. Resettling six million people would be a monumental task in the best organised of countries – in Mozambique it was a joke.

A couple of days later I made my first serious trip outside Maputo. I flew north to Cabo Delgado province with Alex and two of his Mozambican colleagues, Fidel and Paulo, from the Ministry of Planning. The landscape outside Maputo was tinder-dry and the River Incomati, which rises in South Africa and follows a tortuous path through Maputo province to reach the sea just north of the city, was not flowing at all in some of its stretches. Bushfires all around the many mouths of the Zambezi delta sent stalks of smoke into the still atmosphere to feed swathes of mushroom clouds which filled the plane's windows and became a milky haze on the horizon.

At Nampula, capital of the province of the same name, the Linhas Aéreas de Moçambique aircraft landed for half an hour to refuel. The four of us trooped into the terminal building and past an empty ancient display stand for Parker pens into the transit bar. Alex bought beers and we stood leaning on the balcony rail overlooking the tarmac where an Air BP tanker was pumping fuel into our smart new Boeing 737.

The landscape around Nampula is punctuated with huge basalt inselbergs which tower up from among toy green trees. As we gazed at the majestic landscape, Fidel, a man in his early thirties, started to frown. 'What are those things over there?' he said pointing with his chin towards the sugar-loaf domes.

'Mountains,' said Alex.

There was a short pause. Fidel had been drinking beer for most of the day to prepare himself for his first trip in an aeroplane and was feeling slightly the worse for wear.

'Oh yes,' he said, not terribly convincingly, 'I saw things like that when I was in Swaziland.'

Within an hour of leaving Nampula we had landed at the airstrip in Pemba, capital of Cabo Delgado province. The small airport building was being refurbished and we waited for forty minutes inside the sweaty exit hall before someone found a key to let us out. A man from the provincial planning department was there to meet us and we were driven into town where we checked into the Hotel Cabo Delgado.

Over dinner, I asked Fidel how he had enjoyed his first flight. The man who was not sure about mountains put his hand to his high forehead. He wore a virulent yellow shirt and a small beard on his strong jaw. It was fine, he said, but all the beer had given him a headache. This was his first visit to the north of his country and so far he had found it very interesting. It was hotter than in Maputo and all the people here seemed significantly shorter than people in the south.

As if to confirm Fidel's observation, a short waiter came over to our table to pour us some water from the glass jug he carried. Fidel looked at the little man and asked, 'Why are you so small?'

The waiter gave a nervous smile, and said, 'This is a normal question. It is hereditary.' There was a short pause before Fidel made a comment that I only half caught, but it made reference to Cabo Delgado, which means 'Cape Thin'.

'There are also people here who take pills to make them-selves fat,' came the waiter's reply as he filled the last glass with water. We pondered that piece of information for a while as we tucked into our plates of grilled goat, cabbage and chips.

Later, the little waiter came back to hover for a while by our table. He appeared to want to continue the conversation, but was nervous about doing so. Eventually he plucked up the courage and approached our table to ask Fidel, 'Why do you ask this question?'

The waiter nodded with a more confident smile as he was told that people from the south were taller than people here. He had heard as much, he said, but he had never been outside Cabo Delgado so he had not seen it for himself.

It was not just the people who were small in Cabo Delgado. The next day I wandered around Pemba's Mercado Municipal, built in 1940. All its produce backed the province's claim to fame: everything on sale was small. The stalls were stacked with minuscule garlic bulbs, dwarf onions, midget mangoes, pocket-size coconuts and minute tomatoes. Some of the women minding the rows of mini-produce wore face masks made from bark ground to a white paste. Their white teeth gleamed as they smiled and wished me good morning. Many of the men wore Muslim skullcaps on their heads.

Pemba's cement city was compact. Outside the Mercado Municipal most of the shops were run by Indians, as are most of the shops all over Mozambique. There was not a lot going on along the cracked paving stones and pock-marked tarmac of the main streets. Under the shade of the covered walkways, boys sold FN Virginia filtered cigarettes, made in Maputo. The odd four-wheel drive vehicle passed, each one new and bearing an aid agency sticker on its door.

I passed the small port, where the wharf was piled high with battered containers, and moved along the narrow shoreline. Four men, squatting at the sea's edge facing inland, were defecating, each washing himself with the left hand in the Arab mode. A little farther around the bay the beach was littered with human turds. Fishermen were stretched out in the shade of broken bamboo fences, their dhows gently bobbing in the swell. Among the wooden boats were two of the world's oldest rusty steamboats. A fisherman said good morning and asked if I had some money to help him pay for his wife's coffin. I gave him a small donation and as I continued to pick my way through the excrement at the water's edge another fellow approached me and asked straight out for a hundred dollars. When I replied that I had no dollars, he wanted to know whether I had any shorts for sale instead.

Inland from the beach, the central feature in a disused public park and play area was a surrealist-looking monument to the revolution. It featured a plinth with tall column, on top of which the torso of a man in combat gear was punching the air inside a glass box. Below this was an inscription which read: 'Military heroes of Frelimo and liberators of the nation – the struggle continues, the revolution is triumphant'.

Cabo Delgado was the scene of some of the fiercest fighting in the war for independence. The northernmost fringe of the province, along the border with Tanzania, was occupied and run by Frelimo in the late 1960s, and the Portuguese attempted to sap rural support for the guerrillas with a scorched earth policy and a huge programme of resettlement. Thousands of peasants were herded into new villages encircled with barbed wire – *aldeamentos* – to stop them collaborating with the enemy. This strategy continued into the early 1970s, by which time more than 270,000 people had been relocated, nearly half the province's African population. But the strategic hamlets programme was not successful in turning the Mozambicans against Frelimo, partly because many of the *aldeamentos* were in infertile areas, often without water.

In 1970, as the Portuguese saw their grip on the province continuing to slip, a new commander-in-chief in Mozambique launched an outright military offensive. Operation Gordian Knot, as it was known, was an attempt to invade and reconquer the Frelimo-liberated zones. Tens of thousands of troops and an impressive array of military hardware were moved into the province for the purpose. Caterpillar tractors ploughed new tracks into the bush for infantry battalions to follow on search-and-destroy missions, backed by aerial and artillery bombardments aimed at Frelimo bases.

After four months the operation had achieved little and was abandoned. Frelimo had fought off the offensive by holding firm in their ability to mobilise the rural population.

Aerial bombing initially disrupted daytime work in the fields, but peasants soon began cultivating at night. When Portuguese infantry attacks came close to a certain village, people abandoned their homes and dispersed into small groups to reassemble nearer to guerrilla bases. From the bases, Frelimo moved them to another zone. Portuguese advances were met with strong opposition from Frelimo fighters armed with kalashnikovs and mortars, and peasants wielding makeshift weapons. Meanwhile, another group would circle around behind the invaders to plant mines, dig ditches and fell trees across the trails the Portuguese had blazed through the undergrowth. Getting into the liberated zones was a fairly straightforward exercise for the Portuguese troops; making their exit often proved more troublesome.

Portugal was shocked at the failure of Operation Gordian Knot. It is seen as a turning point in the war for independence, since it was the last major offensive of its size which the colonial forces launched in Mozambique.

Given that Cabo Delgado was the scene of such key events in the liberation war as the Mueda massacre, which spurred its initiation, and the victories over Operation Gordian Knot, which spelled the beginning of its end, it may seem surprising that the province remains a backwater. But this is a simple fact of geography: it is a very long way from Maputo, although its remoteness has had its uses. Cabo Delgado and the neighbouring northern province of Niassa are where many Frelimo members who have fallen foul of the latest game of political musical chairs are sent for a tour of duty.

Not all the exiles sent to Cabo Delgado remained in government employment. A long struggle up the hill from Pemba's surrealist monument stood a forbidding edifice surrounded by high concrete walls. It was one of the notorious 're-education camps' set up by Frelimo in the years after independence. Samora Machel, the country's first president, called them 'camps for mental decolonisation' and many of the inmates were political adversaries, old and new, who were sentenced to indefinite terms, usually without trial. But it was not just political opponents who were dispatched to such establishments. Anyone thought to be 'unproductive', or generally in need of a bit of re-education was sent. Vagrants, common or garden criminals and Jehovah's Witnesses, whose crime was a refusal on religious grounds to shout 'Viva Frelimo' at appropriate junctures, were among the thousands who ended up in camps like the one on Pemba's hill. No one really knows how many people were sent to these places to be 're-educated', but estimates range between 10,000 and 200,000. By all accounts the conditions were severe.

Africa Watch, a US-based human rights organisation, interviewed a former Frelimo guerrilla who was sent to the camp at Pemba after deserting prior to independence. For three years, he endured daily beatings, long periods without food and the summary execution of many of his fellow inmates before escaping to Tanzania. Although the worst abuses in the camps ceased at the end of the 1970s with the adoption of the first laws to establish a new legal system, in 1983 you could still be sentenced to eight years in a camp for criticising Frelimo policies in an examination essay, as was one schoolteacher according to Amnesty International's 1987 annual report. The re-education camps became fertile recruiting grounds for Renamo. Some former inmates, such as Afonso Dhlakama, joined Renamo after escaping; others were sprung from the camps by Renamo fighters on recruitment drives.

The re-education camps were one of the ways in which Frelimo alienated some of the people they had fought for and with during the long hard campaign against the Portuguese. Perhaps it is not so surprising that in their efforts to create a state apparatus which could be respected, after such a long history of government being equated with exploitation, physical abuse and murder, they began with some repressive measures. But other forms of state interference in the everyday lives of their people are less easy to understand.

Most Mozambicans are rural people who know little more than to work their piece of land. After Frelimo came to power it seemed that at last peasants would be able to return to their own *machambas* (fields) to get on with their lives, after being forced to work for other people or having their *machambas* stolen from them. In all too many cases this did not happen. Land that had been stolen to form plantations all over the country was taken over and run as state farms, while in the provinces where *aldeamentos* had been established by the Portuguese, Frelimo often told the inhabitants to stay where they were and start working as collectives.

This happened in the Mueda district of northern Cabo Delgado. The chain of events in Ngapa, a former *aldeamento* close to the Tanzanian border, was in many ways typical of the sort of errors Frelimo made in the rural areas where they had won their victory. After independence, the population of Ngapa, who had been forced to live there by the Portuguese, was told to stay put. But as refugees from the independence fighting started to return from Tanzania, tribal tensions in the village encouraged some to move out after the first year, and by 1980 four new villages had been established some distance from Ngapa. The district is remote and difficult to govern, with hardly any roads, no bus, no telephone or radio, so sanctions against the new unofficial villages were not easy to impose. A few attempts were made to encourage people to move back into Ngapa, but when gentle persuasion failed, the new villages were burned to the ground, an act not designed to encourage confidence in government for the people by the people. Each time the villagers were taken back to Ngapa they left again and rebuilt their homes. Eventually, the status quo was accepted and the new villages were instructed to start collective cultivation. Three of the villages complied and their profits were passed to the Ngapa village president, but the money was never put to any use that the new villages could see, eroding further confidence in a system which did not appear to be doing anything for them.

The tribal problems which contributed to the break-up of Ngapa were a particular disappointment to Frelimo. The national struggle against the Portuguese had helped to cement Mozambique as a country not divided by tribal differences. But the post-independence tensions in Ngapa were fuelled by refugees who had not taken part in the liberation struggle. Although Frelimo still claim that their country is not divided by racial differences, most of their senior members are from southern tribes, and the capital is in the extreme south of the country; northerners are thus suspicious of the southern domination of Mozambique.

One morning I woke early and hurried down to the beach for a rendezvous I had arranged the day before with some fishermen. They had agreed to take me out with them on their morning sortie.

Small new acacia trees a foot high had been planted in the pavements to replace mature specimens, many of which were encircled by piles of chopped branches. A woman looked up from her work stripping a tree and smiled when I said good morning. Cement city met mud-hut city where the tarmac road ended abruptly and a dirt track carried on. The streets between the beach huts were made of sand, and children were out in force sweeping in front of their houses in the early morning light. A man was building a new house, filling the double bamboo frame with stones before the application of a mud outer layer. Chickens and ducks strutted and waddled about, pecking at anything that looked vaguely nutritious and quite a lot that did not.

I got to the sea shore and looked up and down for my fishermen. Ropes and nets were being carried into the surf and put into dhows. At one end of the beach, behind a bamboo palisade, two new fifty-footers were being hammered into being. I asked around for my fishermen, but was told that they had already set out into the bay for the morning's work. Two characters who were piling glistening fish into a wicker basket asked me where I was from. I told them England.

'Ha, ha, ha,' one of them laughed incredulously, 'Inglaterra, that is very far away.'

'Very far away', his mate repeated, tossing a large prawn into the basket and studying me with interest. Then the first one asked, 'Do you speak Russian?'

'No,' I said, 'or only a few words, like *ochi karashow* [very good].' They both roared with laughter.

'There used to be many Russians here,' the first man said. 'Bad people,' his mate muttered, 'but now there are not many of them.'

Small children were playing hopscotch outside a mosque as I moved inland from the beach. I followed a line of women and girls who were making their way with an assortment of old paint cans and other metal containers on their heads to a well sunk below the old sea cliff. Near the well was a circular concrete pad where another group of women were washing their brightly coloured *capelanas*, long strips of printed cotton which are worn as wrap-around skirts or on the upper body where they double as baby slings.

I ate some yoghurt for breakfast in a bar in the cement city. It was large and airy and functional, with a counter running along one wall. The prices of food and drinks were chalked on a small blackboard beside a display of Castle and Carling Black Label and Mirinda, 7-Up and Coke cans. Fairy lights which had not worked for at least a generation were strung above the bar's one picture, of palm trees on a beach. There were no curtains at the grubby window panes. A man standing at the counter wore a T-shirt emblazoned with the words 'Saddam Hussein I support you' beside a full frontal portrait of the Iraqi leader smiling in a military beret. The man inside the T-shirt was swilling beer from a Carling Black Label can made in South Africa.

I had been told of a woodcarving cooperative of Maconde sculptors in Pemba and I asked the Saddam Hussein supporter if he knew where it was. He gave me directions and I set off up the hill. When I reached the place, a basic shopfront situated between a general store and the Pemba branch of the People's Development Bank, it turned out to be a retail outlet. All the carvers lived in the villages, the young man

69

in attendance told me, gesturing to some old black-and-white photographs tacked on the wall.

The *Maconde* are a matrilineal ethnic group living on the Mueda Plateau in the north of the province, close to the River Rovuma which marks the border with Tanzania. They have a long tradition of carving. According to Maconde legend they are descended from a man who lived alone in the forest like a wild pig. The man wanted a family, so one day he decided to carve himself a wife from a log, and eventually the couple had children. The first two children were born near the river and soon died, but the third, born on the plateau, survived, and this was taken as a sign that the Maconde should live on the high ground.

The thick forests and steep escarpments of the Mueda Plateau were to prove a haven for the tribe during the nineteenth century when all around them East Africa was being raided for slaves. Indeed it was not until after the First World War that Europeans penetrated the plateau, with the first Catholic mission opening in 1924. So it is only relatively recently that Maconde traditions have been affected by foreign influences.

Carving is a male preserve and carvers, whose skills are passed down from father to son, are leading figures in Maconde society. Their abilities prove that they can control the mysterious world of nature and can enter into contact with the ancestors and spirits. The Maconde word for wood-carving, *machinamu*, also means ancestors, and carvers have traditionally produced human figures used for family worship and masks for initiation ceremonies which integrate young people into the adult world through links with the ancestors and the supernatural beings abounding in nature.

As they became influenced by the outside world, and their carving abilities were hailed by Western art critics, new styles developed. Most of the pieces in the cooperative shop were in these more recent styles: *Shetani* and *Ujamaa*. Both were developed in the 1960s among Maconde living in exile in neighbouring Tanzania. *Shetani* is a Swahili word meaning 'devil' which is used to translate a spirit or group of spirits from Maconde cosmogony. In the singular it is a one-legged, one-armed, no-good spirit which spreads sickness and misfortune like the wind. It also has one finger, one eye and a single hair. But the word can also be used for a wide range of figures or spirits not identified as animals. They are of varying sizes and most of them are nocturnal and mysterious. Each *Shetani* inhabits a specific type of environment and has its own name. Some live in the forests, others on the plains; some eat fish from the river, others live off crops from the fields. Villages and towns have their own specific *Shetani* which prowl the streets at night, and some of them have prostitutes. The carvings arranged on the floor of the shop were tall and gracefully curved, with stylised and abstracted faces and symbols, most carved in heavy jet-black ebony.

The fact that *Shetani* carvings originated in Tanzania is a result of the strength of the Catholic church in Mozambique, which frowned upon, nay forbade, representations of ancestral rites and spirits. By the mid-1960s, Maconde carvers in Tanzania had the status of political refugees, since their country was still occupied by a colonial power, and it was around this time that the *Ujamaa* style developed. *Ujamaa*, also a Swahili word, roughly meaning 'familyhood', was a political style inspired by Julius Nyerere's post-independence drive to organise Tanzanians along African family traditions of cooperation. The carvings are totem-type affairs, showing lifelike people and faces, huts and everyday articles like pots and agricultural implements.

The man in the shop was keen to show me the objects and symbols that appeared in many of the pieces. Water pots appeared in both *Shetani* and *Ujamaa* carvings, he explained, because the Mueda Plateau has no springs or wells and collecting water is a daily drama. This *Shetani* was the spirit of fertility and lovers, with the fertility pot, which looked like a gourd with a stopper, held aloft by a very long foot. That *Shetani* was for keeping evil spirits out of your house,

71

and another, which sprouted things looking suspiciously like angel's wings, was indeed for Christian spirits.

That evening I sat in the bar next to our hotel having a drink with Alex as the light was fading. He was depressed because he had just lost his wallet, containing 200 dollars. The work at the provincial planning department had also been hard going. 'Most of them want to do the job, but they should have started months ago.' Alex held his cigarette over the ashtray and flicked ash which landed on the red and white plastic tablecloth. 'It's been really embarrassing because now I'm telling them that their plans for the province have to be ready for the donors' conference in a month, but I've only just brought the cheque from UNDP to pay for the work.'

The bureaucratic inefficiencies of the UN and other aid agencies was a common gripe I was to hear many times. It had taken the UN Development Programme an incredible seven months to hand over the money. They seemed to work on a geological timescale. The Mozambican administrator in Alex's Maputo office had been working on the national reconstruction project for four months, but she was still waiting for a contract from UNDP and thus had yet to receive her first salary payment. Alex had not received a salary cheque since starting several months before, and had been borrowing money from friends, while his administrator had to moonlight to pay the bills.

The Cabo Delgado planning office had in fact started to draw up their plans, thanks to some creative accounting on their part, using aid money from the Norwegian Ministry for Development Cooperation to pay for the necessary reconnaissance trips into the countryside. But there was still a legion of problems.

'No one really knows *how* to draw up a plan,' Alex said with resignation. 'They've come up with three projects so far, and one of them is to set up a new dance troupe in one of the districts. It's crazy, I was in Sofala province last month and the only project one of their districts had thought of was

72

to buy a new kit for the football team.' He was hunched over the table killing the cigarette in the black plastic ashtray with an unhurried stubbing movement.

I poured some more beer into my mouth. The naivety of the provincial planners was hardly their fault. Few of the staff had been educated beyond secondary school; just three of the country's eleven provincial planning directors had a university education. And throughout the communist period, all the provinces had been doing was paying their own salaries, since virtually all the planning was done in Maputo. Now there was a concerted effort to devolve responsibility from the centralised approach, but the people supposedly doing the job were little more experienced than schoolchildren. The Cabo Delgado department had been given a computer, but no one had been told how to use it.

'There's a really bright guy there who was keen to have a go on it,' Alex said, exasperated, 'but the director won't let him. He keeps it locked away because it's too valuable a piece of equipment to be played with.'

Another problem the government had to face daily stemmed from the harsh realities of introducing a market economy. When Mozambicans were trained in specific useful skills they left almost immediately to work in the private sector, where they could earn several times the amount the government could afford to pay them. We agreed that in the wider perspective this did not matter too much, since the skills were still in Mozambique, but it made the government's job all the more difficult.

A smiling waiter came over and we ordered two more Black Labels since there was no *cerveja nacionale* (national beer) in Pemba. Alex pulled a new cigarette out of the packet. There was still the problem of not knowing when the *deslocados* were going to return, and where they would return to. How could the planners decide where to construct new huts and sink stand pipes in such a situation? 'They can't designate villages because no one would turn up. It smacks too much of Portuguese *aldeamentos* and the Frelimo villagisation programmes. People are fed up with being pushed around and told where to go. The only way of doing anything is just to provide food, seeds and tools and let people get on with it.'

Alex lit the cigarette and sucked on it. He threw the match in the ashtray while it was still burning. As the waiter arrived with our Black Labels Alex blew out a cloud of smoke to one side of the table. 'But even that's not so easy,' he continued as we poured the yellow fizz out of the cans. 'If you don't know how many people are going where, how do you know what seeds to order? I mean they grow mandioca in the north of Mozambique but not in the south.'

It was dark outside now, and part of Pemba's flying insect population was buzzing around the few light fittings that held bulbs. As if he had not highlighted enough problems, Alex pointed out a few more. Many decisions on basic principles had not yet been made by government. 'No one has made any decision about land ownership. What happens when someone returns to their *machamba* and finds someone else working it? Who settles a dispute like that and how?' He was smoking furiously now. 'The government says returning *deslocados* will be allocated land, but who's going to do that? And have weightings been drawn up to allocate different acreages to reflect different soil types? No.'

'Do they even know where the different soil types are?' I asked. 'Probably not.' He sucked down some more Black Label. 'And who's going to build new huts, health posts and schools? Nobody knows . . .' He stared into his beer and sighed.

I said, 'It must make you wonder why you bother sometimes.'

'Something will happen in the end, it always does,' he replied. 'Mozambicans are incredibly resilient people, just look at what they've been through and they still smile at you. All this money the donors are spending trying to make impossible plans, they may as well just give every Mozambican a hundred dollars and let them get on with it.'

74

That seemed a reasonable idea. Perhaps some enlightened aid agency will try it some time.

5

ADRENALIN JUNKIES

One of the common complaints that Alex heard on his tours of provincial planning departments concerned foreign charities, or non-governmental organisations as the United Nations prefers to call them – the inevitable acronym being NGOs. NGOs were running around all over the country doing projects. The planners had little idea of what most NGOs were doing and no control over their activities. What was the point of making plans, they asked, when the NGOs were doing everything anyway and without any collaboration with the local government planners?

There were probably more than 200 NGOs working in Mozambique, although no one knew the exact number. A UN development cooperation report published in 1992 tried to make an assessment of NGOs' contribution to foreign assistance in Mozambique. They contacted nearly 150, but only forty-four bothered to send any data on their activities. Many appeared to be a law unto themselves.

The term NGO covers a wide range of organisations. Some were born out of the old missionary societies while others are linked to newer religious sects; some were established for famine relief, others specialise in helping specific groups such as children or women. Many have a rather anti-government bias on the face of it, because they believe, in many cases rightly, that governments, with their aid agencies and multilateral equivalents, are overly bureaucratic, inefficient and tend to concentrate too heavily upon large-scale schemes which all too often forget to consult the people they are supposed to be helping. But *non-governmental* organisation is a bit of a misnomer in many cases. Although some of their activities are financed by public fund-raising, many NGOs rely heavily upon funding from their home governments, and increasingly these governments are using them as executing agencies to carry out their relief and development work in Mozambique.

It is naive to think that any organisation which sets out to help people anywhere can do so without getting involved in politics to some extent, but the trend towards reliance upon and collaboration with governments worries some NGO members. Acceptance of funds and duties from governments inevitably comes with some strings attached. When NGOs get involved in politics at home, and begin to ask the wrong sorts of questions, governments can make things uncomfortable for them. An NGO worker is often quoted, 'When I give food they call me a saint. When I ask why the poor have no food, they call me a communist.'

One Western observer of Mozambican affairs has suggested that NGOs, effectively working under the guidance of their governments, are akin to the missionaries who went into Africa in the nineteenth century. Just as the missionaries entered Mozambique and other parts of Africa after the wars which followed the carving up of the continent at the Berlin Conference, paving the way for the capitalists, so the NGOs made inroads into Mozambique as the war with Renamo came towards an end, again clearing the way for foreign business interests. Depending upon your point of view and political hue, this idea is either farfetched conspiracy theory or harsh reality.

In the early years after independence, Frelimo was suspicious of foreigners who wanted to help them. Although they were desperately in need of all the help they could get, they were selective about the offers they accepted. Countries and organisations which had supported Frelimo in their struggle against the Portuguese could be trusted, they thought, while others were treated with more caution. Frelimo was well aware that there is no such thing as a free lunch. President Samora Machel, responding in 1980 to an offer of aid from the European Community, is quoted as saying, 'As soon as someone says to me, "We are going to give you five million dollars", I reply, "In exchange for what?" I don't think they will give us something for nothing. God does it. God is good for that. But the EC? Its vocation isn't to carry out distribution, as if it were serving free beer.'

So to begin with Mozambique did not admit certain aid agencies, foreign unskilled volunteers or traditional NGOs. But after Mozambique signed an agreement with the World Bank and the International Monetary Fund in 1987, foreign aid began to flood in, and with it the NGOs, whose numbers leapt after the mid-1980s.

Frelimo was unable to keep out many of the NGOs they considered undesirable, because of their links with donor governments. World Vision International is a case in point. It seems unlikely that Mozambique would have allowed this multimillion-dollar aid charity into the country since it was decidedly anti-communist. It is also overtly Christian, and has often been accused of blurring the distinction between aid work and evangelical recruitment. In the words of the World Vision president, writing in the organisation's newspaper in 1982: 'We analyse every project, every programme we undertake, to make sure that within that programme evangelism is a significant component. We cannot feed individuals and then let them go to hell.' But when World Vision was awarded the contract to distribute some of the US government's food aid in 1984, Mozambique risked losing the food deliveries if it rejected World Vision. Worse still, the contract was awarded at a time when right-wing organisations in the US were accusing Frelimo of repressing religion, and to bar World Vision would have played into the hands of the anti-communist lobby in Washington, jeopardising further aid. As soon as they were in, World Vision began their crusading. On their first project, large numbers of bibles and religious books were flown into the province of Tete along with nearly 800 tons of maize from Malawi.

Losing control over foreign aid money, people and projects is a common concern for all developing country governments. Most have little option but to accept some of the strings attached, because they are up to their eyeballs in debt. In Mozambique, this was certainly the case, and the continuing war with Renamo made things doubly urgent. The aid business is littered with stories of well-intentioned assistance actually doing more harm than good, often due to overzealousness, arrogance or a lack of adequate forethought by those giving. Problems arise when such high priority is given to getting food to those who need it that all other thoughts are secondary, with the result that people can be maintained in a state of dependency for years to come.

An example of this occurred in Inhambane province after Care, a US NGO, arrived in 1985 to distribute food aid. Although there was a drought, and food crops were not growing, tree crops were still being harvested – mafurra fruit, which is used in soap-making, coconuts and cashews. Hence some people had money and just needed food to buy, while others were *deslocados* and had neither money nor food. Until the arrival of Care, food had been transported for sale or free distribution by the state agricultural marketing board, Agricom, who filled their lorries with tree crops for the return journey from rural areas. When Care arrived on the scene, they reorganised distribution on the Agricom lorries, supplying the fuel for their food runs. But they insisted that lorries returning from food-aid journeys should not carry rural produce because the time taken to load it would delay the next delivery of food to the starving.

Agricom protested because it still had to fulfil its role in marketing rural produce. Care retaliated by saying they would set up their own transport fleet, threatening to withdraw with their food if this was not granted by the local governor. Although the government was against setting up different fleets for the distribution of free and commercial food, the governor had little choice but to give in to Care's demands. He took all Agricom's new lorries away from them to establish a new fleet for Care. Agricom was left with four ancient trucks, and since Care was paying salaries in hard currency some of Agricom's staff also moved over to work for Care. With no new vehicles, Agricom's distribution network soon collapsed. Women sat patiently at the roadside by their piles of mafurra, cashews and coconuts while the new Care lorries sped past them down the highways empty. Unable to sell their produce, the peasants ran out of money, and they too were reduced to eating food-aid hand-outs.

To cap it all, Inhambane's soap factory had to close because it could no longer get hold of the mafurra fruit. Donors then began bringing in soap. Renamo were already doing a pretty effective job in destroying and disrupting Mozambique's economic fabric; they did not need well-intentioned foreign aid workers to help them.

This story concerned an NGO, but Mozambique seems to have an almost limitless supply of similar grimly ironic stories about all types of aid organisation. 'Help' from foreign donors often made a step forward in one sector of the economy at the expense of two unexpected steps back somewhere else.

The more I saw and heard in Mozambique, the more I began to question even the most conventional aspects of development theories. Another commonly quoted problem that inexorably plagues poor countries the world over is a lack of spare parts. Machinery of all kinds is bought by developing countries or given to them, often with little consideration for what happens when the machines break down. Text books about development are full of sorry tales of projects grinding to a halt through lack of spare parts or the skills needed to repair the bits that go wrong. But even this doctrine didn't quite fit all the facts in Mozambique. The streets of Maputo were replete with superannuated taxis trundling along in the face of the development theorists. These antediluvian vehicles should by rights have ceased to function decades before; that they continued to defy the laws of physics was a tribute to the mechanical ingenuity of the supposedly 'Third World' old-timers who sat behind their wheels. I don't know anything about car maintenance, but I was sure that the manufacture of spare parts necessary for the antiquated Peugeots and Citroens that chugged around Maputo must have been discontinued years ago.

The most venerable cab I caught was early one Saturday evening when Alex, Noel and I set out for an open-air rock concert, held to celebrate the tenth anniversary of the state electricity company, at a football stadium some miles out of town. Getting around Maputo was often a problem, if the destination was not on one of the set *chapa* routes. The taxis all seemed to congregate at a single taxi rank, a half-hour walk from Alex's house, next to the central market down in town. Apparently a company had recently been established which would send a cab to your house when telephoned, but since Alex didn't have a telephone, this was not an option for us.

The light was fading as the three of us made our way down Avenida Patrice Lumumba, when an ancient Peugeot cab passed at a stately pace. We hailed it and the driver stamped on the footbrake, juddering to a halt in the middle of the road. He kept the engine running as we negotiated a fare. Then, as we climbed in, the engine cut out with a tired popping sound. The driver, an elderly gentleman with a shock of white hair, seemed unconcerned. He took his foot off the brake and rolled down the hill to jump-start his vehicle. Several of the springs were missing from the back seat and I sank into a cavity caused by a thousand bottoms. Through the floor at my feet, a number of sizeable holes allowed us to observe the roadway over which we were passing. I tried to wind down my window, but the absence of a handle made my mission a fruitless one. As we bumped over a minor pot-hole, however, the taxi seemed to have read my thoughts, because the glass from the window bounced neatly out of the door frame and into my lap. Noel laughed. 'It's an automatic,' he said.

We drove gently into town, which was not the route we should have been taking to reach the Costa do Sol football stadium. Alex pointed this out to our driver, who explained that since this was a long-distance trip (it was about eight kilometres) he would have to find sufficient petrol for the journey. This proved a bit of a problem. We chased around several locations before finding a man who gave us some fuel from his jerry can. We set off past the Botanical Gardens and rounded the corner of the bay to proceed at about twenty miles per hour in a north-easterly direction. The driver seemed to be having some trouble with the gears.

'How old is this car, Senhor?' Alex asked the driver.

'Oh, many years,' the old man replied, 'perhaps about thirty.'

'Don't all the gears work?' Alex asked him.

'Oh, all the gears work all right, but not all at the same time,' he replied.

Half-way along the most remote stretch of road leading up the coast out of town we got stuck behind a car driving more slowly than we were and the driver's comment on the gears was justified. He was unable to change down from third and we stalled. We rolled to a gentle stop in the middle of the road.

The driver twisted the key in the ignition. The engine turned over but did not ignite. He tried again. Still no luck. He made several more attempts before we suggested we could give him a push. Fifty metres down the road there was still no life from the engine. A gentle sea breeze rustled the fronds of the coconut palms which lined the beach and a crescent moon was up and shining a clean white light over the proceedings, contrasting with the weak yellow beam from the taxi's headlights. We were stranded on the most remote stretch of the road, a mile from anywhere.

The driver seemed supremely unconcerned. He switched off the headlights, folded his arms and just sat there in the middle of the road, saying nothing. He was in tune with his vehicle, they had both simply stopped. A large lorry

82

appeared around the gentle bend in the road behind us. We were caught momentarily in its forward beam before we moved quickly to the side of the road, expecting the worst. The lorry sounded a lethargic horn as it swerved to avoid the dead taxi in its path. We decided to try one more push and as we gathered speed the engine sputtered into life. We jumped back into the vehicle as the driver revved the engine without comment, and ground it into gear. The back seat had come away from its moorings and was wedged down beneath the front seats, one corner sticking out of my door so that it wouldn't close. I had to hold the door to as we continued our stately progress up the coast road. We all held our breath as we turned off the tarmac on to a sandy track leading the final mile or so to the stadium.

Gangs of kids materialised out of the darkness to sell cigarettes and we pushed our way through the entrance and on to the parched bald grass of the stadium. The main stand was slowly filling up and a small crowd stood in front of the stage at one end of the pitch where a Mozambican group of ten or more were doing their stuff. There were bands from Mozambique and South Africa on the schedule and white roadie technicians, all cowboy boots and pigtails, supped beers at the makeshift elevated stand loaded with mixers and loudspeakers. At its foot, soldiers wearing combat fatigues and white helmets smoked cigarettes while leaning on their AK-47s or nursing their Uzi sub-machine guns.

Eduardo Mondlane's daughter, a well-known singer, took the stage. Her first song was about revolution. As the evening wore on, the entire football pitch was covered in dancing spectators of all ages, shapes and sizes, limbs and joints moving in perfect rhythm to the music. One of the soldiers, who was chatting up a young woman, swayed his hips to the music while propped on his assault rifle. A faint haze of dust rose into the air to catch the flashing lights from the stage.

There are all sorts of motivations for foreigners to give things to Mozambique, as to other developing countries. In many cases there is certainly altruism, a genuine desire to help others less fortunate, to relieve suffering and to improve the lot of the recipients. But there is often a degree of self-interest in the generosity too. Assistance given directly by a particular country, so-called 'bilateral' aid, usually entails goods or services from the donor, so it can be seen as a way of helping employment at home. Other forms of aid are more overtly commercial; they come as loans which must be paid back over varying periods.

All these motivations were mentioned to me when I was talking to people in the aid business in Mozambique. Some I spoke with were adherents of the conspiracy theory: that aid was a tool to recolonise Mozambique, removing power from the government and rebuilding the war-shattered country as the donors saw fit. Several others thought that the billion dollars a year flowing into the country was a form of guilt money – foreign governments paying off their moral debts for failing to prevent the destabilisation of the country through Renamo activities. Estimates confirm the degree of their guilt: between 1980 and 1988, the war had cost Mozambique an incredible fifteen billion US dollars, while the total foreign aid to Mozambique over the period was about a quarter of that amount.

Some aid workers, however, were not convinced that what they were doing was ultimately necessary, although they would never say as much on the record. When I asked one top employee of an international agency how much longer he thought his aid programme should continue after the war ended, he shrugged and said, 'Sometimes I think there was never any need. It's the need of the international community.'

Irrespective of whether or not their country needs foreign help, most Mozambicans are aware that the army of aid workers who have invaded their country are often a good touch in the day-to-day course of events. This realisation starts from an early age. One Sunday morning, a group of us took a stroll down to the beach stretching north of the city. We had lunch among the pine trees at the edge of the beach, within sight of the towering multi-storey skeleton of a hotel started by the Portuguese in the twilight of their rule but never finished. It is a well-known Maputo landmark overlooking the long stretch of golden sands and symptomatic of the country in many ways. The block remains unused because at independence the Portuguese builders poured cement down the pipes and lift shafts before they left.

We ate fried chicken and chips and drank cans of beer, called Laurentina, brewed in Maputo. A small, well-dressed blonde Russian girl played on a broken see-saw and a Mozambican boy, also about five or six years old, approached to rock her up and down from the other end of the see-saw. Alex's girlfriend, Betinha, asked the boy, who wore a torn T-shirt and grubby shorts, 'Why are you pushing her?'

'Because she will give me something afterwards,' the boy replied.

Sure enough, when the girl tired of her game on the seesaw, she gave the boy a sweet as payment in kind.

The employees of aid organisations I met were driven by a diverse range of motivations. At one extreme I came across people genuinely committed to helping Mozambique, by saving lives, training people or building new infrastructure. At the other, there were a few arrogant, self-important individuals who had little interest in Mozambique except as a place which enabled them to make a lot of money, tax free, and have a lifestyle a good deal better than if they stayed at home. I am not sure whether it is fair to expect a high degree of compassion in people employed in a business whose *raison d'etre* is to help others less fortunate than themselves – a job is a job after all, but I was surprised by some of those I came across.

It is easy to be dismissive of people who turn up in the poorest country in the world and check into a flash international hotel while they wait to be fitted out with a smart air-conditioned house and a specially freighted car. Most never ventured outside Maputo, happy to live in a little piece of ersatz Europe and complain about the poor quality restaurants and the price of South African goods in the shops while the people they came to help lived in neolithic poverty, had never been in a restaurant and came across South African produce only when they were staring down the barrel of an automatic weapon.

The contradictions would have been less offensive if all the foreign aid workers were contributing something useful to Mozambique, but this was not always the case. Some were no-good wasters, who did little more than sit behind their desks all day. These desks had a dual purpose: as a surface on which a new pair of shoes could be worn in, or on which pieces of paper, colour coded and in quadruplicate, could be sorted ready to pass on to other no-good wasters. The UN appeared to be best at this – an international bureaucracy which fuelled itself in a perpetual motion of faxes, telexes, requisition orders and special service agreements.

At the other end of the spectrum was a special breed of men and women who thrived on the challenge and endless workload, who were for ever pulling out all the stops to get something done despite the bureaucrats. They were adrenalin junkies who never stopped battling to achieve some progress in a country which is one of the worst messes humankind has yet concocted.

Jean-Luc Friedrich appeared to be one of these people. He headed one of the many disaster-oriented UN acronyms known as UNDRO, the UN Disaster Relief Organization. He was a powerfully built man with an egg-shaped head, a barrel for a chest and a handshake that could have been used for cracking coconuts. I met him in his office on Rua Francisco Barreto in Maputo, where an electric fan was doing its best to carve up the thick humid atmosphere.

His operation dealt in non-food relief, he explained, peering at me through his large round spectacles and speaking with a calm French accent. This covered everything from cooking pots and shovels to electric generators, blankets and tents. UNDRO had been working with the government – he stressed that – for four years. His team was a small one, light on bureaucrats, strong on action. It consisted of himself, a secretary, an assistant, a UN Volunteer and two Mozambican operators in the field. When the UNDRO operation in Mozambique started up in 1989 all their distribution had been by airlift, using DC3s. They had provided disaster relief to 90,000 people in five provinces. By 1993 the operation was working in eight of Mozambique's ten provinces and catering for about 200,000 people in need, with a budget of two million dollars.

'I buy the materials from local markets as far as possible,' Friedrich explained. This avoided a problem caused by many other aid operations, which often succeeded in destroying some of Mozambique's few remaining manufacturing industries by swamping the market with imported products they could have bought locally.

Warehouses had been established in Maputo, Beira and Quelimane so that needs could be responded to as quickly as possible. UNDRO specialised in the more inaccessible areas since they had more money at their disposal than most of the NGOs which did similar work, but at ten dollars a head for the whole operation the cost was still small. UNDRO worked with DPCCN, the government Department for the Prevention and Combat of Natural Disasters, or 'Calamidades' as it was known to rural Mozambicans. In more recent times, agreements with Renamo had allowed distribution to be made with DPCCN trucks rather than by airlift, a far preferable method since truck delivery was a tenth of the cost of an airlift, and far more could be carried by a fleet of trucks.

'But we have had some problems with DPCCN,' Friedrich told me, 'things can go missing. We cannot watch them all the time.' Thieving was at its worst when the DPCCN men were not paid by the government, a not infrequent occurrence. 'So we have to pay their salary for them,' he said.

Corruption and stealing from aid hand-outs is a relatively

recent phenomenon in Mozambique. Many aid workers thought that they were partly to blame because pilfering and corruption had not been stamped out when they first began. The temptation to filch the odd blanket or shovel must have been great for individuals entrusted with large quantities of free goods, particularly when wages, if and when they arrived, were small. If you got away with one blanket on the first occasion, why not take two the next time? And so on. For this reason some NGOs had begun to insist that distribution took place only when one of their staff members could be on hand to supervise. But this often meant that badly needed goods sat in a warehouse for weeks awaiting the arrival of a supervisor while the need outside was infinite.

'We have a very detailed distribution method,' Friedrich told me. He opened a drawer in his desk and pulled out a sheaf of dog-eared papers. 'Every family in a district is listed,' he said as he pushed the wad of paper across the desk, 'with number of members specified, and children by sex and age. We need to know this data so that we can bring the right amounts of clothing in correct sizes. But no system is fool-proof,' he continued. 'This family says they have eight children,' his finger followed a row across a series of columns on the page I was holding, 'it is in a Renamo-held district. Families are larger on average in these areas, where polygamy is common. If we count only six children with the mother and she tells us one is sick and another is away fetching water, how can we know these children exist?' He gave me a Gallic shrug with his wide shoulders. 'Always some things will go missing. I see our materials on sale in a local market, but it is impossible to control totally.'

The free goods that end up in a market are not always the result of procuring a bit extra by devious means, however. 'We bring bars of soap, but some people have never seen soap before. They don't know what to do with this thing, so they sell it.'

'Can't you tell people what it's for?' I asked.

'There is usually someone who will know that soap is for washing, but not everyone will find out.'

He rummaged in his desk drawer and brought out a pile of large format colour photographs which he passed to me. 'These are taken in Zambézia province,' he said. The photographs showed Friedrich and his team handing out clothing, soap and utensils to queues of patient Mozambicans. 'For this convoy we used a private transport company – they are protected by private soldiers who pick up a gun each, ride on the trucks and hand in their weapons on return to base. These companies insure the convoy in transit,' he told me, 'anything that is stolen the company pays us three times its value in compensation.'

The presence in Mozambique of Mr Friedrich and his UNDRO troubleshooters was of course a reflection of the country's poverty-stricken status. Mozambique was broke, and bankruptcy had forced it to go cap in hand to the international community for cash. One of the central strings attached to the provision of this money was the adoption of a 'structural adjustment program', a ruse thought up by that global economic double-act, the International Monetary Fund and the World Bank. The petty corruption, and some not so petty, which Friedrich had to deal with, the growth of private companies competing with government set-ups, and Mozambicans' low wages, which were often not paid at all, were all results, intentional and otherwise, of Mozambique's structural adjustment programme.

The IMF and the World Bank are extremely influential institutions in the developing world. Both grew out of the 1944 Bretton Woods conference, which was called to sort out the global economy in the aftermath of the Second World War. They are in reality quite different institutions. The World Bank is a specialised agency of the UN, although in practice its links with the UN are pretty tenuous, and provides cheap loans for projects in developing countries. The IMF is not an aid agency but is so intimately involved in providing finance to the world's poorer countries that it has become an integral part of the whole aid game. Both institutions have their headquarters within spitting distance of each other in Washington, DC, and both are largely controlled by the world's rich countries. They work closely together, and agreements with these bodies are virtually essential to poor countries wanting aid. Without such agreements, most other potential donors show little interest.

Structural adjustment is one of the prices most poor countries pay for joining the IMF/World Bank club, and it is supposed to get the country going again. It means less government, freer trade and more private enterprise. In practice, it is usually a bitter medicine: public spending on health and schools is cut and prices for food, housing and transport rise because of the removal of subsidies. These programmes are being implemented all over Africa. Their critics (including some in the World Bank itself) say that they do not work; that all they do is 'screw the poor' and allow the rich to get richer. In Mozambique there was a still larger question-mark hanging over the wisdom of the men in smart suits from Washington. Mozambique was a country in the middle of a civil war, and the World Bank had never tried a structural adjustment programme on a country at war before.

Alex and his colleagues at the Ministry of Planning had already come up against the inconsistencies of the situation. One of the conditions of the programme was to curb the numbers of government employees, and under its terms the government was not allowed to take on new staff. The questionable wisdom of this rigid philosophy can be illustrated in just one area: education. The war with Renamo had resulted in the destruction or closure of close on 3000 schools. Rebuilding schools was thus an important aspect of the post-war reconstruction programme, but while new schools could be built, the government was not allowed to employ teachers to teach in them.

To some extent, it seemed that corruption was also an offshoot of structural adjustment. The value of salaries had fallen because of the programme. A free market meant that there were more goods in the shops, but they were available only to those who could afford them. With structural adjustment fewer could. For the large majority of Mozambicans all it meant was that they could now enjoy a new pastime while they went hungry: window-shopping. Many families could only manage on two incomes, or with the bread-winner doing some moonlighting on the side. In such an environment corruption became an increasingly attractive proposition simply to survive.

There was no question that people in the cities were being squeezed hard. A friend of Alex's was a personal secretary to a top administrator in the Ministry of Agriculture, a good job by any standards. She earned 120,000 meticais a month, about £25. She lived with her five-year-old son in a two-bedroomed apartment in Maputo's concrete city, for which she paid 8000 meticais monthly in rent. The cost of water and electricity had been hiked from about 10,000 meticais a year before to 43,000 meticais a month. This left her with 2,300 meticais a day, about 50 pence. She could afford to buy bread and rice and a few vegetables, but meat was a luxury; other basics such as shoes and clothing were beyond her.

This young woman had a well-paid job, and she did at least receive her salary each month. Many others were not so lucky. Shortly after I arrived in Mozambique, the headline news in the Maputo daily newspaper *Noticias*, described a demonstration by *mutilados*, Frelimo war-wounded. Several hundred disabled veterans had massed on National Highway Number Two to protest at not having received their state disability pensions for the past eight months. Their recompense for losing limbs for their country was 6000 meticais (just over £1) a month, only they weren't getting it. Alex had been there and he described the bizarre spectacle. A squad of fully limbed soldiers had been sent to stand guard over the crippled protesters. Alex had exchanged a few words with one of the active servicemen.

'Life is hard for them,' he said gesturing towards the *mutilados*.

'Life is hard for everyone in Mozambique,' came the reply, 'it is just a bit harder for them.'

Squeezing the people living in cities was one of the basic ideas behind structural adjustment, the notion being to provide more for those in the countryside. This might be a good philosophy in many poor countries where urban-based politicians focus too much on the cities, but in Mozambique the city was the only place where the government had any serious influence. To redistribute resources to the rural areas was meaningless, since the government controlled hardly any rural areas. But it made little difference to the sharp-suited loan sharks from the First World. They called the shots, and structural adjustment was what they were selling. If Mozambique didn't like it she knew what she could do.

Numerous studies had shown that the programme was making large numbers of people poorer and less healthy, so the World Bank tacked on a charity component to help out a few target groups. That children were now out on the city streets selling cigarettes and chewing-gum when they should still have had schools to go to – well, sorry. It was not relevant that during World War Two European governments intervened in the market to control prices of essentials, while Mozambique, facing a war twice as long, was being told to loosen up. That was different (no it wasn't, except, you have to say it, World War Two was a white man's war). Hang on in there, the World Bank was saying, things do get worse before they get better. It was not sufficient that Mozambique had been brought to its knees by the war with Renamo, a war fuelled by the bully boy rich world. Life was miserable for many Mozambicans who had been victims of atrocities or driven from their homes, but it was not bad enough for those lucky ones in the cities, whose friends and relatives in the countryside had been hacked to pieces or reduced to starvation. Now it was their turn. If the war hadn't got you, structural adjustment would.

In their own way, the World Bank gurus were adrenalin junkies too. They could identify a screwed-up economy when they saw one and they had the answer. Lending money was their business and structural adjustment was their gospel. To the cynical observer, it seems that their idea of a good time is to fly into a country, check into a five-star hotel which costs more for one night than the average Mozambican earns in a year, and force a government to make their people, already the poorest in the world, even poorer. It must be quite a buzz.

The longer I stayed in Mozambique, the more tenable the conspiracy theory became. Structural adjustment seemed to be putting the final kibosh on Frelimo's dreams; the Western white world was going to push Mozambicans around until they came to their senses. For a brief eighteen years they had got above themselves, dreaming of free schools and health care for all, an equal society. They had to learn to lie down and take it again like proper black people.

I had seen the situation in the city and was keen to get out into some rural areas. I was already beginning to feel the customary guilt and moral dilemmas that all well-brought-up, sensitive white people are supposed to face when they go to a poor black country. The feelings were stronger in Mozambique than anywhere else I had seen, and I was sure they would get worse still in the countryside. In a sense I was no different from the aid workers who I felt high and mighty enough to be rude about; but perhaps not quite so bad. I was not pretending to help directly, I was there to observe. By writing a book about it, I was making some small contribution by showing people what it is like in Mozambique. That was my excuse anyway. Observing was all I could really do; I could never be a part of it since I always had the option of jumping on a plane and getting out should it get too awful. And, if I was going to be a voyeur I might as well do it properly. I had not seen any starving children yet or any serious war damage. I felt cheated. I went to see Oxfam.

They have their Maputo offices on Avenida Patrice Lumumba, a long straight tree-lined street which descends diagonally across the old cliff face towards downtown. Thabi Mngadi, their bright country representative from South Africa, was in her office in the ground floor of a building which overlooked the container ships in the bay. As I sat outside her office waiting for her to become less busy, I flicked through a copy of *Oxfam News*. It carried a report about modern-day slave traders operating in Mozambique's war-torn southern provinces. These people were offering jobs in South Africa to men, women and children who were not aware that they were being sold into slavery. Girls were sold as concubines, boys were made to work in township liquor stores in return for food and clothing, and labourers worked for 'starvation wages' on white-owned farms. Just like old times again.

Thabi Mngadi had been in Mozambique since 1987, and things had changed a lot in that time, she told me. 'Mozambique has been lost,' she said. 'When I first arrived, people I met wanted to know me to form a relationship, they wanted to know me as a person rather than for what I represented. Now I am never sure whether a friendly approach is entirely without hidden motives.'

Oxfam was one of the longer-standing NGOs in Mozambique, having arrived in 1984. In those early days, their programme was geared to emergency response in central and southern provinces. They now have a two-pronged programme, continuing with emergency aid but also doing longer-term development work. For instance, 'We try to respond to grassroots needs,' Thabi told me, 'to supply a community with a grinding mill, or some scythes to cut reeds for basket-making.'

Oxfam's relationship with the government was tricky at times; there were clashes over their different approaches to development. Some government employees were still geared to a 'mega' approach, wanting to concentrate on huge prestige projects. Thabi felt there was also still some resentment towards NGOs, since it was often they who had a better idea of what was going on outside the cities. Many were richer than the government, they could afford to hire planes to fly to remote places cut off by the war. Without lifts from NGOs, local government administrators would not have been able to do nearly so much. The reliance upon foreigners inevitably bred discontent at times.

I saw Thabi Mngadi a couple of times before she agreed to let me visit one of Oxfam's workers in the field. Now that she had spoken to me, she felt that a trip would be OK. She had to be careful; in the past Oxfam had been accused of taking Renamo agents into the bush, masquerading as journalists or writers.

6

THE EDGE OF THE WORLD

I flew to Niassa province in the north-west. One aid worker I spoke to called it the 'Siberia of Mozambique'. A Western diplomat in Maputo told me that there was a saying about Lichinga, the provincial capital: 'If it's not the edge of the world, you can certainly see it from there.'

It seemed like just the place I was looking for.

I was awakened in the early hours of the morning of my flight by the sound of small-arms fire in my bedroom. I climbed out of bed smelling the acrid whiffs of cordite on the air as further loud cracks echoed from the shots fired outside, but it was impossible to see anything from my room, so I returned to my bed. Just as I got back to sleep the howling, barking and squealing of a cacophony of dogs woke me again. These were the usual sounds of the small hours in cement city Maputo.

One of Alex's colleagues picked Alex and me up from the house in his Lada at five thirty and we drove to the airport for the flight to Lichinga in one of Linhas Aéreas de Moçambique's new Boeing 737s. The café was not open for an early morning shot of coffee and we left at seven. A kid on the flight was dressed in a Colonel Gadaffi sand-coloured military outfit complete with peaked cap. We were served with LAM breakfast, the same as LAM lunch and LAM dinner: a round cotton-wool roll containing a sliver of omelette, and a sad, dry cake.

The flight touched down at Beira where the tarmac was choc-a-bloc with Antonovs commandeered for emergency food airlifts, their huge engines mounted above the wings.

New United Nations and World Food Programme markings had been slapped on alongside their former Aeroflot insignia.

We met a Polish friend of Alex's during a brief stopover at Nampula. He told us that the previous day's UN mission to Lichinga had been cancelled for fear of unrest, as the army in Niassa had not been paid for several months. Throughout the continuing flight north-west to Niassa the view from the window revealed endless fires, their smoke blending to give a milky background to the candyfloss clouds. As we descended towards Lichinga I could see blocks of coniferous plantations surrounding the town, standing in sharp contrast to the brick red soil. I was to learn that these trees were under increasing threat from firewood-hungry *deslocados* holed up around the provincial capital.

There was no one to meet us at the airstrip in Lichinga. Outside the small terminal building stood two lines of government and aid agency vehicles and a four-wheel drive pick-up full of government soldiers awaiting the arrival of the provincial governor. The troops looked docile enough beneath the blazing sun, clutching their pieces of heavy iron and not about to cause unrest. Alex was here on a visit to the provincial planning office, and I was supposed to be meeting the Oxfam representative. All I knew about her was that she was Dutch, and that her name was Els. I strolled around the groups of people waiting in the midday heat, trying to identify suitable candidates, and drew a complete blank.

We waited for half an hour. A man sitting in a truck told us that Lichinga had been without water and electricity for the last week. Food was not a problem, he said, there were always potatoes and beans to eat.

A diminutive, middle-aged white woman appeared from the direction of the airstrip with a spring in her step. She had a small button of a nose and her hair was up in what had been a bun before it had started to unfurl. She seemed to be looking for someone. I moved over to her and asked if that someone was me. It was. Els pushed some unruly locks back up on to her head and asked if I was ready.

'We are going to Cuamba,' she said.

I grabbed my hold-all, bade farewell to Alex, and followed her back to a corner of the airstrip where a cream-coloured, six-seater Piper Cherokee sat on the tarmac.

Niassa is Mozambique's largest and least populated province. It is the size of three Belgiums and a Holland but has only enough people to fill two Wembley stadiums. It is mostly made up of a high plateau, and its remoteness was accentuated by the fact that the railway line running to Lichinga, an offshoot of a main track which links the Indian Ocean port of Nacala with the Malawian city of Blantyre, was in poor repair thanks to Renamo attacks. A train struggled up to Lichinga every few months, and the journey of around 250 kilometres often took several weeks. People joked that, to allow the train to pass, the passengers had to spend most of that time carrying sleepers from behind the train to patch up destroyed stretches of track in front.

Our small aircraft followed the track south-eastward to Cuamba, the town at the junction with the main line, where Oxfam had their operational base for work in the south of the province. From the air, bundles of cut rushes gave fields a braided pattern, echoing the plaited hairstyles of Mozambican women. Other fields were littered with patches of white ash where newly felled trees had been burnt to return some goodness to the soil.

Cuamba was a pleasant little railway junction town. It was also a government military base, so it was safe and operated as normally as anywhere could in war-torn Mozambique. Trains running on the stretch of track from the Malawian border to Nampula were protected by the Malawian military and Cuamba was one of their bases too. Off-duty soldiers wandered to and fro along the sleepy streets, the Malawians distinguishable from government troops by their dark green fatigues, as opposed to Frelimo's camouflage variety. Many of Cuamba's consumer goods supplies, such as soap, drinks and cigarettes, were brought in from Malawi, and the town's shops and kiosks were well stocked for a remote Mozambican settlement. There was a pretty reliable electricity supply too, generated by a small hydroelectric installation built in 1988 with Norwegian aid. It sat high in the towering granite range which rose abruptly to overlook the town in its pancake flat landscape. But hardly a stretch of Cuamba's roads could boast tarmac and there was no telephone link with the outside world. Els had to communicate with the Oxfam office in Maputo by radio.

Oxfam's programme in southern Niassa was largely concerned with emergency work, organising and monitoring food and non-food relief. The priority was to help people displaced by the war by providing them with seeds, tools and clothing. The situation was changing rapidly in the period when I visited Naissa in September 1992, since hopes were high that the Peace Accord would be signed in Rome and refugees from camps in Malawi were beginning to return to their villages. Oxfam did not distribute food aid in Niassa, but they did pay for some of it, and so were involved in monitoring distribution to make sure that it got to those who needed it. All the villages in their remit were accessible only by air because of the security situation, so the chartered Piper Cherokee Six was in constant use and its pilot, a willowy man of about thirty named Artur, was effectively one of the Oxfam crowd.

Els, the only European, had quite a large team: a young assistant named Bernado, a smiling driver, and Senhor Marcelino who cooked meals in the makeshift headquarters housed in a former tea company's building where Els lived and a large room served as dining room, lounge and office. Most of the team were therefore support staff, and since Bernado had only recently begun his job, Els was effectively a one-woman whirlwind of energy. She seemed to work virtually nonstop, her stamina was endless, and she was invariably good-humoured. She smoked heavily and drank beer to relax in the evenings, although she told me that she would have preferred sherry if it had been available. She was also remarkably open and trusting with me. Shortly after I arrived she told me that she had played host to several journalists since she had first come to Niassa in 1988. She had not found many of them particularly sympathetic characters, and the dangers for her and for Oxfam of opening up too much to the press had been brought home to her when a Dutch film crew had followed her around. Els was divorced and had two children at home in the Netherlands. The film they shot was broadcast in a 'mother abandons her kids to work in the Third World' vein, which had upset her. She would much rather have had her children with her, she told me, but their education would suffer if they lived in Niassa. She had been away from Europe for so long now that she could not imagine living there again during her working life. The materialism and preoccupation with things she considered unimportant would have got her down. She saw her children when she was on home leave, and they visited her in Mozambique during their summer holidays.

Much of Els's time was spent shuttling back and forth between Cuamba and the villages which were in the Oxfam programme. The use of the plane meant that this was an expensive business for Oxfam, but travel overland would have met with ambushes, and the speed of air travel meant that a lot more could be done. The day after I arrived in Cuamba we took off for Mecanhelas, a sizeable village to the south-west about fifteen kilometres from the Malawian border.

As we approached Mecanhelas at about 5000 feet, a gigantic puddle which was marked on the map as Lake Chilwa shimmered beyond the village. Cattle were grazing in the marshes at the edge of lake and three canoes were grouped around a large gossamer fishing net. The first white man to see Lake Chilwa was David Livingstone, the Scottish missionary, who spent several years exploring in and around Mozambique in the nineteenth century. He 'discovered' the lake in April 1859, approaching it from the south on a little sortie from his central mission, which was to explore the Zambezi River. His sortie was not an easy one. No sane guide could be hired to take him there for love or money, he wrote in his diary, so he had to rely on a succession of madmen to lead him. When he reached the shore of the lake, he found leeches, fishes, crocodiles and hippopotami wallowing in the waters, which tasted like a solution of weak Epsom salts.

We landed at Mecanhelas on the rough airstrip beside the village. A small gaggle of children congregated to watch as we taxied to a halt and climbed out of the aircraft. Els was buying seed from local farmers to give to *deslocados* in the area, and she was here to check on how the scheme was going and to see how many refugees were returning to the district from camps in Malawi. Mecanhelas's position close to the border meant that it was a major entry point for returnees.

Our first stop was the small office of DPCCN, the government natural disaster agency, which was a three-minute stroll from the airstrip. The Mecanhelas DPCCN representative, a man in his late twenties wearing a smart lemon-yellow sweatshirt with a thistle embroidered on the breast above the word 'Deeside', sat behind his desk made of old wooden crates. Around his neck a medallion of the Pope hung from a thick golden chain. His well-spruced appearance was in stark contrast to his poky office. Two curling, sun-bleached posters advertising past Frelimo Party congresses decorated the grotty whitewashed walls.

Els greeted him and got straight down to discussing the numbers of returning refugees and *deslocados*. The DPCCN man's assistant, also a young fellow, whose short-sleeved shirt said that he was 'Colin from Paper Mart', dug out a sheaf of dog-eared school exercise book pages from a wooden box and handed them to the man from Deeside. He held them sideways on his desk for Els to see and leafed through the pages of neatly written figures. The numbers of refugees crossing the border from Malawi and entering his district had increased significantly in recent months. The data showed that nearly 500 had arrived in the previous month alone, compared to a total of 2233 for the entire previous year.

Els lit a cigarette and opened the pages of her notebook to jot down the figures. Then she turned to me. 'I am suspicious of this man's figures,' she said in English, 'they inflate the numbers and so they get more relief which they can then use for themselves. I do not believe this number for last year's total returnees.'

She took a drag on her cigarette, swept some loose hair from her eyes, and looked squarely at the man from Deeside with a half smile. The clean-cut man in yellow returned her stare. She was like a schoolteacher quizzing a mildly naughty schoolboy and waiting for the truth to be told. Els stabbed her finger at the dog-eared pages on the desk. 'These are real figures?' she asked.

'Real figures,' the man from Deeside said unequivocally. He understood what she was getting at. 'There is no fiddling of numbers here in this district to get more aid,' he added with an emphatic wave of his hand.

A child of maybe two or three years of age had wandered into the little office through the open door and squatted on the floor picking its nose. The child's mother sat in the doorway chatting to a group of women huddled against the building's overhang to escape the hot sun.

'Are there any Malawians coming here with the returning refugees?' Els asked the DPCCN man. She had heard rumours in other districts that Malawian peasants were leaving their homeland to move to Mozambique now that the war was nearing its end. Malawi is a heavily populated country and the prospect of being given a plot of land in Mozambique, where population pressure was much less intense, was an attractive one. The man from Deeside shook his head.

'There are no Malawians coming to this district,' he said.

In practice it was often well nigh impossible to distinguish between a returning Mozambican refugee and a Malawian who was after a new start in life. Few of either group had identity documents of any kind and Malawians from the area near this part of the border would be from the same ethnic group as Mozambicans from Niassa; they would look the same and would speak the same language. Asking people who turned up in the Mecanhelas district which of the two country's official European languages they could speak – English in Malawi's case, Portuguese in Mozambique's – was also a pretty ineffective way of distinguishing between the two groups, since few peasants spoke their country's official language.

A young girl entered the office and strode across to the kid who had finished picking its nose and had started to totter towards the piles of packing cases at the end of the office. She plucked the infant up, sat it on her hip and left the room.

'And *deslocados*?' Els asked.

The man from Deeside flicked through his wad of paper and pointed to some figures. About one hundred had arrived in the last couple of months, having fled the fighting in the neighbouring province of Zambézia. Els noted the number down in her notebook.

We left the man from Deeside and Colin from Paper Mart and squinted as we walked out into the glaring sunshine. We passed a group of women dressed in vividly patterned *capelanas*, who were standing patiently beneath a spreading mango tree waiting to use a maize grinder powered by a petrol generator which chugged along in a half-built brick building. A small market sold needles from China, plastic bowls, pencils and Lever Brothers soap from Malawi, and finger-long fish from Lake Chilwa. I commented on the size of the fish to the boy sitting behind the length of matting on which they were displayed and he told me that they would start catching bigger fishes the next month.

Els and I walked down a long dusty track towards the house where the official from Agricom, the state agricultural marketing agency, had his office.

'Always I have to let the DPCCN man know that I will not accept figures which he just makes up,' Els explained as we passed a large peppermint-coloured stone church with a yellow bell tower. 'On one occasion he told me there were six hundred returned refugees in various villages in this district. I went to four of the villages and didn't find a single one.'

We turned off the track and headed towards a neat little wooden house. 'We have a seed-buying programme operated by Agricom,' Els told me, 'we supply a float and they have a team of buyers who go around the farmers and purchase their surplus grain which we then give to returning refugees and *deslocados*.' We were inside the building now and a young man wearing a yellow Fred Perry T-shirt and bright white plimsolls shook our hands. Posters warning of the dangers of pests and the proper precautions to take when using pesticides were hung on the walls. The young man ushered us into his office and went to sit behind his desk. I sat on a wicker two-person settee and Els positioned herself on a chair at the desk opposite the Agricom official. Silhouettes of lions, zebra and water buffalo were picked out in green on the dirty white curtain which hung from a piece of string above the mosquito mesh at the window. It was dark inside the office after the bright sunlight, but there was no point in switching on the single light bulb which hung from the ceiling because Mecanhelas had no electricity.

Els asked to see the seed-buying records. Each purchase was recorded on a standard form, the seller filling in the amount of grain sold to Agricom and the price received, signing for the transaction in the end column. Els produced a pocket calculator from her bag and began to key in the amounts. She asked the Agricom official how much he had left in the float. He unlocked a drawer down to his left and started to pile wads of grubby meticais notes on to his desk. As Els keyed in the numbers he began to count the money.

Time passed slowly as they became engrossed in their counting missions. The air inside the Agricom office was still and every now and again a bead of sweat trickled from my armpit down the inside of my upper arm. A solitary fly glided back and forth from a scabby tropical ulcer that had developed on my shin, lazily avoiding my attempts to brush it off and floating in a wide arc to return to the target of congealed blood on my leg. Neat piles of meticais were mounting up on the desk top beside the plastic pen holder. Eventually, Els jotted down the total spent in her notebook. She asked the Agricom man how much he had left in his float, and she wrote that figure down too. There was a pause as she bashed away at her pocket calculator some more. She looked at him.

'Are you sure that's how much you have left?' she asked him.

He nodded, 'Yes senhora,' and he gestured to the piles of cash sitting on the desk between them.

'That means there is 350,000 meticais missing,' Els said.

The Agricom man shrugged, he did not seem too concerned at this announcement.

'What has happened to this money?'

He shrugged again. 'It is impossible to record everything,' he said weakly.

She looked at him sternly. 'I suppose I shall have to count it now,' she said picking up one of the piles of notes. She handed me another and we set about confirming the figure Mr Agricom had come up with.

As we neared the end of our recount another Agricom official appeared. The two men conversed in low tones. Our count confirmed the shortfall and there followed a mildly heated discussion as to the whereabouts of the missing 350,000 meticais, a sum which was probably equivalent to about a third of their annual salaries. The two Agricom men kept insisting that it was impossible to record every transaction. The second man adopted a rather obstreperous attitude, and implied that Els was being unreasonably pernickety. The man in the yellow Fred Perry shirt maintained an unconvincing air of hurt innocence throughout, as if it did not really have much to do with him and any suggestion that it did would be taken as a personal slight on his character, which of course it was. They kept insisting that the odd lapse in recording a transaction was a completely normal state of affairs. Between outbursts, they would look into various corners of the room as if in hope that Els would give up on the issue and they could all forget about it. She did not give up, and each time she asked again where the money had gone she was met with a fresh outburst from the Mr Nasty and Mr Nice routine. Then one of the men suggested that maybe the money had been stolen. They could not keep it in their sight all the time and perhaps someone had crept off with it while their backs were turned. Els looked unimpressed. They both shrugged again.

'We have to find this money,' Els told them, 'we can't just forget about it.' More shrugs and another pained expression from the man in the Fred Perry shirt.

This time it was Els's turn to shrug. The Agricom men were paid a daily allowance for travelling and board and lodging while they were in the villages buying grain. She told them the missing money would have to come out of their daily allowances. They appeared to be unhappy about this, but Els said it in such a firm manner that they had no option but to accept. We left the Agricom building after a rather strained farewell.

Els was in little doubt that the men had pocketed the money. It was a fairly common occurrence, she told me as we made our way back towards the airstrip. Oxfam would not bear such losses, since they considered them a sign of bad management by the field worker. Els had learned the hard way to hold the daily allowances back until after a buying programme had been completed, since she had paid out of her own pocket for similar disappearances of Oxfam money in the past.

It was depressing to see how much of her time was spent keeping an eye on petty local officials and their pastime of stealing aid. Els was of the opinion that some of the blame for this was to be laid at the feet of the aid donors for not stamping it out when it first started. Now there seemed to be a continual game to see what freebies they could siphon off without being found out. Certainly all the local officials I met who were involved in aid in some form or another, and that meant all of them, were markedly better dressed than most other rural Mozambicans I came across; this was probably an indicator of some success in their activities. But at the same time I had some sympathy for their situation: life was difficult for government officials who often went many months without being paid. Besides, it could be argued that the odd bag of sugar here or bottle of oil there was one of the perks of the job. Most people working for organisations the world over have taken office pens home or made personal phone calls from work and thought little of it. Drawing the line between a legitimate perk and corruption was often a matter of personal morality. The sad aspect of Mozambique's case was that corruption of any kind had been virtually non-existent until a few years before. Several foreigners I spoke to, who had known the country for a long time, told me that corruption had been absent at all levels, from government ministers to the lowliest bureaucrat, in the early post-independence years, but there was now an increasing feeling of everyone for himself. The sense of working together and helping each other which had characterised the first years of independence had been eroded.

Corruption was by no means limited to the local level or the small scale, however. Oxfam had had several run-ins with the provincial chief of DPCCN in Lichinga, whom they alleged had ripped them off to the tune of fourteen million meticais in 1989. Oxfam in Maputo had asked for the removal of the man in question, whom I had also heard described as a drunkard who spent more time in the bars of Lichinga than in his office. The request was not granted, and Els still had to deal with the man. Some of his subsequent actions suggested that he was responding in kind to Oxfam's accusations. When Els requested that new DPCCN administrative people be appointed to two districts to oversee Oxfam aid, this DPCCN head had surveyed his operation in Lichinga and chosen a telephone operator and a warehouse worker for the jobs and sent them to the districts without any training.

The same man was interviewed on Radio Mozambique when I was in Niassa. He called for more aid to Niassa since the drought was biting hard, particularly in the southern parts of the province. The claim was simply untrue; there was no drought in Niassa. Everyone I spoke to about this said he was after more aid which he could take his cut from.

During her day-to-day tasks, Els also had to be aware of other sensitivities while trying to limit the corruption. Being reduced to living off aid hand-outs did little for the self-respect of Mozambicans, and given the country's history the dominance of foreigners in the running of Mozambican affairs was unfortunate. Many of the local government officials I came across in Niassa relied heavily upon income from Oxfam schemes in the form of daily allowances, which meant they were additionally beholden to European powers. There was no room at the aid frontline for the faint-hearted. Els needed to be firm in dealing with corruption, but she did not want to cause unnecessary humiliation. She was also well aware that one of the dangers of giving aid over long periods is creating a dependency on hand-outs and removing the incentive for people to help themselves.

Els made every effort to scotch the idea that she was simply a representative of the latest generation of white people here to order Mozambicans around, but she would always be open to such an accusation. She was a representative of both a foreign power and the aid business, and it was distressing to see how many times the trust she was continually building with Mozambicans was undermined by her fellow aid workers, particularly those well away from Niassa, in the aircon offices of Maputo and various European capitals.

There had been several recent instances of this nature relating to grain buying. The owner of the small pension that I stayed at in Cuamba, a businessman with varied interests, had been commissioned by the European Community to purchase a hundred tonnes of grain locally which the EC would use as food aid. He was promised immediate payment when he had bought the grain, so he confidently borrowed money from the bank to do his purchasing. One evening as we were finishing our dinner the man knocked at the door of the makeshift office-cum-dining room in Cuamba. Nervous strain was written all over his face as he sat down to explain the situation to Els. Two weeks previously, he had sent a message to the EC in Maputo to say that he had now bought the hundred tonnes. He was still waiting for an acknowledgement of his message, let alone his money. The bank was hassling him for his loan to be repaid, since the bank manager knew that he had completed his side of the bargain and the businessman had told the bank manager that he would be paid immediately. Furthermore, the banks in Niassa had started to come down hard on debtors; only the previous week another businessman who had been unable to repay had most of the contents of his home taken as collateral.

The businessman was under pressure to repay his debt, the food was sitting in the warehouse while people in the neighbouring province of Zambézia were starving and the likelihood of their ever getting this particular hundred tonnes was rapidly diminishing since the businessman was now on the verge of selling the grain to Malawi, where he knew he would be paid immediately. This was by no means an isolated example. It was enough to bring tears to the eyes to see how easily confidence could be destroyed and ultimately people could die simply because someone was not doing their job properly.

Some days later, I travelled with Els to a village named Maúa to the north-east of Cuamba. As we drove the few kilometres to the airstrip, a Malawian military Dakota took off and banked over the town with a long-drawn-out drone from its engines. The plane was a regular visitor, flying in supplies

109

to the Malawian troops stationed at Cuamba, but rumours abounded in town that the Mozambican army had made an arrangement with the Malawians to sell them aid supplies meant for Mozambique; maize and blankets were spirited away from the Agricom warehouse on the edge of town to sell to the Malawians. Since the military had the guns and had not been paid for months there was little anyone could do about it.

We loaded up the small Oxfam plane with some blankets and clothes and climbed aboard. As usual we had a small contingent of people who were hitching a lift. Els was continually approached by people asking for lifts. There was a private light aircraft service which operated between some of the towns in Niassa, but it always seemed to be full and anyway Maúa was not one of the settlements served. Today, we had a large mother and her son, and a young nun on board.

Artur, the pilot, who was always meticulously turned out in well-pressed bush shorts, khaki shirt, dark glasses and a felt hat, went through the procedure of setting his compass and checking dials and asked if we had fastened our seat belts. He let in the throttle and taxied out to the runway. Two small children waved at us from the tall grasses at the edge of the airstrip as we sped along the black ribbon of tarmac and our wheels left the ground. As we turned north-east and climbed to our cruising altitude, Artur passed me his chart on which the route and compass bearing for Maúa were marked. The chart was made by the Defense Mapping Agency Aerospace Center of Saint Louis, Missouri. It was compiled in 1973 but had been revised in 1986, according to a small printed note at the bottom, and yet when I looked at the Niassa border region the frontier with Tanzania was marked 'Mozambique (Portugal)'. I pointed this out to Artur, who eyeballed the printed sheet. He smiled, and shouted above the sound of the engine, 'Eleven years after independence and the fucking Americans still say we belong to Portugal.'

As we circled Maúa, Artur cursed again, this time at a large termite mound which he had asked to be removed on his previous visit but still stood near the middle of the rough landing strip. The strip itself was short and I had to open my door to help slow us down as soon as our wheels touched the bumpy ground.

The nun we were carrying was joining a small group who called themselves the Missionary Sisters, and one of their number, dressed in a grey habit, met us at the airstrip to drive us the kilometre or so into the village. Government soldiers who were lounging by mounted machine guns, their AK-47s propped against nearby trees, took little notice as we bounced along in the Land Rover and crossed a narrow wooden bridge.

The nuns, most of whom were South American, were welcoming and offered us lunch in their airy house. We served ourselves spicy chicken and rice from the pots on the stove in the spotlessly clean kitchen and drank real coffee ground from beans which they grew in their garden. They ran a small girls' school in the village and a night shelter where villagers came to sleep, since the security zone around Maúa was very narrow. There was a large Renamo base just thirty-five kilometres away by foot and attacks were frequent. One of the sisters took me to see the girls who were sitting cross-legged beneath an open-air rush-roofed shade in the compound behind the house. They were singing a song as we approached and all stood to attention when they had finished and I was introduced. Each small face looked sincere and respectful. The kindly nun who was with me explained that they were unlikely to have much of a clue as to where England was. Few of the girls had been outside the Maúa district, and even Cuamba might have been on the moon as far as they were concerned.

We were in the Land Rover again, heading for a small village just beyond the edge of Maúa, outside the security cordon. Els had heard that this village was low on food. The poor security situation meant that many of the fields were too dangerous to cultivate, and peasants from other villages in the district were also congregated in and around Maúa for fear of being killed or kidnapped by Renamo. We arrived at a group of half a dozen neat huts with rush roofs near a well. The place seemed deserted. The huts were a health centre and maternity unit, but there did not seem to be any homesteads within sight. The local health worker materialised and led us down a slight incline towards a distant granite sugar-loaf dome. We came across flimsy reed huts with the odd woman and child milling around. There was no point in building more substantial mud huts since the village was often attacked at night and villagers had grown tired of returning from their safe sleeping in Maúa to find everything destroyed.

Els stopped at the first hut and called out to see whether anyone was at home. A woman emerged dressed in a *capelana* which depicted Mozambican bank notes on a red background. A second was wrapped around her waist to hold a baby tight to the small of her back. The woman did not speak Portuguese, so Els asked her through the health worker whether she minded telling her how much food she had. The woman looked unconcerned as she led us into the shack to see her larder, a wicker platform raised above the earth floor. On the platform sat a pile of dried mandioca, thick dark wizened tubers, and a few dried maize heads. Was that it? Els asked her. She nodded. We emerged into the sunlight once more and Els took a look at the baby sleeping on the woman's back. We thanked the woman and moved to another small compound of rush huts. 'That was about one month's food,' Els muttered to me as we approached the next hut.

A woman was sprawled in its shade, staring at a tiny baby which lay making slow-motion jiggling movements with its arms on a piece of dirty cloth spread on the dry clay. The woman hardly looked at us as we greeted her. She had given birth to the baby three days before, here in her hut since she had not been able to make it to the hospital in Maúa in time. Her breasts were wrinkled and wizened like the dried mandioca we had seen in the previous hut. Els asked her if she was feeding the infant. She nodded mechanically.

'Do you have enough to eat yourself?' Els enquired.

The woman continued to stare at her baby as she explained that she had eaten nothing today or yesterday, but had found some mandioca leaves to boil the day after the birth. Her husband was handicapped and they had lost their store of dried mandioca in a hut burnt in a Renamo raid the week before. Els asked why she had not tried to get to the hospital since there they had milk which the baby could drink and food for herself; the woman said that she had no money to pay for the hospital. Gently, Els explained that she did not have to pay, and told the woman that we would take her there when we drove back to Maúa.

We walked to other huts and looked at their stores of food. Most of them had the same piles of dried mandioca, sometimes with maize, in other cases with some dried black beans. But each hut also had separate stores of seeds, often wrapped in bark, which were being kept for the following year's planting. In some huts the seed store was kept at the bottom of dried mud vessels, in others it was preserved in a separate sealed mud container like a piggy bank. Els told me that she had never seen people resorting to eating the seed store. Even when they ran out of conventional food, they would not broach this precious hoard, since they knew that when they reached that stage, they were finished. In the meantime they gathered leaves and grubs from the bush to keep themselves going.

But the food situation was soon to become critical in this village. The piles of dried mandioca would last only a month or so, and the next harvest would not be for another five months. Dried mandioca had no vitamins, and the proximity of the Renamo base meant that gathering famine foods from the bush was a dangerous business.

We came upon another woman who was walking between huts en route to gather firewood. She was wearing a jute sack to cover her dignity and carried a child in a bundle on her back. Els looked at the large anaemic-looking head poking out from the roughly woven fabric, the eyes puffy and unseeing. The infant hardly moved as its mother released it from her back and unwrapped it like a mummy excavated from a tomb. Its little hands and feet were pock-marked with eczema and its belly was bloated.

I felt a strong sense of embarrassment at being a voyeur of the woman's distress as Els asked her how much food she had to give her child. She was reticent and uncomfortable when asked if she had any other offspring. We persuaded her to lead us to her hut where she said she had another, slightly older boy. By this time news of our presence had passed around the village and a fair-sized crowd of mostly young healthy-looking kids had gathered around us. We proceeded through the huts to this poor woman's home and she ducked into it to produce her other son. This child was in a worse condition: veins were protruding from his head, and although I hated myself for having such a thought, it looked as if he had been designed to appear in a film about semi-human creatures from outer space. The boy would die soon from severe malnutrition if he did not receive help. Els told the woman that we would take her too to the hospital.

As we continued to walk through the village, followed Pied Piper-like by a growing crowd of healthy juveniles, we found the same picture of one month's food. The early victims of malnutrition were, like the veiny-headed child in the hut, all hidden from view. There seemed to be a point at which people gave up and hid their children to die slowly in dignity, unaware that help was available free in the hospital in Maúa.

In only one hut did we find an old man whose food store was brimming. He had two large storage containers made from woven sticks and stuffed with mandioca, maize heads and beans, raised on rough wooden stilts outside his hut. He stood slightly bent from a life tilling his *machamba*, dressed in a torn blue shirt, tatty brown shorts and no shoes. He explained that he had filled his store by collecting food from the abandoned fields well outside the village. Els asked him whether he was not afraid of meeting Renamo soldiers. The man smiled to reveal a few brown stumps protruding at a variety of angles from his gums, 'This is a possibility,' he replied, 'but there is much food out there.'

It was getting late. We passed a small circle of roughly hewn quartz pebbles, arranged around seven low cacti outside the hut of the village medicine man. It was a place where villagers came to offer words to the gods when they were sick, Els told me. A procession of women, supporting huge piles of wood on their heads, was silhouetted against the sugar-loaf dome hazy in the distance across the dry grasses of the savannah. We met the village chief and Els told him that his people should be informed that the health centre and hospital were free and were there to help them. He said that his villagers did seek help for fever and diarrhoea, but they were reluctant to go when they were hungry, even though he insisted that they knew there was no need to pay.

His village was on the brink of starvation, about to don the media mantle of Third World misery. The villagers were starting to become hungry, but they had not yet reached the photogenic starvation stage. With only a month's food left, they were heading that way, however, and there was the constant threat that what food they had in store could be stolen or burnt by Renamo at any time.

Els was in thoughtful mood as we walked back to where we had left the Land Rover. These people would need an airlift of food to tide them over to the next harvest. Airlifts were expensive and took time to set up. Els explained the procedure she would have to put in motion as soon as we returned to Cuamba. She would write a report to send to Maputo. This was usually sent back to her with comments and requests for further information before it went to Oxfam's headquarters in Oxford, England. There, the Emergencies Unit would scrabble around for money, some of which would usually come from Oxfam's own funds, the rest raised from government aid organisations, such as the British government's Overseas Development Administration (ODA) or the European Community. Meanwhile transport tenders would have to be called for and food located.

The sun was setting as we prepared to leave Maúa for the forty-minute flight back to Cuamba. It was a fiery red orb in the sky behind the decaying exterior of an old cotton factory which lay in ruins beside the airstrip. Black mould and bullet holes pock-marked the crumbling yellow façade, and a small boy wearing an aid hand-out T-shirt inscribed with the words 'Big Boys Bonking Kit' smiled a wide smile and said goodbye to me.

Visibility declined rapidly as we left the little village on the edge of disaster and the giant granite sugar-loaf domes faded into the dusk to become shadowy hazards to flight. We climbed to 7000 feet and everywhere below us pinpricks and small rings of fire trailed exhaust plumes into the evening haze, at acute angles to the flat savannah plain.

The airlift arrived at Maúa in January 1993, four months after my visit. Nine hundred tonnes of food were supposed to be delivered, although some of this was for another village in the east of Niassa, but only about seventy per cent of that total arrived in January. Oxfam had located food in a World Food Program warehouse in Nacala, the port at the end of the railway line from Cuamba, but it had been sitting there for so long that part of it was deemed unfit for human consumption. In May 1993 Oxfam was still looking for an alternative source of food to make up the delivery.

Other than the normal bureaucratic procedures involved in organising an airlift, for which the time lag of four months was about standard, an Oxfam representative in Oxford told me delays were also experienced because the ODA was reluctant to stump up half the £450,000 bill which Oxfam requested. Airlifts were too expensive, they argued, and this one was for a relatively small number of people. They did eventually pay up after pressure from Oxfam's head, Frank

Judd, was brought to bear on Linda Chalker, the British Minister for Overseas Development.

The Oxfam representative I spoke to said she thought it unlikely that mass starvation had set in at Maúa in the meantime, or they would have heard about it. It seemed that Els's assessment of one month's food supply was an underestimate. Some of the villagers probably had died, but their bravery in the face of no other options had forced them into the bush in search of famine foods.

7

KALASHNIKOVS AND ZOMBIE CUCUMBERS

We circled Metarica early in the afternoon before deciding to land. The previous time Els had tried to visit, a month before, the village was in ashes and Renamo soldiers had fired at the plane. This time Metarica seemed quiet, its rows of reed-roofed huts tranquil and undisturbed in the midday sun. As we bumped along on the runway, children materialised to stare and wave, and a small crowd had gathered to greet us by the time we were climbing out of the aircraft.

A grinning military man with long sideburns, dressed in combat fatigues and high black boots, pushed his way through the crowd to meet us. A beret with red dagger insignia was perched almost vertically on the side of his head. This was the commander of the thirty or so government troops stationed in Metarica. He was full of smiles and bon-homie, and he sized us up with eyes that could count the money in your hip pocket. He shook everyone's hand and said the situation was calm, but his carefree smiles barely concealed an atmosphere of expectancy in the village. It was 24 September; the next day was the anniversary of the start of the armed struggle against the Portuguese, and an attack by Renamo was expected.

Renamo usually picked Frelimo red-letter days for their offensives, and Metarica was a regular target. It was the first district centre on a road that runs north-east from Cuamba, joining it to several other districts, so was of strategic import-ance. It was also the centre of a district which had enjoyed a bumper harvest in 1992, so the prospect of rich pickings made the village doubly attractive. As we walked the few hundred metres from the rough airstrip to its centre, we crossed the shallow trench which had been dug all around it. Metal beds were positioned by heavy machine gun emplacements and bored soldiers sat by their weapons. The remains of several huts lay in piles of grey mud and charred remnants of reed roofing.

The village centre was no more than a hundred metres across. Several single-storey concrete buildings stood on the bare earth: a school, health post and hospital, the district administrator's house, an Agricom office and a couple of small warehouses. You could have been forgiven for thinking that apart from the medical buildings, which looked complete, everything was in the early stages of construction. The cement floors were there and the bare walls, but the shells had no roofs, no window frames or doors, and only holes where electrical light fittings would go. In fact, the buildings had been stripped of everything that could be destroyed or carried away and only the bare shells were left. Bullet holes left a trail across a slogan on the school wall which read, 'Long Live Marxism–Leninism – Scientific Ideology of the Frelimo Party'. The brilliant green leaves of a papaya tree stood in odd contrast to the gutted building, and a few feet away armoured personnel carrier number 729 sat beneath a spreading mango tree in anticipation of tomorrow's onslaught. Kids, blissfully oblivious of the next day's threat, ran in and out of the disembowelled primary school, their shouts echoing from the bare walls.

Els's local buyer of grain in Metarica, a man named Awuha, seemed completely out of place in this sad settlement. He looked as if he had sauntered in from a beach in Jamaica, wearing a sleeveless T-shirt with a slogan about weight training, white shorts, wrap-around dark glasses and a straw hat. So far, he and his team of ten buyers had purchased forty-eight tonnes of maize from the local population, he told us. Els was here to check on his neat lists of counter-signed purchases and to ask him to step up his work, since there were rumours that people were about to burn the maize remaining from last year to make room to store this year's crop. Oxfam was the only buyer in this district, as DPCCN had no money, and to destroy food here while people were starving a few hundred miles to the south and on the brink in the neighbouring district of Maúa would be criminal – if just another bizarre contradiction in a country full of bizarre contradictions.

We walked through a doorway and into the health post, recognisable by the two pairs of crutches propped in a corner next to some old weighing scales. Els and her assistant, Bernado, sat down on benches at the wooden desk and went through Awuha's accounts. While they were doing this, Awuha took me to see some of Metarica's destruction at first hand.

We asked permission of the military commander first. He was still smiling and ultra-polite, but in a way which made me feel that he might at any moment decide to relieve me of all my personal possessions. He said that he was happy for us to look around.

The paved path up to the former residence of the district administrator lay smashed into a million pieces. Inside, boxes of ammunition of the Frelimo troops could be seen beneath reed mats, and kalashnikovs stood in corners of the empty rooms. Awuha pointed to where the light fittings had been methodically removed and explained that this had been the bathroom. Each ceramic tile had been torn from the wall and the toilet and bath had been ripped out and smashed, he said. This destruction had occurred in an attack a year ago tomorrow. Later, Els told me that she remembered having dinner with the administrator in this house some years before. Its floors had all been parquet, but not a single slab of wood remained. Everything had been smashed, hacked to pieces or carried away.

Renamo raids usually aimed to obliterate predictable targets: the cement buildings that represented Frelimo presence.

Samora Machel wags a knowing finger in front of the house that Eiffel built in Maputo. Behind is the spire of the Catholic cathedral built by the Portuguese, partly with child labour.

The wall mural near Mavalane airport depicts Mozambique's turbulent history.

Cement city Beira, in need of a coat of paint.

Street life: a good game for the streets of Beira; a cigarette vendor.

Schoolchildren are urged to 'Study, produce, fight'.

Mother and child in Beira.

By appointment to the local *curandeiro* community, purveyors of magical equipment in Xipamanine market.

Street traders in Pemba, Cabo Delgado, a province where everything appeared to be small, including the people.

Collecting firewood beneath a granite sugar loaf near Maúa, Niassa.

A boy at Metarica, Niassa.

A transit village for returning refugees and *deslocados*
outside Cuamba, Niassa. No one expects to stay in these
villages for long, so the huts are flimsy.

Ilha de Moçambique's nineteenth-century hospital, the country's oldest.

Pumping water in the sixteenth-century fort on Ilha de Moçambique.

Assado gives the thumbs up as his uncle (centre) finally appears to take us to Cahora Bassa.

Some proud young men display the products of their handiwork in Songo, Tete.

The *chapa* stop in Tete: Peugeot and Jesus combining forces for a safe journey.

The dam on the Zambezi at Cahora Bassa. About 10 per cent of its electricity generating capacity is enough to supply all of Mozambique's needs.

A new *capelana* design marks the signing of the Rome Peace Accord.

This pathologically methodical destruction was typical; the stuff that was carried away was either something that could be sold or used in a Renamo camp, or simply a trophy to prove the success of an operation. Two European technicians, captured by Renamo in the mid-1980s, have related how on one occasion they saw a Land Rover dismantled, carried in pieces to the Malawian border, and reassembled to be driven across the frontier and sold. The Renamo headquarters, at Gorongosa in Sofala province, was reputed to be littered with worthless junk: rolls of rusting barbed wire, great heaps of coins, damaged bicycles and motorbikes, broken chairs and useless pieces of machinery. They were all souvenirs of missions accomplished, a ritualistic accumulation of knick-knacks which represented the tearing down of Frelimo civilisation. The Gorongosa HQ was known to Renamo as Casa Banana, but a UN official who had visited the camp explained to me that the name was perplexing: there were no casas and no bananas, just a lot of rubbish.

Government employees were also prime targets for Renamo gunmen. Schoolteachers, administrators and health workers were representatives of the opposition and often the first to be dispatched. Awuha told me about a friend of his who had been Metarica's health worker. When the village had last been attacked, many villagers fled into the surrounding bush to hide. Renamo did not usually stay long, just the time it took to wreak destruction, carry out their killings and select souvenirs, but on this occasion they remained longer and lured the runaways back by sounding the village all-clear drums.

Awuha's friend, still clutching the medical bag he had grabbed on leaving his health post, returned with other villagers to be met by the Renamo soldiers. Sometimes Renamo decided to kidnap people with medical training to work for them, and on this occasion the captors radioed their base to ask whether this man should be killed or kept. Awuha's friend had already decided in his own mind that he would rather die than be taken prisoner, so his heart sank when the answer came back that he should be escorted to the nearest Renamo base.

For two days he and his armed escort walked through the bush. They built up a rapport of sorts, and on the third day Awuha's friend asked the Renamo soldier whether he did not get tired of being on the move. Yes, he was told.

'We get tired too, of running from Renamo all the time,' the health worker said to him, 'but we have some strong medicine which makes it easier.'

The guard's eyes lit up at the mention of strong medicine. Witchcraft, sorcery, magic and potent potions play an important role in everyday life in Mozambique, both in the bush and in the cities.

'I have some of this strong medicine here,' the health worker told his guard, 'would you like some?'

The Renamo man jumped at the chance of a dose of strong medicine, and Awuha's friend took a syringe from his bag and injected it into his guard's arm intravenously. The guard died instantly of a heart attack, and Awuha's health worker friend ran away, eventually returning to Metarica.

We had reached the old Agricom building, destroyed several years before, where fragments of white tiles still clung to the bathroom wall. The building had been reroofed and its windows bricked up after government soldiers had stolen the seed stored there the previous year. Charred bookshelves had been nailed together to block another window. Other planks had been brought in by plane from the neighbouring district to make new doors, Awuha told me. This was where he had stored the sacks of maize which he and his team had bought. It seemed like a ripe target for tomorrow's attack.

We emerged from the Agricom building and bumped into the military commander again, smiling like an alligator. He admired my camera, and trying not to look hesitant I gave it to him to look through the zoom lens. He was impressed as he focused on one of his men a hundred yards away, leaning against a tree smoking a cigarette. Then he carefully handed it back to me.

On our return to the health post, Els and Bernado were coming to the end of their sums. Els handed over large wads of notes for Awuha to continue his buying; she had carried the cash from the plane in a *capelana* for fear that the soldiers might decide to help themselves. A white coat and stethoscope hung from a rough hook in the wall beside some stained medical posters. The handover of the money, which Awuha transferred into his camouflaged rucksack, had the atmosphere of a shady deal being done in a doomed town on the edge of another disaster.

Bernado was quiet when we left the health post. He paused by the eviscerated school building and told me in a soft voice that he remembered taking an exam in that classroom more than ten years before. He wandered into the concrete shell and stared at the blank walls; his mind must have been a tumult of reflection and memories. He had been back in Niassa province for only a couple of months, after nine years studying in Cuba. Ten years before that he had moved from his village of birth to Metarica, to study in this school. During the twenty years away from home, he had lost contact with his parents and relations, but since his return to the province as an Oxfam employee Bernado had been learning of the events of the last decade. His father had been killed by Renamo and his mother had lived on in the remote village of Nipepe until that year when, tired of the struggle of life in a village continually prone to attack, she had walked a hundred miles through the bush to Cuamba. She had arrived with blistered feet and swollen legs, a forty-six-year-old woman who looked more than seventy, to be told that her son was there. She had long thought that he was dead, and had wept at his feet when they met.

Bernado was a gentle and fun-loving man, but the bombardment of childhood memories, and of seeing his lost relations, was having an effect on him. He also bore the added pressure of being a returning hero who had benefited from an education and was now a well-paid grown man. Rediscovered friends and relations were asking him for help which he could not always give. He had started to drink heavily, and sometimes he would go missing for hours without explanation. Els was worried about him. When I returned to Mozambique in 1993 I learned that Bernado had lost his job with Oxfam; he had been dismissed after being caught stealing Els's underwear.

Artur, the pilot, who had been sitting beneath the large mango tree near the armoured personnel carrier, stood up as we emerged from the school building and said that we ought to get going. The military commander walked with us to the plane, smiling all the way.

On the international front, Renamo dealings often took place in that twilight zone between governments, private enterprise and the criminal fraternity – a murky underworld occupied by secret services, innocent-looking front companies, hidden bank accounts and post office box numbers. At meetings in public places, or behind doors with no plates, men without faces decided the sources of finance and arms shipments. Casualties of the covert procedures could, and did, meet with accidents, often in mysterious circumstances.

But in other ways Renamo was an unorthodox rebel movement. It was different in several ways from umpteen other anti-government guerrilla forces fighting all over the world; its central distinctive feature was its lack of a political ideology. The organisation had been furnished retrospectively with a political manifesto, by a group of German academics, but it did not count for much in practice. That Renamo president Dhlakama had been talking to Frelimo in an effort to establish peace, and that Renamo would become a political party competing in democratic elections, was an anachronism. Apparently neutral people I spoke to who had been involved in the Rome negotiations and in the subsequent dealings leading to elections, agreed that Renamo were a bunch of bandits not really interested in politics.

The war in Mozambique had become so politicised that it was difficult to distinguish between truth, rumour and propaganda. Another commonly held impression about Renamo was that, unlike most other guerrilla groups, it lacked popular support. Dhlakama has been quoted as saying that his soldiers were like fish in the water: the people were the water and, like fish, Renamo would die without it. But Renamo's support from the peasantry was not usually voluntary, it was obtained through terror and coercion. Violence is the central tool of all wars, and the government targets of Renamo raids were calculated and planned. Early on Renamo had singled out clothes and consumer goods as symbols of Frelimo influence; peasants were made to bury their clothing, so that anyone who appeared in an area wearing clothes was recognisable as a Frelimo sympathiser and killed. Food was destroyed, to show that Renamo could do that too if they wanted. When Renamo troops turned up in your village, they would burn your food, steal it or sit down and eat it. To some they were known as the 'locust people'.

Their soldiers also routinely mutilated civilians in a gesture of intimidation. Ears, noses, lips and sexual organs were often hacked off living victims to leave an ever-present advertisement of the power of Renamo. Such atrocities were probably also carried out by Frelimo soldiers, on civilians thought to be collaborating with Renamo, although not on an equivalent scale. There was another side to Renamo's violence which made it distinctive: it had a terrible random element. On occasions, the killing took place in a frenzy which defied logic. Random ritualistic butchery left terrified civilians with their minds blown, and personal accounts of horror stories are legion. I quote one, told by a woman from northern Tete province: 'Renamo soldiers arrived in my village saying they were extremely hungry. We told them we had no meat to give them with their *nsima* (mealiemeal). So they grabbed my child, chopped it up, and forced me, trembling, to cook it. They even forced me to eat some. I have vowed never to eat meat again.'

Killing and mutilation were often used as an initiation for new Renamo recruits. Until their first blooding, trainees

125

would be kept under guard, and thereafter they were afraid to leave because of their complicity in atrocities. Many recruits were boys captured in raids. I met a young former Renamo fighter in a refugee transit camp in Cuamba. The camp, built by returned refugees and *deslocados*, using local materials, was clean but deliberately spartan to encourage people not to settle there but to go back to their villages. Such camps also housed former Renamo people who had responded to an amnesty offered by Frelimo in the months leading to the signing of the Peace Accord in Rome.

A young man was standing at the window of one of the shelters. As I passed, I nodded hello to him and he said simply that he had been with Renamo for the past seven years, since his capture at the age of sixteen. Latterly he had been a commander, but had decided to run away. He looked indistinguishable from a thousand other Mozambican youths I had seen. He introduced the woman standing next to him as his wife. She had been the partner of another commander before he had been killed. Considering the horrors he must have experienced, this man's normality was more disturbing than if he had looked like a mass murderer. The only thing that gave him away was his eyes, which showed that he had been emotionally gutted. They were black, and as shallow as a sheet of paper, or as deep as a hole to the centre of the earth. They did not say anything either way, and probably hadn't since the day he had chopped up his first baby.

That this man was in this camp was just another facet of the extraordinary goings-on in Mozambique. It was feasible that he would be sharing accommodation with the friends and relatives of his victims. Some feared the tensions that such a juxtaposition would inevitably throw up, and not surprisingly, there were stories of retribution, though none that I heard in the camps. However, captured Renamo fighters had been stoned to death in Metarica.

Most of those I spoke to in the Cuamba transit camp were uncomplicated country people, forced to spend several years away from home in a refugee camp in another country because of a war they did not understand. One man had returned after seven years in a refugee camp in Malawi. He did not know why Renamo had maimed his fellow villagers and killed his wife. He sat in the dirt in the shade of the rush roof of one of the accommodation centres, weary and uncomplaining. He wore a red and white crocheted woollen hat on a head of kinky hair greying at the temples. The thick lenses in his heavy black-framed spectacles made his peering eyes look tiny and deformed. He had lost all the fingers from his calloused hands. He told me that all he wanted was to get back to his *machamba* again.

I think the war stopped simply because Mozambicans were tired of all the killing.

One aspect of the war that I found particularly interesting was the important role played by traditional religious and other beliefs. Although religions brought to Mozambique by outsiders, particularly Christianity and Islam, have a firm foothold, most Mozambicans are more concerned with their traditional beliefs, and these are not necessarily at odds in their minds with the imported doctrines. They are based around the importance of ancestors, and are tied up in a complex cultural package which includes witchcraft, sorcery, spells and magic. For me, a European outsider, the mix of traditional African mystical powers with the hard, gun-metal reality of the kalashnikov was fascinating and slightly unnerving.

Renamo had successfully played on people's traditional values for a long time, proclaiming its struggle as a 'war of the spirits', intimating that they were fighting on behalf of the ancestors and harnessing the forces of the spirit world to help them. It was a tactic that generated some support among Mozambicans who were often dismayed at Frelimo hostility to traditional beliefs. Some believed that Renamo and its actions were expressions of the ancestors' anger at certain Frelimo policies.

Many Renamo units included resident spirit mediums in

their ranks, whose job it was to divine dangers before going into battle and to dole out fortifying potions of goat's blood, mixed with potent herbs, before fighters entered the fray. Dhlakama told his men that the spirits of Renamo would pursue and kill anyone stupid enough to break ranks and defect. Renamo had often claimed to be able to turn bullets into water, and their soldiers were routinely vaccinated against bullets. This practice was drawn from a long history of magical military powers; it also occurred during the Barue rebellion against the Portuguese in 1917. But Renamo had gone further. To counter the weaponry of modern warfare, their mediums had developed effective vaccines against helicopter gunships and Mig fighter aircraft.

In the later years of the war, Frelimo buried their hostility to such 'primitive' practices and responded in kind to the success of Renamo's collusion with the spirit world. Frelimo officials have been quoted as saying that the government's military success in Zambézia province during the late 1980s was because they had managed to kill Calisto Meque, a Renamo commander described as a 'strikingly weird personality' by one Western researcher and certainly a leader with serious magical properties. Some also believed that Frelimo soldiers were given the anti-bullet vaccine.

Such forces were not only used for military advantage. In a peculiarly Mozambican phenomenon, Renamo had been driven out of limited areas of the countryside by supernatural powers harnessed to create peace zones. In southern Mozambique, stories began to emanate in the late 1980s from a small pocket of territory known as Mongoi, which was blissfully free of the fighting, rape and pillage all around. The area was named after a powerful spirit medium who had got the measure of Renamo and talked them out of entering his land with evil intent. Renamo and Frelimo forces could come and go as they wished, he said, but not if they were going to indulge in violence. So influential was Mongoi that both sides agreed to his embargo, and the people of his land have lived in relative peace and harmony since.

A similar story is told of an area close to Renamo head-quarters, where a spirit medium called Samantanje estab-lished a neutral zone on a hilltop in the Gorongosa mountains. Samantanje, a close confidant to Dhlakama, con-vinced the Renamo leadership that anyone entering his terri-tory with a weapon would be bitten by a cobra or killed by a lion.

Another development in the pacifist magic vein began in Zambézia province in 1989, when Manuel Antonio, a young traditional healer, founded a movement known as 'Nap-rama', which means 'irresistible force' in Macua. Manuel Antonio said that he had died of measles, but had come back from the dead after a meeting with the spirits who gave him a mission to rid Mozambicans of war; the movement attracted large numbers of supporters. Members were initiated in an elaborate ceremony involving much singing and ritual, and recruits were vaccinated against bullets, using a special *muti* or magic potion. To convince them of their invincibility, they were then hit hard across the chest with a vicious knife, a *panga*, with no ill effects. The vaccine's potency lasted as long as the recruits adhered to certain taboos. These included no sex before battle, avoidance of certain types of meat and, most importantly, no killing. Anyone breaking the taboos would be wounded or killed in battle, or would become a victim of spontaneous madness.

Naprama pacifist forces, described by Manuel Antonio simply as people tired of war, marched upon Renamo bases dressed in loincloths, wielding spears or knives decorated with red ribbons, beads and animal skins. They rattled tin cans and marshalled an impressive inventory of unconven-tional battle tactics. Opposing forces were locked in a com-plex magical encounter of spells and counter-spells. An account of one such battle tells of how the first two Naprama assaults on a Renamo base were foiled by evasive Renamo sorcery, but on the third occasion 250 Naprama approached the base by turning into anthills and long grass at a hundred metres. Twenty men then flew into the base as bees and stung the Renamo soldiers, who had been transmogrified into snakes.

Manuel Antonio was killed in a clash in December 1991, after the development of a new vaccine to make Renamo warriors immune to Naprama assaults. His body was literally riddled with bullet holes and bayonet wounds, but his Naprama cult had overrun a string of Renamo bases, allowing thousands of people to walk back to their homes in relative safety.

The rise of the Naprama movement and the creation of peace zones are symbols of the extraordinary resilience of Mozambican people. By drawing on their rich spiritual heritage, they were able to cling to some semblances of normal life and to counter the horrors of their bloody civil war.

The magical aura surrounding Renamo forces was to some extent due to the tribal origins of their leaders. Most senior Renamo personnel were N'dau, a subgroup of the Shona long noted for their fighting skills and well-known as dealers in powerful magic.

Liaison with the supernatural began with their first leader, André Matsangaíssa, a former Frelimo soldier who had been convicted of stealing a Mercedes Benz and sent to a re-education camp from which he escaped. He gained respect and support from the local population by employing a spirit medium, who is believed to have given him magical powers. Matsangaíssa was supposedly killed in 1979 during a Renamo raid on a government position, but several versions of the story are told and no one seems to know what became of his body. According to one version, his supernatural energies protected him when he was shot, at point-blank range with an automatic rifle; the bullet bounced off him. The Frelimo soldier who had tried to kill him, puzzled at the failure of his kalashnikov, picked up a bazooka and tried again. Matsangaíssa fell dead, but the Frelimo man paid dearly for dispatching Renamo's Mr Big: he went insane, courtesy of a witch's spell. Variations on this theme have entered the realm of folklore in central Mozambique; some believe Matsangaíssa is alive and well and wandering around as a living-dead man. So influential was the legend that many country people referred to Renamo as the 'Matsangas'.

Refugee accounts tell of the use of truth potions by Renamo at their headquarters in Casa Banana, where a soothsayer would administer a herbal drink to people accused of casting bad spells. If the potion provoked convulsions the accused was found guilty, but if the accused vomited up the liquid, he was declared innocent.

I came across another version of this ordeal, described in great detail by a Swiss missionary named Henri Junod, who worked in Mozambique at the turn of the century. Junod's detailed work on the life of the Tsonga people is still the most cited account of southern Mozambican ethnography, and his description of the 'Mondjo ordeal', used to identify purveyors of black magic, and fatal to the guilty party, identifies the key ingredient of the potion as a member of the genus *Datura*, part of the potato family.

Datura is a hallucinogenic plant which has been called the number one drug of poisoners, criminals and black magicians the world over. One of its species, *Datura stramonium*, is known in Haiti as the 'zombie cucumber'. It induces a state of psychotic delirium, characterised by disorientation, confusion and total amnesia. Ethnobotanists believe that Datura is the mind-blowing active ingredient in a drug administered to zombie victims after they have been poisoned by another concoction based on tetrodotoxin. Tetrodotoxin is one of nature's most toxic substances. Tests in Western scientific laboratories have shown that it is 160,000 times more potent than cocaine, and as a poison it is 500 times stronger than cyanide. A well-known source of this deadly neurotoxin is in the skin, liver, ovaries and intestines of puffer fish and I had seen many puffer fish on sale at the witchdoctor suppliers' stalls in Mozambican markets. The fact that they were said to make a good potion for preventing people from stealing ties in with the effects of tetrodotoxin at extremely low doses, which is how it is administered as the zombie poison. It paralyses the victim physically, while allowing the mental faculties to remain normal, which would indeed stop anyone from stealing.

The total immobility of someone poisoned by tetrodotoxin to the correct degree, in which breathing stops, makes the border between life and death uncertain, even to trained physicians; the zombie victim can appear to be dead and is buried alive. The advanced stages of tetrodotoxin poisoning also fade into what Western scientists call near-death experiences, in which the victim feels that he is floating contentedly and travelling timelessly in several dimensions outside the physical body. The creation of a zombie then takes several stages. A poison containing tetrodotoxin is administered to the victim, who appears dead in every respect, goes through out-of-body experiences and, because he is *compos mentis* throughout, witnesses his own funeral and burial. Such an ordeal must be a little disturbing, but after the victim has been dug from his grave he is force-fed a paste containing the hallucinogenic Datura, the zombie cucumber. The result is a zombie.

I came across most of this information only after my return to Britain, and I cannot say whether there are zombies in Mozambique. Henri Junod makes an interesting reference in his section on black magic to the activities of people with the evil eye. One of the rather unpleasant ways they bewitched victims was to turn them into mindless servants to plough their fields or chop wood. Several individuals told me of people in modern Mozambique who fitted the descriptions given by Henri Junod of those possessing the evil eye. Such characters are known as *feiticeiros*. They lead a double life which, rather as in the Dracula story, is divided into night and day. During the day they appear to be normal citizens, and are usually unaware that at night they turn into something sinister. Like miscreants who operate at night anywhere in the world, their nocturnal activities consist of criminal practices directed against innocent folk. These include thieving and murder and, as often as not, cannibalism. *Feiticeiros* ride on the backs of bats or owls, and everyone in Mozambique knows that if an owl or bat arrives in your house someone will soon fall ill or die, or you will shortly receive news of illness or death in a family member. The dreadful energies held by a *feiticeiro* are hereditary, according to Junod, sucked in at the mother's breast. The holders of this power all know each other and are members of a secret society which holds regular nocturnal board meetings where intended targets and victims are discussed. Victims, who can be members of the *feiticeiro*'s own family, are often eaten. In several cases, people told me that when you were targeted, you could expect two or three days of fever, stomach pains and generally feeling awful until you died. When you had been taken to the cemetery and buried, the *feiticeiro* came along to eat you. The truth potion used at Renamo headquarters, which probably contained the zombie cucumber, was the recognised method for identifying and dealing with *feiticeiros*.

When I first heard these stories I was intrigued but sceptical. Those of us brought up in a Western tradition are taught to be dismissive of phenomena which cannot be explained scientifically. Although some of the drugs used in such mystical practices have been understood by Western science, I was initially unconvinced by troops being vaccinated against bullets and nocturnal hitmen riding around on bat-back practising cannibalism. I did not think of them as mumbo-jumbo, more as unfamilial local beliefs and superstitions. But the more I thought about it, the more I realised that such phenomena were no more or less improbable than my belief, for example, in an extraordinary British creature which lived in brick walls and spat money at you when you fed it plastic biscuits and punched its eyes in a certain sequence. The more I heard, the more I realised that Mozambican society was underpinned by this magical subtext. I heard stories about the spirit world from people in all walks of life, including those educated in Western norms and traditions, such as schoolteachers and senior government employees. There was no doubt that for them these goings-on, which to me seemed weird and unlikely, were real. As my stay in Mozambique progressed, I realised too that they were real. Matsangaíssa may indeed be wandering around Mozambique.

8

UNDER THE INFLUENCE

Niassa province had the reputation of being a hotbed of black magic. By the time I had reached Cuamba I was beginning to understand the spiritual background to Mozambican life. *Feiticeiros, curandeiros* (variously described to me as healers and witchdoctors dealing in white magic), *espiritistas* (spirit mediums) and *profetas* (prophets) were figures of prestige and authority and could be found in every village, town and city in the country. Their roles varied enormously – from the macabre activities of the *feiticeiros* to being medical men, insurance salesmen, loss adjusters, psychiatrists, weathermen and priests. Whereas *feiticeiros* were bad people often incapable of controlling their misdemeanours, the services of *curandeiros* were for hire. If you got wind that a *feiticeiro* was after you, you went straight to a *curandeiro* for help. While *feiticeiros* inherited their terrible powers, *curandeiros* learned their craft by apprenticeship.

Curandeiros also dealt in dodgier activities, however. If, for example, you wanted someone knocked off, the local *curandeiro* was your man. A village operator would charge perhaps 10,000 to 25,000 meticais (£2–£5) for this service; his counterpart in Maputo would cost up to 200,000 meticais (£40). The victim would usually meet with an accident, or simply become ill and die.

Another speciality was the preparation of spells to facilitate social or financial advancement. The most common method was sacrifice, ideally of a young family member. You went along to the local *curandeiro*, told him that you wanted a leg up in life, and paid your fee. At an unspecified later date one of your offspring would meet with an accident and soon after your advancement would come about. There was an alternative method which did not involve your child meeting with a fatal accident. It was described to me as either driving one of your children insane and/or practising a sort of social deprivation where they were denied all the normal things in life – friends, education and the like. The mayor of Maputo was reputed to have five daughters locked up in a lunatic asylum as proof of the effectiveness of this approach.

One evening, after a fine dinner of gazelle and spaghetti served up by Senhor Marcelino in the Oxfam headquarters, I asked Els about Mozambican magic. She confirmed the impressions I had collected and added some of her own stories.

The *curandeiro*'s social advancement technique was commonly practised in Niassa, she told me. She knew of one man who had been in prison for some crime who on being allowed a weekend's home visit, went straight to consult a *curandeiro*. The man had a simple child whom he was prepared to sacrifice to get out of prison permanently, but he was told he could not choose his victim. For the rest of the weekend the man forbade his favourite son to leave the house in any circumstances, for fear that he might be the one to meet with an accident. On the Sunday afternoon however, the favourite son crept out to play with his friends by the river as he often did on Sundays. On finding his son missing, the man rushed out to find him. He arrived at the river where his son's friends were splashing about and diving, but the favourite son, an excellent swimmer, was nowhere to be seen. Some of his friends thought that he had run off to hide in the long grass on the river bank. His father found him drowned in a knee-deep pool around a bend in the river. The father was allowed out of prison for the boy's funeral and never had to go back.

We were alone in the large room which served as dining room and lounge, sitting at the table with two bottles of Fanta between us on the plastic tablecloth. Outside, the cicadas were playing their usual background accompaniment to the still tropical night. Els pulled the cellophane from a fresh pack of Malawian cigarettes which were inappropriately called 'Life'.

'The *curandeiros* here mostly deal in spells,' she told me, as she pulled a cigarette from the red pack. 'They work,' she said simply.

She struck a match, lit the cigarette and placed the dead match in the severed beer can which was the ashtray. People often died without any medical explanation, she added, and the power of the *curandeiros* was a dangerous force to be reckoned with. 'People are frightened of this magic. All the time I get people coming to tell me of corruption, but they will never confront those they accuse because they fear that a spell will be cast on them.'

Els looked tired, but her eyes were bright and alert. She smiled when I urged her to tell me more of what she knew.

'I too was interested in this magic when I first came here to Niassa,' she said, 'but now I do not dig too deeply.' She took a slug of Fanta from the bottle in front of her. 'Let me tell you what happened to me when I was first in Niassa.'

Els had been sent to Niassa by the French medical NGO Médecins sans Frontières, in 1988. She was a nurse by training and had been involved in an emergency airlift and medical rehabilitation programme. She had stayed for six months, and although she had benefited from the experience, she had no particular intention of returning to Mozambique.

'One day, near the end of my contract, I was approached by the sister of one of the Mozambican nurses I was working with. I had never met her before, but she asked me to meet her on the edge of town that evening. She did not say what this meeting was for, but I went. It was a stormy night; no rain, but a lot of lightning and sometimes some thunder. You know: it was like a spooky horror film.

'This woman asked if I would follow her, and she led me through the night. We passed several villages and whenever there was a lightning flash she pulled me towards her so that no one would see me.'

'Weren't you frightened about where she was taking you?' I asked.

'No. The storm was kind of frightening, but I just wanted to see what would happen when we got to wherever we were going.'

Els swept some of her hair back to the top of her head and took another drag on her Life cigarette. 'Then we came to a hut. The woman asked me to remain outside. It was totally black, but when the lightning flashed I could see inside the hut there was this pot of liquid, like a witches' brew. And outside there was a large cauldron of water boiling on a nearly dead fire next to a small pit dug in the earth.

'The woman asked me if I would take off my clothes and put on a *capelana* as she wanted to give me a bath.'

I expressed surprise with my eyebrows.

'Yes, it was a bit weird, but it was very interesting and exciting, and I wanted to see what was going to happen. There were two other people there, and they placed me in the pit and gave me this bath with the herbal brew, and then they vaccinated me.'

I wanted to know just how this vaccination business worked.

'They make an incision with a fresh blade, here in the chest, and here,' she held a finger to the centre of her forehead, 'and they rub in herbs.'

'What was it for?' I asked.

'They told me I would be returning to Niassa. They also gave me a root which they told me I should bury in a grave-yard. They gave me very specific instructions where, in relation to which grave. And I had to do it at night.'

Els moved in her chair, 'I didn't do that bit,' she said. 'Anyway, the next day I got this radio call from MSF in Maputo saying Oxfam was interested in asking me to apply for a job. So I went to Maputo and spoke to Thabi, and she asked me to apply. But my contract with MSF was finished and I returned to Holland. There, some weeks later, I was invited for interview in Oxford. There were perhaps forty people. We stayed for several days of interviews and tests and round table discussions. Most of these people had degrees and I think I was the only one without a degree. I felt very inferior at the discussions and didn't say much. I thought that I had done very badly at the interviews and that there was no way I could compete with all these graduate people.'

Els made a shrug and opened the palms of her hands towards me. 'So I returned to Holland. Then, some days later, Oxfam rang me in Amsterdam and offered me a job. There were three jobs and they offered me the choice: Cabo Delgado, Quelimane or Niassa. Straightaway I said Niassa. They asked me: don't you want to think about it? And I said no, I want to go to Niassa.'

She stubbed her Life cigarette out in the beer-can ashtray and looked at me through her bright eyes. 'I have been here ever since.'

There was a pause, then Els got off her chair and walked to the exterior door which led to a concrete balcony. She pushed the door shut and switched on the antiquated air-conditioning unit which made a lot of noise and did not do much to cool the room.

'This woman asks me for money sometimes,' Els continued. 'She returned a few weeks ago and said that she knew that my contract with Oxfam was coming to an end. There was no way she could know that.'

Els opened the fridge and took a plastic bottle from inside the door. 'Would you like some water?'

I nodded.

Els poured the water into two long glasses which she took from the sideboard, and returned to her seat.

'She told me that she could give me another bath, or she could put a spell on my children so that they would come to Niassa. But I want to decide for myself what will happen. It is all rather scary.'

She smiled. 'I have been here a long time, but I shall never fully understand how the people work. If you want to learn more about this magic you should talk to Ivandro Artur, he is a local artist who paints very well. He has had a difficult time with witchcraft and many of his paintings are inspired by these magical things.'

Els said she would try to arrange a meeting for me. We moved on to talk about other aspects of Niassa and the need to know what makes people tick in order to do a good job as an aid worker. She began by telling me about a nutritional programme for expectant mothers which had been started in the province in which the women were encouraged to eat more eggs. But none of the aid workers knew that pregnant mothers in this region never ate eggs, because they believed that the child of a mother who ate eggs during pregnancy would never grow any hair. Although mothers would always agree vigorously when told to get more eggs inside them, none took any notice.

It was the afternoon of 25 September, a national holiday to commemorate the beginning of the armed struggle against the Portuguese. Artur the pilot was on edge; this was the day Renamo was expected to attack Metarica, and since his was the only small plane in Cuamba capable of landing there, he was expecting to be asked to fly out the wounded as on previous occasions. He had not drunk any beer the night before so that he would have a clear head.

It was not strictly accurate to say that his was the only suitable aircraft. The Dutch branch of MSF also had an operation in Cuamba and they had their own plane, but they would not allow it to be used as an air ambulance. Artur, normally a man of few words, did not think much of their attitude, particularly since MSF did use their plane to fly members of their expatriate staff out to Zimbabwe for holiday breaks.

'MSF only work in the comfortable places,' he said with

scorn in his voice, 'here and in Lichinga. They aren't interested in the villages.'

I had sat in on a late-afternoon MSF meeting a few days before, with Els, in an open air bamboo shelter outside their centre in Cuamba, around the corner from Oxfam's makeshift headquarters. The MSF operation was larger than Oxfam's, its personnel consisting of two middle-aged Dutch doctors and a young red-haired English nurse under the direction of an El Salvadoran. As they discussed their programme, which consisted of health work, caring for *deslocados* and more recently food distribution, I kept wondering whether the anti-malarial pills I was taking would provide any protection against the fatal strain of cerebral malaria the mosquitoes in this part of Mozambique specialised in. I would soon find out, I thought, as the sun sank behind the old colonial building which housed the MSF operation, and the mosquitoes materialised for an evening's blood-sucking.

One of the MSF projects, a Canadian-financed initiative to sink wells in accommodation centres for returning *deslocados* and refugees, was facing problems. Few of the people in these villages were willing to help collect sand and stones and dig the wells. This was hardly surprising, I thought, since no one was sure how long they intended to stay in these transit villages, by definition settlements in limbo. Els had taken me to see one of them; it was like a surprise visit to the palaeolithic period, the most motley collection of flimsy grass huts I had ever seen. But the headman in one village revisited by the red-haired English nurse (who had spent the previous year in southern Sudan and the previous evening lecturing me on the subtleties of media manipulation in Britain) had found an answer to the problem of those evading the work: the local militia rounded people up and forced them to help with the construction. MSF were worried that this approach smacked of a return to forced labour, which of course it did.

Artur and I were on the concrete balcony of the Oxfam room. Across the road boys were enjoying a game of football

141

on the bald patch of earth next to the school. A couple of small black pigs were rummaging beneath a tree at the edge of the pitch. Artur was a proud man, and had some strong opinions about the foreigners here to help his fellow Mozambicans. I could never quite make out what he thought of me, however, since he played his cards very close to his chest. He was an air force pilot, but since the Mozambican Air Force did not play a significant role in the war, he was on secondment to the charter company which ferried Oxfam around. He obviously had great respect for Els and her work, although he had an acid sense of humour which he used to provocative effect. At lunch he had asked me to pass the salt which was right beside Els: 'Nick, can you pass me the salt please? If I ask Els she will start talking about emancipation.'

Many of the missionaries and religious charities involved in aid work were high on Artur's list of foreign helpers Mozambique could do without. He knew of too many such operations which used their religious credentials as fronts for seedy activities: monks who ran mission schools for young girls whom they saw as a pool of innocent flesh with which they could have their evil way, for example. There was too often a hidden agenda, he told me. Even the Missionary Sister nuns we had met at Maúa, who were good women, were flying in food to distribute only to Catholics.

I agreed with Artur. I have come across missionary types in several parts of the world, and in many cases I have found their motives and activities suspicious. One of the most horrific examples of misguided religious fervour in Mozambique concerned the building of Maputo's cathedral. The Portuguese authorities had routinely picked up teenage girls from the streets of the capital and taken them to the city's central administration where a woman examined them to establish whether or not they were still virgins. Girls who had lost their virginity were fined for their immoral behaviour, but the majority were unable to raise the money and had to pay off their fines with their labour, helping to construct the cathedral and two other churches in the city.

As we stood on the balcony, overlooking the football match below, we were continually interrupted by citizens of Cuamba after lifts in Artur's plane. Artur and Els were for ever passing such requests back and forth between them. The usual preamble was a story about a preoccupation of some sort. Knowing the pressure for free places, people went to extraordinary lengths, often returning day after day, to embroider a story which made their particular case for a seat impossible to refuse. It had been some time since Artur had flown to Lichinga, and people were queueing to fill any spare seats for the next trip. For the last three days a man had been coming to tell Els and Artur about his child who was in hospital in the provincial capital. Els had already reserved a place for the man's wife so that she could visit the child, but her husband kept returning to remind Els of her promise. Then the wife had turned up and asked for a lift. Els told her that she already knew about her child in hospital and that there was a place for her on the plane. The woman looked shocked. 'My child in hospital?' she exclaimed with alarm. Their place was cancelled.

A small round man whose head was shaped like a lemon, with a pointed beard on the bottom, appeared at the balcony door. He was all smiles and very deferential. Did Senhor Pilot know when he might be going next to Lichinga? Was there any chance at all of a lift? Artur said he didn't know. Perhaps he should ask Els. The man smiled even wider, so that his lemon head became a beaming beacon. He bowed to Artur in mock ceremony, and said that he knew that weight was a problem on Artur's small plane, but he was prepared not to eat breakfast on the morning of the flight if he could have a seat.

Artur sent him packing. 'That was the head of Cuamba's police intelligence service,' he said.

We were joined on the balcony by a tall man dressed in a white short-sleeved cotton shirt and well-pressed blue trousers. He was also a pilot, who had been stranded in Cuamba for most of the week waiting for a mechanic to arrive to fix the landing gear on his aircraft. His continued presence in Cuamba had become a minor source of amusement. Each day when we left to fly to one of the villages we would bid farewell to this pilot who hoped to be able to leave, but each evening when we returned he would greet us, still waiting to be airlifted out. He had been flying for the national air charter company for six years, after attending a civil aviation course at Bath, England, and spending a year with Ethiopian Airlines. He flew all over the country, with occasional flights to carry Mozambican contract labourers to work in the South African mines when the security situation meant that it was too dangerous for them to travel overland. I was surprised when he told me that in all that time he had not been shot at once.

'I can fly for two or three hours and see not one hut, not one person,' he said, 'there is plenty of room in Mozambique, and water too. Often I ask myself, why are people fighting out there?'

As the afternoon wore on, bottles of Portuguese red wine were opened. The stream of visitors continued, either angling for a lift or simply passing the time of day. Two military men appeared, and drank Coca-Cola with their walkie-talkies beside them on the easy chairs. There had been no news from Metarica; it seemed that their radio had broken down.

When the sun was setting, Els, Artur and I decamped to a small bar along the dirt road past a mango tree. The pilot was already at a table outside the small bar. Bernado and his girlfriend were with him and two very pretty teenage mulatto girls wearing party dresses. Their table was crowded with empty brown beer bottles. The pilot hailed me as we approached, gesturing to the table-top. 'This is Mozambique. This is what Mozambican people like.'

He did not turn up to dinner that evening. Senhor Marcelino served us another royal meal from his small kitchen across the corridor; Artur and I tucked in to some more gazelle, while Els piled a salad made from huge tomatoes on to her plate. There was a snigger from Artur when I asked for the tomatoes, and he explained that 'tomato' is only used in the singular there since 'tomatoes' was a word used for the male genitalia.

Els asked if I had noticed the two mulatto girls at the bar, and told me their sad story. They had lost their innocence five years before, at the age of ten or eleven. A Catholic NGO had hired a South African charter company to carry out an emergency airlift and the pilots, after completing their job, had spent a night in Cuamba before flying home. The men had a penchant for very young girls, and had rounded up half a dozen in the town with promises of sweets if they came to their hotel rooms. The girls were all mulattos (white men seemed to prefer half-caste girls, Els thought), and the two at the bar had been prostitutes ever since. I met one of the girls the following morning, emerging from the pilot's room at my pension. I said hello and asked how she was, but she didn't respond. She just looked at me with expressionless eyes and went on her way in her party dress.

We had moved to the easy chairs and sofa to drink chicory coffee when Ivandro Artur, the artist, arrived. He was a tall, thin unassuming youth in light blue jeans and matching T-shirt. His hair was cut very short and he had an affectionate smile and long fingers which he used constantly to reinforce his words in the air. Els had shown me some of his paintings which I told him I liked very much. Slightly embarrassed, he thanked me and curled his toes inside his dark blue deck shoes.

I asked him about his technique and his paintings and gently led him towards the subject of magic. I explained that I was interested in magic, and wondered whether he would mind telling me about his experiences. Ivandro Artur curled his toes some more and began to relate his stories.

Women often put spells on their husbands so that they could only perform sexually at home, he told me. When the mother of his child did this to him, he felt a real difference

145

in his body every time he was in a bar or at a girlfriend's house. He eventually left this woman because she refused to have the spell cancelled. He moved away from where they had lived in Nampula to Cuamba, but for the first six months he had suffered from diarrhoea every day. He was becoming badly dehydrated and doctors could do nothing for him. He was flown back to Nampula on a drip.

'But the moment I arrived back in Nampula I felt all right. I pulled the drip out of my arm,' his long fingers grabbed an imaginary needle and yanked it from his forearm, 'and I walked away from the stretcher.'

He went to see the mother of his child and she agreed to have the diarrhoea spell removed, but she told him that he would never have a child by another woman. He had a girlfriend here in Cuamba, and he said that they had been trying to have a child together for a long time. Then happily his girlfriend had become pregnant. Two months later she had a miscarriage.

The traumas Ivandro Artur was going through were expressed in his work. One of his paintings, a large work in raw-coloured oils, stood against the wall of the room. It depicted a man and a woman in front of traditional village huts. A foetus was visible inside the woman's womb, but her body was spiked around the edges, and the man's penis was limp. A small pile of maize flour on the ground beside the couple was an offering to the spirit of the dead child, he told me, his toes still curling.

I asked Ivandro Artur how long he had been a painter. He had begun four years before, after losing his job. The incidents with his wife had inspired him: 'Suffering forces you to make things,' he told me simply, emphasising each word with his nimble fingers. He was visibly less nervous when he told me how he had been having difficulty finding a studio in Nampula before the governor of the province had taken him under his wing. The governor had offered him a scholarship to study art in Hungary, but Ivandro Artur needed a ninth-grade school certificate to go and he had not progressed that far at school. When the governor offered to give him one, he had refused because he was worried that the deception might cause him problems in the future.

He had been moderately successful with commissions and sales in Nampula, and had supplemented his income by teaching art. But he had discovered that his students were against him, another reason for leaving town, when he smelt potions underneath his chair and the public had inexplicably stopped purchasing his work. He smiled for a moment and then his toes began their curling once more. 'Magic is everywhere here,' he said, 'people bury a corpse under the floor,' he waved his long fingers below his chair, 'in a new office for good luck. When on the radio there is a broadcast that someone is missing from a family everyone knows what has probably happened to this person, since the magic is strongest when a relative is buried.'

After Ivandro Artur had left, I made my way back around the corner to my pension. The street lighting in Cuamba was haphazard, and although I knew the route by now the town seemed to be dark with something more than just night. Somewhere in the blackness someone was playing what sounded like an electric guitar. The same seven chords, over and over again, echoed endlessly in the humid night shroud. I reached my room, stripped off and lay perspiring on my bed. The seven chords twanged repeatedly in the still air. A lone mosquito had somehow penetrated the windows which I always kept closed. I turned on the light and occupied myself with a search-and-destroy mission which passed a few minutes. The same seven chords kept reverberating through my head. I was reminded of William Bendix in his role as a war veteran in the 1940s film, *The Blue Dahlia*. He had a metal plate in his head which vibrated with a big-band sound penetrating the walls of his room. 'That monkey music' was driving me insane. An afternoon of alcohol and all the talk of magic was engulfing me. Black Africa was swallowing me up. The seven chords were an African version of the Chinese drip torture, designed to drive me demented.

Sweat was trickling off my brow, and I wanted out. I felt I was losing something to the juju music inside my head.

The following day was a Saturday, a day Cuamba's inhabitants had been building up to for some time, because it was a wedding day. Another member of Cuamba's tiny Dutch community was marrying a local girl, whom he had been seeing for two years. They had decided to marry when she got pregnant. The Dutchman was in his early thirties and his bride was half his age.

On the morning of the wedding, long tables in a reception room on the ground floor next to my pension were groaning under the weight of more than thirty garishly coloured cakes laid out for the wedding reception. The Dutchman was found laid out in bed, horribly hung over, and the town was full of confusion. A boy had died that week, and his funeral was to take place that morning. Many of the funeral guests were also due to attend the wedding, so the wedding would have to be postponed. The funeral was supposed to have happened the day before, but the coffin had not been made in time. No one was quite sure which outfit to put on.

So Els and I went shopping. We sat in a small café drinking Coke as the sun was cranking up for another scorching day, when the funeral cortège crawled by on the way to the graveyard from the small church with the neon cross. Someone said that the wedding would happen that afternoon, when the bridegroom had sobered up. Dusk was approaching when the same collection of motor vehicles transformed itself from a funeral procession into a wedding convoy. Every vehicle in town was packed to the gunnels with laughing people processing along the streets with horns blaring, faces smiling and white palms waving. I jumped on to the outer step of the white Oxfam Land Rover, with Els at the wheel and Bernado and his girlfriend packed inside with half a dozen small children wriggling in their Sunday best. The convoy made a stop for photographs outside the houses of the bride's parents and each of her sisters. The young bride, looking slightly nervous, was resplendent in white lace and her four tiny bridesmaids were beginning to get mischievous while still clutching their posies.

The reception room was mild pandemonium as the guests trooped in. Paper chains and balloons were festooned through the air and the cakes sat on the tables in a phenomenal display of catering ingenuity. There were red ones and blue ones, square ones and heart-shaped ones, and cakes with several podia poking out at angles. Bottles of Carlsberg beer and Fanta lined the tables, between plates piled high with biscuits and sweets. At one end of the room the Indian community had set up shop. Stern-looking fathers watched hawk-eyed over their pretty daughters in spangled dresses sitting in a row beside their fat mothers. In the middle of the room, between the two long tables, groups of Indian and mulatto youths wearing black stone-washed jeans smoked cigarettes. Kids rushed up and down the long room making new friends and women popped large breasts out from under their blouses to suckle small babies. Donna Luisa, a huge woman who seemed to run most of the town, cruised up and down the aisles carrying bottles and plates. She wore a billowing pink dress and reminded me of a tank on guard duty, keeping everything under control. Over the hubbub, a worn tape played Elvis singing *'Love me Tender'*, and when the bride and groom kissed beneath a bunch of balloons, a ripple of appreciation ran through the buzzing crowd.

Artur, the pilot, whispered to me that there was still no news from Metarica.

9

THE MONSTER WITH SEVEN
HEADS

I saw in the New Year at Beira, and I arrived with four hours
to find a party. Three months had elapsed since my last
visit to Mozambique, since the signing of the Peace Accord
and the official end of the war. I was back to see whether
the guys with guns had given up killing people.

There was something odd about the hotel I was checking
into, but I couldn't put my finger on it. A man sat in the
shadows behind the desk in the foyer, an old flickering hurricane lamp the only source of light between us. I could just
make out rows of switches on an antiquated telephone
switchboard to one side of the man, and scrolls of a fleur-
de-lis painted on a wall behind him.

'Do you have any rooms?' I asked him. There was a pause
as he sized me up. Then he looked away.

'Senhor, we have one hundred rooms,' he replied.

'Do you have one for me?' I enquired. There was another
pause. I couldn't understand why he was being so cagey. To
me it seemed like a normal enough question to be asking at
a hotel reception desk. But then it was New Year's Eve.
Perhaps the hotel was full.

'Which one would you like, Senhor?' came the reply.

'One with a bath, overlooking the sea,' I told him.

He waited. It was as if I had said some coded phrase
and he now expected me to hand over a secret package of
microfilm. At last, he fumbled about underneath the counter
in front of him and pulled out a key. 'Come with me,' he

said, his voice still full of suspicion, and he took the hurricane lamp by the handle and emerged from behind the desk.

I followed him into the shadows, up seemingly endless flights of stairs and along a corridor to room 310. He opened the door, and as we entered a refreshing sea breeze was strained into our faces through a mosquito mesh on one of the windows.

Automatically, I tried the light switches. Nothing happened.

'No electricity,' I said feebly.

'At the moment, no,' the man replied apologetically. He dug a candle out of his pocket, handed it to me and left. A few moments later he returned with a plastic bucket full of water.

'Water,' he said, and he left again, for good this time.

Despite the lack of most of the usual amenities associated with a hotel, I was thankful that I had found a bed to rest my head on. I had been travelling for twenty-four hours and I was exhausted. I had arrived in Harare early the previous morning, supposedly to meet Alex and his girlfriend Betinha for New Year. After sitting on a wall outside Alex's mother's apartment block for most of the day, I gave up and jumped on to an overnight train headed for the Mozambican border. Harare railway station was plastered with posters telling you to report suspicious persons to railway security immediately, the instruction printed above a pale photograph of a guard finding a man behaving suspiciously beneath a carriage seat. Suspicious persons obviously posed a serious threat on Zimbabwean trains. As I was wedging my hold-all beneath the seat in my compartment a railway official entered.

'Now gentlemen,' he said in a grave tone, 'you know we are living in a different world. You must beware of thieves.' He looked at me to make sure that I was paying attention, and he eyed my bag with concern. 'Even you must look under your bed, because the culprit may be there.'

I checked that I had not inadvertently covered up a transgressor with my bag, but resisted the temptation to open the

151

zip to make sure a felon had not secreted himself inside. Through the carriage window, which still bore the two inter-twined R's of Rhodesian Railways frosted into the glass, a sliver of a moon was trying to peep through the ragged black clouds as the 111 Down train pulled out of Harare station. One of the men I shared my compartment with told me a cautionary tale about a heavily pregnant woman with whom he had shared his previous journey. She had begun to go into labour while they were travelling on the Harare–Mutare line and he and his fellow passengers had rushed her to the toilet. The woman actually gave birth to her child and it had fallen straight through the toilet on to the line below. Amazingly, the baby had survived virtually unscathed. 'I pulled the communication cord,' my fellow-traveller informed me, 'and the baby had not even been squashed a little bit.'

The train arrived at the border town of Mutare early the next morning. A new matt–brown armoured troop carrier stood outside the station entrance to remind me that I would soon be re-entering a war zone. A taxi took me the few kilometres to the border post and I walked into Mozambique as the morning sun was starting its daily fry-up. I jumped on to a yellow Peugeot *chapa* which was going to Chimoio and it sped off along the tarmac strip which stretched all the way along the so-called Beira Corridor to the Indian Ocean coast.

I was voyaging into the unknown. It was three months since the Peace Accord had been signed in Rome, but I had no idea whether or not it had been successful in stopping the bloodshed. That had been one reason for my rendezvous with Alex in Harare, to get the lowdown on the security situation. The Beira Corridor had been relatively safe during the last two years of the war, but there was no way of telling whether the Peace Accord had maintained that status quo. I also had no idea whether the places en route down the Beira Corridor would have hotels, or if they did whether they would be booked up in the holiday season. I had visions of spending New Year in a ditch somewhere, and of being rudely awoken by a Renamo attack.

I assumed Beira would have hotels, but again I didn't know for sure, and I also had no idea whether I would make it to the coast in one day. There was no option but to travel as far as I could and stop when it seemed a good thing to do.

The *chapa* shot through a succession of maize fields sewn on to the landscape like patches over a network of tree stumps. Small round huts with rush roofs were dotted about the gentle slopes as far as the eye could see. The relative safety of the corridor, protected by Zimbabwean troops, meant that *deslocados* had flocked into the zone and population pressure was high. We drove through a eucalyptus plantation, where the tall thin trees stood like giant pencils with their bark peeling off in sheets.

We reached Chimoio, about one-third of the way to Beira, at around midday, and the *chapa* driver said that he would continue on to Beira. By the time we stopped briefly at Muda the sun had disappeared and the sky was full of a leaden light which etched the edges of the sombre clouds. Cicadas were screaming in a mango tree by the roadside and a fresh wind blew up. Lightning streaks split the skyline in the misty grey distance and angry rain lashed the windscreen as we crossed the Pungoe River where Zimbabwean heavy machine guns pointed from the bridge out into the deluge. The moist air was fresh and sweet-smelling as we crossed the railway line at Dondo, a junction which boasted the deadest collection of rolling stock I had ever seen: the carriages looked as if they had spent the last fifty years on the sea bed.

Dusk was falling by the time we pulled up at a roadside in Beira and a throng of people converged upon us. I asked the driver where I could find the Hotel Dom Carlos. It was a shot in the dark but it was the only name I knew. I had seen it mentioned in a 1965 guidebook to southern Africa and I had no idea whether it still existed. A helpful man in a straw hat told me to follow him and he led me to a truck full of people which he said would take me there. The area I wanted was called Macúti, the man said. It was another half hour out of town, up the coast, and it was dark by the time we arrived.

From the window of room 310 I could hear the gentle crashing of the waves on the beach somewhere beyond the kiosk opposite. Although the Hotel Dom Carlos had a problem with water and electricity (there wasn't any) it was at least still there and I had at least arrived. Now I felt hungry. I went in search of the hotel restaurant. The hotel also had a problem with food: there wasn't any of that, either. The man at the desk was back in the shadows. He considered my request for food. He was getting accustomed to my unusual requirements, and he asked me to follow him again, this time leading me out of the hotel and across the deserted road to a long low-slung aircraft hangar type of building which had a mock crazy paving concrete floor inside. Two neon strips lit the bare interior which seemed to be some sort of disused canteen. The man from the shadows conversed in hushed tones with a man behind the canteen who smiled at me and said that he could probably find something for me to eat. I sat at a table near the door where the sea breeze was and I was soon presented with a large plate of goat and rice.

Two small black cats turned up to envy my supper. One was content to chase its tail, but the other sat patiently at my feet, reaching up gently to bat my elbow every now and again to remind me that I was not the only hungry one around here.

Later, after a lie-down on my bed, and thinking that this would probably be one New Year I would spend on my own, I wandered back to the beach. Music throbbed from the direction of the hangar as a few firecrackers jumped on the road outside. It was midnight. I entered the hangar to find it full of Mozambicans drinking and dancing to a music system which had been set up at one end of the large space. I soon got talking to some young men who thought it was just great that I was here for New Year. We bought each other beer and they kept asking whether I needed a woman, in a very matter-of-fact way, as if a woman were a type of drink. I told them I had a girlfriend. They nodded, then looked around.

'Where is she?' one of them asked. In England, I told them. They all looked puzzled. 'Then you need a woman now,' I was told. One of the youths was dispatched to find suitable candidates.

'Is your girlfriend beautiful?' a guy wearing a white T-shirt asked me.

'Yes,' I replied. The guy asked me to describe her. She was blonde I said, and they nodded sagely. I went through some other qualities.

'Do you love her?' the white T-shirt man asked.

'Yes,' I said.

'Will she make good babies?' he asked. I smiled and said we hadn't made any yet, but we had discovered how it was done. They burst out laughing. The white T-shirt man slapped me on the back and I nearly lost my front teeth on the beer bottle.

'And when will you be married?' he asked. It wasn't quite that simple, I explained. The group jumped at this, there was no doubt then that I needed a little something for this evening. At that moment, their friend returned with a little something, a girl in a red satin dress whose name was Tina. I said hello to Tina, who looked about seventeen and was very thirsty. She told me that bit herself, as her bright brown eyes picked out my bottle of beer on the table in front of us. Tina asked if she could drink some, and plonked herself down on my lap, grabbed the bottle and emptied its contents into her mouth without letting the bottle touch her lips. She wiped her mouth with the back of her hand, jumped off my lap and ran back to join the dancers.

Tina was mine if I wanted her, I was told. I said I didn't think I did and the group looked perturbed.

'Don't you like black women?' the white T-shirt man asked. I said I did but I was thinking about my girlfriend. Other women were brought, I danced with some, we drank more beer and I staggered out of the hangar some hours later to scramble up the dark stairs to my bed, alone.

Beira is Mozambique's second city, and has a population of about 300,000. It is also a large port, linked by road and rail to Zimbabwe and Malawi. Although it has never been the best of ports, since it has always needed constant dredging to stay open, in colonial times it was the one closest to Rhodesia and a good option for parts of Zambia and Malawi. Through these transport links, the city prospered during the 1960s and early 1970s and tens of thousands of Rhodesians regularly drove the 200 miles down the corridor to lounge on the beach and wolf seafood at Beira. The Dom Carlos was one of several hotels built to serve this booming tourist trade.

Beira's bubble burst after Mozambique became independent and the Frelimo government enforced United Nations trade sanctions against Ian Smith's Rhodesia. The border was closed, 10,000 jobs were lost in Beira and the tourists stopped coming. Rhodesian soldiers began visiting Mozambique instead, to blow up bridges, railway lines, dams and oil storage facilities. They even attacked a refugee camp, leaving 600 dead bodies behind them. At the same time, Ian Smith's military intelligence service was busy setting up a Fifth Column to operate inside Mozambique, developing its functions to include terrorism. Renamo had been born. Frelimo propaganda against the Smith regime likened the Rhodesian leader to a mythical monster which was particularly difficult to kill. Smith became known as the 'Monster with Seven Heads'.

Even after the border was reopened in 1980, when Rhodesia became Zimbabwe, the tourists did not return. By then Renamo had made Beira a rather dangerous holiday destination; today its hotels were empty and no one had painted a building for seventeen years. Its roads needed repairing, the garbage needed clearing and everyone who lived in Beira looked as if they could use a holiday before starting again, now that the war was over.

Yet I liked the place, or at least the Macúti part of town where the Dom Carlos was situated. There was something appealing about living in a hotel which had just ground to a halt, and I stayed for a week. The last serious residents the hotel had accommodated had been Soviet military personnel two years before and throughout the week I stayed there, they had no other guests to occupy their hundred rooms. I later discovered that the electricity and water had been cut off six months ago, after the owner of the hotel had run off without paying any of the bills. He had left the hotel staff to fend for themselves. The man from the shadows turned out to be a friendly and accommodating gentleman. It seemed that his suspicion on my arrival had simply been because he could not understand why I wanted to book into the hotel. His incredulity was shared by other staff members, who turned up for work each day, even though there was no work for them to do. None of them could understand what on earth I was doing there, and I wondered the same about them, particularly after I discovered that they had not been paid for six months. The reason was that they had nowhere else to go and nothing else to do.

The whole place was like a semi-living museum. The dining room, replete with chandeliers and thick velvet curtains, was permanently set with crisp white tablecloths and cutlery, and there was usually someone on duty. But there was never any food. The smiling waiters seemed to be constantly ready in case a freak event should come about when food and customers were simultaneously available. Meanwhile they languished and chatted, and one would occasionally wander into the lounge with its plush blue carpet which didn't quite tickle your ankles when you walked across it, and its white and gold stucco ceiling. Surrounded by gilt mock Louis XIV furniture and pictures of Portuguese conquistadors in armour on horseback, he would tinkle the keys of a small piano, most of which had lost their ivory long ago.

One day the man from the shadows explained that with no electricity and no water he could hardly expect any customers, and with no customers there wasn't much chance of paying off their huge debts and getting the place running again. He said that now the war was over there was a chance that the original Portuguese owners might return and the Dom Carlos would once more grind into action. I hoped so, I told him. I also hoped that the staff's loyalty would be recognised if such a day ever came.

But food was still a problem when I emerged from my room late on New Year's day. One of the waiters in the hotel restaurant said that there were no other restaurants in Macúti. But he thought that there might be some goat at the Estoril. Where was that, I asked him. He pointed out of the window overlooking the front. Just next door he told me.

The Estoril was also a former hotel, built for the Rhodesians in the 1960s. No one seemed to know exactly when the hotels had been built; everyone I asked would pause and say 'ooh, many years ago'. While the Dom Carlos had continued, be it with a severely reduced clientèle after the fall of the Monster with Seven Heads, the Estoril had been taken over by the government after independence and turned into public housing. The ground floor was a series of broken windows, decrepit shopfronts which had not sold anything for more than a decade, the old hotel reception area, its tropical timber counter faded but still imposing, and a restaurant-cum-canteen.

I wandered into the Estoril, towards the canteen. Kids scrambled up the crumbling staircase and black faces peered from the broken windows at the first floor. The canteen looked run down and gutted. All the chairs had rips in their olive-green plastic covers and the tables' Formica was chipped and grubby. The salmon-pink walls were peeling and crumbly. The place looked as if it had not been used by anyone but the flies for many years. I approached the counter and called hello. A man appeared from behind the bare aluminium shelving and looked at me. He had a kindly middle-aged face which shone slightly with sweat. The face had a deep scar beneath its left eye where his cheek bone should have been, and above it his hair looked like a piece of short pile carpet. He wore a brown shirt, with frayed collar and three different buttons down its front. A darker brown patch on his breast indicated where a pocket had once been.

I bade him good day and asked whether he was open. He looked at me as if I were insane, then his face broke into a smile. His eyes surveyed his broken-down canteen, as if what he was looking at should be answer enough to my question. I said that the people at the Dom Carlos had told me he might have some food. He broke from his reverie and said, 'Yes Senhor, I can get you some goat.'

I said goat was fine and he led me to one of the tables by the window. He asked if I would like something to drink while I was waiting and then said could I give him the money now since he would have to go across the road to the kiosk to buy my Coca-Cola. I said that I could go, but he wouldn't hear of it, so I handed him some notes.

The man returned with the drink and a rag that had probably been clean once, which he used to redistribute the dirt on the table-top. He moved about his old canteen gently, making less noise than the flies that shared it. Forty minutes later he brought me a magnificent plate of black goats' meat in a sweet sauce placed between two large neat piles of steaming white rice. As I tucked into the food, a small boy who said his name was Pepito clawed at the broken window by my elbow. He was wriggling in the way small boys are wont to do. Pepito had small brown stumps for teeth and big brown eyes. He smiled a lot as he squirmed in his torn shorts. He said he lived upstairs and that he too had eaten rice for lunch.

I had no idea where the canteen man had rustled up the goat from, but when I left I gave him a large tip. I asked him whether he would be open that evening. He smiled and let out a small chuckle. Then he thought a bit and offered to bring some more goat to me in my room at the Dom Carlos, say about 5.30?

I became a regular visitor to the Estoril canteen, and the man with the hole in his cheek who moved like a fly often provided me with food in my room in the evenings, which I ate by the light of my candle. It was always goat and rice. The man seemed more pleased to see me each day, and our encounters took on the quality of visits to an old friend who had been lost for many years. He had worked in the canteen for twenty-seven years, he told me one day after I appeared early for lunch to find him laid out across some of the chairs sound asleep in a pink polyester shirt the colour of the walls. He became animated when he told me how busy this place had been before independence, waving his hands around slowly to express his words like a slow motion mime artist. He asked me whether I was from South Africa.

'No, from Inglaterra,' I said. This information drew the usual response, a huge smile and a sigh: 'Ooh, Inglaterra? That's very far away. Ah yes, very far.'

'Do you get many visitors from Inglaterra?' I asked him.

'Not now,' he sighed, 'before, there were many. They stayed in the Hotel Dom Carlos, but then the war.' He gave me another wide smile and opened out his white palms to wave them gently about his torso. 'Then nothing,' he said, 'nothing.'

My visits to the man with the hole in his cheek were part of the daily routine which involved rising with the sun since room 310 had no curtains. The dawn would come up like a huge painting outside the window, with pink and orange glows on the clouds above the lighthouse, which must have been on the blink the night the now rusting freighter *Macúti* had been beached directly below it. The lighthouse was bricked up and looked as if it had not operated for many years, but each evening a weak pencil of light shone forth in a feeble effort to prevent further *Macútis* from being wrecked on the golden-grey sands.

Slowly, the sounds of the morning would begin outside

my window. Bouncing music from a limited selection of cassettes began to play from the kiosk opposite as people assembled by the bus stop for the trip into town. A motor would whoosh by, and the driver of a bus or converted lorry or pick-up would announce his arrival by leaning on his horn. The occasional bird would tweet and children's voices could be heard calling the odds over the first game of marbles in the dirt. In the audible background the Indian Ocean continued its lapping of the beach.

I would pull on my clothes and descend the deserted staircase of the Hotel Dom Carlos to drink a Coke and have a chat with the woman who ran the kiosk across the road. She was usually busy doing something else, like peeling boiled potatoes or sewing a button on to her children's clothes. One morning a man who was waiting for a bus told me that he had been a welder for ten years in Berlin and was now looking for a job in Beira. He asked me for a cigarette and I bought him a packet. He told me that these Kingsport cigarettes from Zimbabwe were usually past their sell-by date, and if you knew this you could peel one side of the pack away to reveal the date, which in this case was eleven months old. 'They know that Mozambicans are poor people so they will buy them anyway,' he said as his bus arrived, and he ran off clutching the out-dated packet.

After my Coke, I would continue fifty metres to the beach and plunge into the sea, and spend the rest of the day lounging about reading, often in the company of some small boys who would sit next to me, sometimes for a talk but as often as not just to sit and play in the sand. Some days I summoned the energy to catch a bus into town myself, since I intended to make a trip across the estuary of the river Pungoe to Buzi, an old sugar plantation. But I never made it to Buzi, the boat had always either just gone or wasn't going at all; I never quite got it right.

Beira was tired and run down. I could see that the cement city had once been noble and even beautiful in places, but now it was just another collection of decrepit buildings decaying in a network of pavements which looked like the scenes of mini-earthquakes where the tree roots had burst through the concrete slabs. Urine and rotting refuse vied with the sweet perfumes of the frangipanis, and crushed Coca-Cola cans embossed with the words 'Do not litter – keep South Africa clean' should have had 'Throw it away in Mozambique' added to their dictum.

Some people were prospering, like the Indians in their smart cars and fancy clothes. As in other cities in Mozambique, they had the commercial sector sewn up and could now afford shiny BMWs and Mercedes-Benzes which the young Indians drove with too much speed and screeching of tyres.

One evening I decided to forgo the candlelit goat and rice routine and went in search of somewhere with a more extensive menu. I jumped on to a wagon which was headed for town as the sun was about to set, squeezing in next to a man wearing a mock US army khaki shirt, and we took off. A sack on the roof was leaking maize and when a man climbed aboard with two ducks dangling from his hand the US army guy next to me said that he had come at the right time because ducks were very good with maize. Everybody inside the cramped vehicle laughed at that and I pulled my lighter from my pocket and said we should start the fire now, and everybody laughed some more.

I got out of the *chapa* when we reached the centre of town and crossed over towards a square. Beneath a street lamp a small group had gathered to watch a game of draughts played with beer and Coca-Cola bottle tops. It was difficult to tell in the dim light whether the approaching motorcyclist deliberately tried to mount the central reservation à la Steve McQueen in *The Great Escape*, or for some reason lost control. He hit the concrete kerb at speed, the machine went over on itself and crumpled like a piece of cheap metal. Sparks flew and I heard some crunching noises. The man took about a hundred years to fly through the air, bend in the middle and hit a tree with his head. The head on the tree made a dull thump and I might have heard a cracking sound which would have been his neck breaking, but I wouldn't swear to that. He slumped sideways, still hunched, his head at an unnatural angle, his eyes wide open and blank.

His denim shirt with embroidered pocket was frayed at the collar and his trainers were tied with bits of string. He looked like a hundred other guys you see every day on the streets of Mozambican cities. Only this one was now dead. A human being with blood and a brain and emotions, and perhaps a few friends. It was odd to think that the only dead person I saw in Mozambique, a country with more than its fair share of dead people, was the victim of a traffic accident.

I cut through the square as people were running towards the dead man from all directions. I had heard of and seen situations like this, in which an innocent foreign bystander is accused of involvement in an accident he has just witnessed, so I didn't want to stay. A small crowd had gathered at the scene and someone was bent over the body looking for signs of life as I turned a corner. I was looking for the only restaurant I had been able to identify during the previous day's wanderings. The PicNic was hidden down a grubby little sidestreet towards the docks. Down the ill-lit, smelly, rubbish-strewn alley you go and then this flunkey in a red top hat and well-pressed jacket materialises to invite you in and open a door. You step inside and enter a world of over-attentive waiters in white shirts, maroon waistcoats and bow ties, where a general manager floats around to ask if everything is allrightsir and a stern maitre d' disapproves of your clothes and scowls when you ask for *cerveja nacionale*. There was even a guy whose job it was to light your cigarette with a flamethrower.

The lights on a small Christmas tree flashed on and off on a three-second time switch and soft Hispanic muzak filled the subtly lighted room. There was a red carpet which was just a carpet, with potted ferns placed on it at strategic locations, and a piece of matting painted with an unpleasant curved abstract pattern hanging on one wall. A large beaten brass gong shielded the bar from the dining area which had room for nine tables covered in red and white check tablecloths. I ate olives and bread and a tournedo PicNic since the prawns were off. The tournedo shared the plate with some over-cooked french beans and chips. As I stepped back into the street it was like being covered with a hot wet blanket. A street light across the road lit a couple of boys dressed in rags playing in the puddles of fetid water which would not drain away. The vacant lot next door to the PicNic was full of the carcasses of dead cars and there was a smell of fresh excrement in the air. Frankly, I preferred the goat and rice.

I passed a restless night in a sweaty sheet in the company of several cockroaches, a single bloody mosquito and a rat which was trying to gnaw the door away. But when I woke there was a crisp zing in the air which was enough to make anyone feel that life was worth living. The morning light filled my room as I lay there. The Hotel Dom Carlos must have been a rather upmarket place when it was first built, I thought. There was a marble floor in my bathroom and big brass lion-headed towel rails and soap-holders, more marble on the ornately carved tables in the bedroom, and a large coat of arms in plaster behind a glass screen above the window. The walls were covered in gilt candelabra light sockets, though none of them now held bulbs, and the white stucco ceiling looked like hoof marks in dry mud around a waterhole. There were gilt-edged mirrors everywhere and an oil painting of a ballerina hung slightly cock-eyed on one wall. I had tried to straighten it several times, but it preferred an angle.

It was Sunday and I was going to spend it on the beach. I had more company than on other days. There were the usual groups of small children and bands of people hauling fishing nets out of the ocean, but Sunday was also the day that Beira's forsaken Russian population came out to play. There were several parties of them looking burly and slightly awkward as if they had been given an extra stone of muscle overnight and were still getting used to moving inside their expanded bodies. The troubles of the world, many of them theirs, were etched on their thick white faces, and they were drinking a lot of beer to forget them.

I was settling down to read my book when a young Mozambican approached me, sat about two towel lengths away from me on the sand and said hello. He was a tall young man, with long expressive fingers and delicate arms. He wore a white straw hat with a wide brim which threw a shadow on to a sensitive face. He pulled off the canvas shoes from his feet and sifted sand through his fingers. He said that he was a student from Tete studying here in Beira and his name was Assado.

Assado and I spent much of the day together, chatting about this and that. This was his holiday period and he was waiting to travel to Tete, in the north-west, just as soon as his father had finished fixing his old Ford lorry. Assado wanted to go to university in Maputo when he had finished school, but this would be difficult since he would have to pay a lot of money which he hadn't got. Towards the end of the afternoon, Assado and I took a walk up the beach, beyond the lighthouse and the wreck of the *Macúti*. Set back from the sands were lines of bungalow beach houses which belonged to the Estoril.

'Before, when tourists mans coming and they want to play on the beach, they take one of these,' Assado told me in his broken English, which was, none the less, better than my Portuguese. Now workers from the hotel lived in some, while *deslocados* lived in others.

Long heavy wooden boats were drawn up on the sands and a group of boys, perhaps five- or six-year-olds, were catching terns for their supper. Their traps were ingeniously simple, comprising two sticks stuck vertically in the sand at the water's edge eight inches apart. A length of filament fishing line was strung between the two sticks and a small silver fish placed beneath the line. Once the traps were set the boys retreated to the wooden boats to wait for one of the white seabirds to arrive, hovering along the coast above the gentle breakers. Swooping to catch the silver bait, the bird would get entangled in the line and two of the boys would rush to the water, one to grab the tern by its wings and carry it up the beach, the other to reset the trap. The boys were gentle with their prey, but they enjoyed allowing the bird to peck at their fingers with its long orange beak. I chose not to stay to see how they killed their dinner.

Later that evening, after I had eaten, Assado and I met up and took a lorry into town to drink coffee in a café called the Scala. We sat down at a table near one of the doors. I had been to the Scala a few times during the day when its clientèle consisted of elderly Portuguese men who read the newspaper or discussed topical issues in gruff tones, middle-aged businessmen in short-sleeved shirts carrying folders, and young women who looked as if they had been up for much of the night. Ferns and elephants' ears in pots lined the low split hardwood window sills which they shared with the upturned corpses of a thousand flies. Some bedraggled Christmas streamers adorned the windows behind stickers advertising Lucky Strike cigarettes, 'An American Original'. A central thick red pillar grew out of the mock crazy paving concrete floor like one of the trees in the pavements outside. Its trunk was adorned with a black metal relief sculpture, abstract but reminiscent of a disorganised line of different sized beer bottles. The radio played a mixture of jazz which was so laid back it could put you to sleep and African dance music which passing women of all ages, shapes and sizes could not help swinging their hips to in a way that European women simply can't do.

Among the evening's customers were the same girls as in the mornings, only now they were spruced up and ready for the night ahead. The Scala's waiters all wore ancient white tunics and trousers with a sky-blue trim. Their outfits were frayed at every edge possible and more besides. All had pockets which sagged from years of being filled with small change and some had ragged holes in the shoulders.

Assado left me to people-watch over a second coffee, brought in a sachet with a small pot of hot water and another two sachets containing sugar. The café had the carefree atmosphere of a student bar where most of the customers knew each other and would pop in to pass the time of day with or without buying a coffee or a beer. Small boys patrolled the tables, some to sell cashew nuts, others just to ask for a hand-out. Some took time out from their routine to sit on the pavement or to play tag in the street. A youth of perhaps eighteen, in a white bush hat, white T-shirt and white shorts, hung around on the street corner on crutches, his useless stick legs dangling. The upper ends of his crutches were made from wooden gun-butts. He smiled a lot to himself and to anyone who noticed him.

After some minutes a young woman in a T-shirt, a pair of tan cut-off dungarees and open-toed sandals approached my table and asked whether she could join me. She said her name was Maria. Maria's face, which was handsome but not pretty, was mostly forehead, but that was probably only because her hair was scraped back so tightly over her scalp that it didn't really look like hair at all, more like a shiny black patina on her shapely skull. Below her neck her hair was tied in a cascade of thin plaits; her skin was smooth, with a sheen like polished ebony. She looked to be in her early twenties and must have been about five foot three in her bare feet, which judging by the hand on my knee was how she spent a lot of her time.

Maria held a neatly folded handkerchief in her other hand, which she sniffed at from time to time and otherwise waved about in an ineffectual effort to fan herself. She said she had a cold, which surprised me for some reason. She spoke slowly and lazily in Portuguese.

'You are from Zimbabwe,' she told me.

'No, I'm from Inglaterra,' I said.

'Aah, Inglaterra, that is far away,' she replied sniffing at her hanky. 'What are you doing in Beira?'

I told her and she feigned interest while keeping an eye on other tables.

'Are there many English people in Beira?' I asked her.

'No, not many,' she replied.

A waiter approached our table and Maria ordered a Fanta.

'How long do you stay in Beira?' she asked me.

'Just a few days.' Assado had offered me a lift with him to Tete in his father's truck. They were hoping to leave in two days' time.

'Do you want me to go with you to your hotel room?' Maria asked, looking directly into my eyes.

'I'm very tired,' I told her, 'I want to sleep.'

'I can leave afterwards,' she said helpfully.

The waiter put the Fanta and a glass down on the table between us. The orange can carried a picture of Donald Duck who was giving me a mischievous sideways grin.

'I don't think so,' I told her. She looked crestfallen but kept her hand on my knee just the same. Her eyes wandered across the café. I felt sorry for her.

'I don't like those men over there,' she said without turning back, 'they all think I'm a prostitute. They don't respect Mozambican women.'

'Are there many prostitutes in Beira?' I asked her.

'Yes, some of these girls here are prostitutes, they are all my friends.'

She got up from her chair suddenly and swayed her hips as she walked over to a table at the other side of the room. She took a cigarette from a packet on the table, which was occupied by two young women both with dyed blonde streaks in their afro hair. Maria talked to her friends for a minute as she lit her cigarette and returned to where I was sitting. Donald Duck was still grinning sideways at me. Maria looked bored.

'Do you live near here?' I asked in an attempt to make conversation.

'Yes,' she said through her handkerchief, gazing at nothing in particular in the street outside. She sipped some Fanta.

'With your parents?'

'No, my mother is dead. My father lives in another town.' She was still staring outside.

I drained my coffee cup. I didn't really see why I should be made to feel guilty because I didn't want to go to bed with this woman.

'I live in my house, I pay for water, electricity, food. I'm not a prostitute.'

'I didn't say you were,' I told her.

'You are thinking it,' she said, 'I just come in here to take a coffee or a Fanta and if I meet someone I like I might walk with them.'

A boy with a severe crewcut came up to our table and looked at me. I looked at him back. He asked for my sugar sachets and I gave them to him. He took them and said something to Maria in a language I didn't understand. She smiled and he walked out of the café to sit down on the pavement and tear open the sachets. He poured the sugar grains into his mouth from about six inches above his nose.

Maria turned to me and asked, 'Are you married?'

'No.'

She sniffed. The boy with the crewcut screwed up the empty sachets and dropped them in the gutter. The youth with the gun-butt crutches and the useless dangling stick legs was on the move. A middle-aged man at a table on the pavement gave him a red 1000 meticais note and the youth looked at it from below the brim of his bush hat. He moved his head to look around and hobbled over to our table just inside the door. He proffered the note to Maria, saying that he wanted to buy a beer. A thousand was not enough, so I chipped in the difference, but he still wanted Maria to buy it for him. She called a waiter who shuffled over, threw the youth a quick disparaging glance and told him sharply to stay outside. The youth smiled and hobbled to a free table

169

on the pavement to sit down with some effort. The waiter eventually brought him his beer.

Maria was waving her hanky aimlessly again, staring up the street outside towards two kids dashing along the pavement in front of a decaying concrete apartment block guiding old bicycle wheels in front of them with sticks.

'Do the girls here have men who take a part of their money?' I asked her. 'Prostitutes are often controlled by a man in other countries.'

'No,' she said, 'why do you always speak of prostitutes?'

'Sorry, let's talk about something else. Do you like dancing?'

'Yes,' she said, smiling at me.

'Are there good dancing places here in Beira?'

'Yes, there is a place not far from here.' She pointed out into the night.

'Shall we go?' I asked her. Maria smiled again and stood up.

'Come on,' she said, tucking her handkerchief into the top of her dungarees.

I paid the bill and we walked for ten minutes, across a patch of waste ground and over a small bridge. The night was thick and humid and the cicadas were playing at full strength. Small boys hung around the entrance to the night spot trying to sell cigarettes and chewing gum. The dancing place was an open-air compound with rush-roof parasols over the tables and fairy lights on the rush roofs; it was fairly empty. Maria had a long chat with the waiter who brought us our beers, and we danced on the central concrete dancing pad to African music with a strong beat. Soon some of the other women from the Scala began to appear and set up shop at other tables. But it was not a busy night. Everyone seemed to be bored and just going through the motions. When I left at one in the morning, Maria asked me if I could buy her another beer. I did.

10

FISH ISLAND

I waited for another three days in the hope of hitching a lift to Tete with Assado and his father. They kept being nearly ready to leave, but never quite; I could tell that I might spend another month waiting for them, so I moved on, not to Tete but to Nampula province in the north-east. I flew to Nampula, the provincial capital, and after sitting by the roadside for two long hours I jumped on to the first *chapa* which was headed towards the coast. I was aiming for Ilha de Moçambique, or Mozambique Island, capital of the country for much of the time of Portuguese rule.

It took three rides and most of the day to travel the 180 kilometres. On the first *chapa*, a lorry fitted out with wooden benches in the back covered by a tarpaulin, the driver called me to join him in the cab after we had passed through a perfunctory military checkpoint on the outskirts of Nampula. He introduced himself as Alberto and told me that he had been a driver for eleven years, since his sixteenth birthday. He said he had a wife, two children and a headache, and had I got anything for him? I gave Alberto some paracetamol and asked why there was still a checkpoint on this road. Was it because it was still attacked? I asked, trying to sound casual.

'No,' he replied, 'the purpose for these roadblocks is gone now, but the soldiers have nothing else to do. They are waiting for demobilisation.'

I left Alberto at the point where he turned off the main route towards Ilha de Moçambique, a place called Namialo. Huge soft bales of cotton were piled up on a concrete pad beside the road and there were a lot of people milling about waiting for rides. The next leg of the journey was in the back of another truck fitted with benches, but this one was uncovered and the driver sped through the lush green landscape at such a pace that I had to remove my glasses to prevent them from being blown away in the wind. This lorry dropped me and some other passengers at the turn-off which led to the port of Nacala, north of my island destination. A small group of children sold the usual display of goods by the roadside: cigarettes, cashew nuts roasted in their husks, home-made snacks, piles of mangoes and pineapples. Nearing the coast, more of the people climbing in and out of the trucks I was riding were wearing headgear, the women brightly coloured headscarves and the men Muslim skullcaps. The colour of people's faces was changing too, from black African to a mixed-race, lighter-coloured stock.

I travelled the final fifty kilometres to Ilha de Moçambique in an ancient dark blue Mazda lorry which belonged to Mohammed Abibo Haji Cassano. The going was more leisurely than the gale force winds of the previous truck, and I was quite happy to ride in the back until Abibo asked me to join him in the honoured cab seat. The foam padding was oozing out of the torn covers and at the windows the blue paint had been worn away to the metal by years of elbow rubbing.

Abibo presented a neat, clean-cut figure in his pink-and-white striped short-sleeved shirt and blue slacks. His closely trimmed black beard and large brown eyes gave him a Middle Eastern appearance. He told me that he was glad the war was over as we passed what was left of a Toyota pickup silent and crumpled beside the road in the afternoon sunshine. 'War has no eyes,' he said. 'This is an old Swahili saying. Many innocent men and women were killed on this road.' Now people could go back to their *machambas* and get on with their lives, and he could conduct more business and meet people like me from faraway countries. This was good because he had always been interested in faraway countries.

'Inglaterra has much industry and many machines, I have heard,' he said to me, 'what about fruits? Are they the same as in Mozambique?'

I told him that we imported many of the same types of fruit, but we didn't grow things like mangoes, pineapples and papayas.

'The mangoes here in Mozambique are very good,' Abibo said, 'there are many different kinds.' We were approaching a village and there was a call from the back of the lorry which meant that one of the passengers wanted to get out. Abibo slowly drew his vehicle to a halt at the roadside, opposite a clearing surrounded by reed huts.

'Come on, I want to show you,' Abibo said, and he climbed out of his door, leaving the engine to pump black exhaust fumes into the still air. We crossed the road to the clearing where numerous piles of mangoes were on display. There were tiny orange ones each the size of an egg, slightly larger versions in red and small rugby balls in green.

'These are the best to eat,' Abibo said, crouching down to pick one of the green rugby balls from the pile in front of a haggard woman in a matching green scarf tied tightly over her head.

'How much are they?' I asked the woman.

'Five hundred for six,' she told me with an expectant smile.

'In England you would pay five thousand meticais just for one,' I said. Both Abibo and the haggard woman looked amazed.

'Five *thousand*?' Abibo repeated in an astonished tone.

'Five thousand.'

Abibo drew a five, a comma and three noughts with his finger in the dirt in front of the mango pile. 'Five thousand?' he said again.

'Yes, that's right.'

Abibo shook his head incredulously, but the woman looked unimpressed. I had quite obviously got it wrong, there was no way that a single mango could cost that much. I bought some green mangoes as Abibo moved over to another woman sitting behind a heap of large tiger prawns on a banana leaf. We walked back to the blue truck, now enveloped in a suffocating cloud of black smoke, and climbed into the cab. Passengers in the back were hanging out of splits in the tarpaulin waving hands across their faces, but no one complained that their bus driver had taken a notion to buy a few provisions and left them to asphyxiate in a cloud of fumes. Abibo placed his prawns carefully on their banana leaf in the cracked dusty dashboard, gently let his vehicle into gear and we pulled away from the village.

Mango and cashew trees lined the route, interspersed with bundles of wood for sale as fuel, each tied neatly with a long strip of bark. Small boys waved as we passed and proffered their junior-sized plastic bowls of roasted nuts. We chugged along at a constant forty kilometres an hour, past a defunct sisal plantation, its ranch house gutted and roofless in the distance, the rows of spiky sisal plants still discernible but almost engulfed in long grasses and stumpy shrubs. Every so often we drove over a blackened and blistered piece of asphalt where a truck had been attacked, its driver shot, its contents carried off and the vehicle left to burn.

I got my first glimpse of the sea and Abibo said that we would arrive soon.

'Look,' he cried suddenly, 'there is my new house.' He pointed across to my side of the road towards a shell built in red brick which was set back from the road and full of undergrowth. 'M. Abibo Haji Cassano' was daubed in pink paint on the inside back wall.

'I am still building it,' he added, 'it should be finished soon.' There was no way of my telling how long 'soon' meant to Mohammed Abibo Haji Cassano.

As the road continued along the coastline, he pointed out huge rectangular cleared patches which were too brilliantly white to look at directly. 'Salt,' Abibo announced, 'do you have salt in Inglaterra?'

Ilha de Moçambique was connected to the mainland in 1966 by a single lane concrete causeway with passing places, and as we crossed it Abibo waved and called out to almost everyone we passed. 'That is the administrator of the island,' he said of one middle-aged man we trundled past.

Abibo was smiling broadly. He took one hand off the steering wheel to gesture at the long low landmass we were approaching.

'On this island we have fish,' he said lovingly, 'not much else, but there are a lot of fish.'

Ilha de Moçambique is a long thin, slightly curved island a couple of miles in length and about a quarter of a mile across. On a map it looks like a banana leaning over and pointing out into the Indian Ocean.

There were about 7000 people crammed on to it the last time anyone counted, which was in 1980. There are probably more now, but I shouldn't think many of them are terribly bothered about it. The inhabitants are a pretty laid-back lot, most of them fishermen, and as Abibo said, there are plenty of fish. The people live in two distinct zones, a stone-built area which takes up much of the northern end of the island and a reed-hut zone to the south. The two zones meet in the middle of the island, facing each other along a perfectly straight dirt and rubble roadway. The dirt and rubble, like the stone dwellings to the north, are made of limestone. In fact, the whole island is made of limestone.

It was here that Vasco da Gama landed in March 1498, starting almost five hundred years of Portuguese rule over Mozambique. Da Gama was by no means the first foreign maritime visitor to drop anchor at Mozambique Island. Greeks, Persians, Indians, Chinese and Arabs had been here before him. During the island's long history as a port and commercial centre it has been laid siege to, invaded, pillaged and razed by countless seafaring nationals. But it is the last four hundred years of history that are reflected in the stone buildings of the island.

In 1609, the Portuguese appointed a governor for its east African colony with a capital at Ilha de Moçambique, and that

175

administration became self-governing in the mid-eighteenth century, after a period in which it was administered with Portuguese territories in India. The eighteenth century was the ivory century, and ports like Ilha de Moçambique were thriving, busy places. Tusks, traded principally by the elephant hunters and merchants of the northern Yao tribe, were exchanged for cloth brought from the Indies. As the 1700s progressed, the Portuguese also became interested in package tourism. Mozambicans were offered trips to exotic locations such as Brazil, North America and the Caribbean, and by the dawn of the nineteenth century Ilha de Moçambique and the port of Quelimane down the coast became the Gatwick and Luton airports of their time, dealing with 10,000 passengers a year. The only differences between the Portuguese version of package tourism and its twentieth-century equivalent was that the tours lasted a lifetime. And the tourists were involuntary. It was called the slave trade.

This repugnant commerce was not entirely the fault of the evil white man. The Yao were keen enough to keep the slave ships supplied with their African kith and kin. The coastal Makua tribe swept the north-east clean of spare able-bodied Africans, and the Chikunda spread their net into Zumbo and the Luangwa Valley in present-day Zambia. Until the 1860s, most of the unfortunate victims were probably obtained through negotiation with local rulers, but after that time the trade became more mercenary, as European merchants started swapping guns for slaves, making raiding and conquest a more profitable mode of acquisition. David Livingstone, an ardent anti-slavery campaigner, reckoned that for each person sold into bondage four others died either in the raids or on the march to the coast.

Lisbon had outlawed the slave trade by this time, having realised that kidnapping people from their homes, marching them in chains to a ship, cramming them into the hold and giving them a hideous trip to a life of misery on another continent was not an acceptable way to behave. But the practice continued illicitly for another fifty years. Labourers were collected in the interior, marched to the coast and then asked in Swahili – the language of the coast which they did not understand – whether they objected to going to the French island colony of Réunion. If they did not reply, which of course they could not since they didn't understand the question, it was assumed that they had no objections.

For the merchants of Ilha de Moçambique these were profitable times, and their fortunes were ploughed into the stone dwellings of the island. If you could conveniently forget that these buildings were constructed by slave traders and elephant murderers, the tranquil tree-lined streets with their render-and-lime façades, carved cornices and rhythmically placed windows in restrained walls evoked all the romance and mystique of the Arabian Nights. Or had done. Most of them are now falling to bits.

Today, the stone town of Ilha de Moçambique looks more like war-torn Beirut or Mogadishu than any fairytale city. Gaping holes yawn from the wreckage, small fans of rubble are piled against the crumbling walls, and black and green lichens swarm across every surface like creeping lurgi, slowly digesting the calcareous façades. The dereliction is not due to the war: Ilha de Moçambique was pretty much cut off from the death and destruction on the mainland, its causeway easy to defend. Simple economic impoverishment is the reason.

The island's hospital was one of the sorriest looking buildings I had ever seen. It was in the middle of the stone part of town, on one side of a leafy square. It looked as if it had been sitting there since Noah's flood and had come out of that badly. Its ornate wrought-iron gate led into spacious grounds which still displayed the bones of a classical layout, with empty flower beds and derelict fountains. A once-grand sweeping stone staircase fed into the main building through six slim columns holding up a crenellated portico, its doorway permanently open because one of the doors was missing. I was so moved by the sad exterior that I ventured in one day and asked whether I could look around. The director appeared and took me on a short tour.

It was a large complex, and the oldest hospital in Mozambique, the director said. He was a youngish man, perhaps in his late thirties, and most of the staff whom I saw were ten years younger. They were all bright and friendly and dressed in white coats as clean and smart as they could be, given their obvious age. Their hospital was as clean as circumstances allowed, and some of the rear buildings had freshly white-washed walls beneath their sagging terracotta roof tiles. There was room for forty patients in the various wards, the beds metal-framed, some with mattresses, some without. The well-swept floors were uneven with cracked tiles, the ceilings and walls mouldy in places, doors hung from their hinges and many of the window frames no longer had glass. All the rooms were equipped with a bare minimum: I only knew I was in a hospital in one consulting room because there was a dog-eared poster on the wall, behind an ancient desk and a wooden chair without a back, which said 'vaccinate and prevent'. In another consulting room, equipped with a metal-framed bed with foot traps which made it look like a medieval instrument of torture, a small girl in the clutches of her mother was having a gammy leg dabbed with iodine by an orderly. The little girl looked grim and very determined not to cry. In the pharmacy, another young male orderly smiled and waved his hand around the airy high-ceilinged room with its bare shelves.

'We have almost nothing,' he said. The comment was both a cry for help and a statement of pride that the hospital was still functioning, despite the desperate lack of resources.

The strange non-existence of clues as to the function of some of the hospital rooms, a simple reflection of the absence of objects, was echoed in many of the island's stone buildings. Bars were spartan and functional: an old wooden counter, battered chairs and tables in various states of disrepair, sometimes an old calendar adorning one wall, occasionally a refrigerator. The dwellings too were bare. I met a student named Silvano who took me to see his sister in her apartment along one of the debris-strewn streets. The wide stone staircase up to the first floor was swept but crumbling. Inside the two-room apartment Silvano's niece and nephew played on the stone floor beside a single old black settee with torn plastic upholstery. A sideboard stood against one peeling wall. There were no carpets, no pictures on the walls, no books and no bookcases, no radio or TV. A lack of material comfort gave the apartment a Zen quality in which wall-gazing could become an attractive proposition.

Yet the absence of so many of the possessions we take for granted in the rich countries did not seem to faze the inhabitants of Ilha de Moçambique. As in the hospital, they just got on with life and made do. It was ironic that the most cluttered rooms I saw on the island were those of the art museum, a small, solid eighteenth-century building with stone crucifixes above its rounded windows. Its display cases were full of the paraphernalia of the ruling Portuguese: silver candlesticks, incense boxes in the shapes of galleons, caskets, Catholic costumes and images of Christ.

The island's importance as a port and as the seat of Portuguese governance meant that many descriptions of the place and its surrounds have been written by residents and passing travellers over the centuries. HM consul in Mozambique in the late nineteenth century was a man named Captain O'Neill, who hated his desk job on the island and took every available opportunity to explore the mainland in an effort to drive out 'a few of those elephants with which – upon the authority of Swift – mappers are wont to bedeck the blank spaces of the earth'. The reports of his expeditions into the blank spaces, in search of new routes and uncharted mountains, lakes and rivers, were discussed regularly by geographical gurus at the Royal Geographical Society in London. In a report read to the Society in 1885, O'Neill noted with incredulity that although the Portuguese had been on Mozambique Island for nearly four hundred years, they had only just discovered the harbour at Nacala, considered by O'Neill to be one of the finest on the east African coast, and within a day's sail of Ilha de Moçambique to the north.

It was the discovery of Nacala that sapped the island's local importance as a port, and this was followed by the shift of the colony's economic centre of gravity southwards, culminating in the movement of the capital to Lourenço Marques in 1897. Altogether, the dawn of the twentieth century spelt the beginning of the end of Ilha de Moçambique's significance. Today it is a sleepy backwater with a lot of fish and reminders of times gone by. Some suggested in the early post-war days of 1993 that the country's capital should be transferred back to the island, but few took the idea seriously. It remains for Mozambique's government to find the cash to renovate and conserve the island's heritage, a plan they have already started in a minor way.

Another explorer who visited Ilha de Moçambique was Henry Salt, who stopped off on his way from Portsmouth to Abyssinia in the first decade of the nineteenth century. Salt saw great numbers of fin whales in the Mozambique Channel as he sailed up the coast from the Cape to dock at the island, and his ship was hailed as they passed the fort, which still stands at the northernmost tip of the island, by a trumpet three feet in circumference. Salt's description of the fort, built in 1508 from gargantuan chunks of limestone which are now honeycombed by centuries of salty spray on the seaward sides, could almost have been written the day I wandered into its compound. He saw eighty pieces of cannon mounted, a lot of rusty cannon balls lying around on the battlements and, apart from a few sentries, the only people to be seen were two or three old women selling cakes. The cannon and the cannon balls were the same nearly two hundred years later. There were no sentries, but in lieu of the cake sellers, I said hello to two youths who immediately ran away, to return half an hour later clutching a leopard skin and a turtle shell which they offered for sale.

Salt mentioned in his diaries an interesting local method for catching turtles which involved tying a particularly odd species of fish to a line and trailing it in the water behind a boat. Salt referred to it as a 'sucking fish', because of the incredible suction it exerted with its mouth. The sucking fish was particularly drawn to turtles, Salt was told by a local bishop, and once it had slapped its lips on one there was no pulling it off. To catch your turtle you simply pulled in the line once the fish had started to suck on the nearest large marine reptile.

I tried to ask the boys whether they had caught their turtle in this way, but my confused questioning succeeded only in drawing confirmation that turtles did indeed live in the sea, and that the sea was also full of fish. My attempts to mimic the sucking fish left them with the impression that Englishmen enjoyed amorous encounters with turtles whenever the opportunity arose.

I gave up trying to confirm Salt's story and told the boys that I didn't want the turtle shell after all, which confused them even more. Then they proffered the leopard skin instead; perhaps a dead cat would be a more suitable object for my curious desires? No, I told them. They were undaunted, this was useful market research information. How about a live turtle then? No. Was it the fish that interested me? No. Things had got out of hand. I left them looking perplexed, re-examining their merchandise in a totally new light.

My hotel, the Pousada de Moçambique, was the only one on the island and situated near the fort at the northern end. It was fitted out with the usual dust and cobwebs I had come to associate with hotels in Mozambique and, like the island as a whole, it suffered frequent power cuts. The staff, most of whom had been working there since Portuguese times, were businesslike and friendly, and each morning a man brought me a bucket of fresh water drawn from the well inside the fort's compound. They had welcomed very few guests during the war years, the water man told me, but now that it was over they were almost full most weekends, although during the week when I was staying there were only two other guests.

On the evenings when power cuts hit the Pousada de Moçambique, I ate my dinner by candlelight, although there was only ever one candle, which was passed between the tables by whoever finished first. The waiters, all wearing blue shirts which were more darning than original material, were so used to operating in the dark that they never needed artificial assistance. They walked silently in bare feet on the rich red-brown parquet floors.

Meals were usually fish, occasionally squid, always grilled or fried to juicy perfection. Sometimes the waiters would nod knowingly when I asked about dessert and bring a small crème caramel, the only type of pudding I ever ate anywhere in Mozambique and was always referred to as 'puddim'. The excellent food was eaten from white tablecloths which were so thick and starched they could have stood without a table beneath. The dining room had a high, formerly white ceiling with huge beams, and water marks and mould above ornate square metal lamps dangling from thick chains. Tangled grubby thin cables wound their way up and down the walls leading into candelabra fittings and across the beams like trapeze wire to feed into the lamps. If all these lights had been lit at once, which they never were since most lacked bulbs, diners would have had to be issued with sunglasses and parasols to eat their meals. After dinner I would take my coffee outside on the terrace overlooking the fort and the rocky foreshore, where the stone columns of the low wall had been eaten away to their rusting braces by the salty ocean breeze.

One day, Silvano, the student, offered to go with me across the causeway to the mainland in search of a British war cemetery I had been told of by the third secretary at the British Embassy in Maputo. The Lumbo British Cemetery was looked after by the War Graves Commission, said Keith Shannon, a small bright Scottish chap in his early thirties. I left the hotel early in the morning and walked the length of the island to meet Silvano at the start of the causeway, the place to hitch a lift. I strolled along the narrow palm-lined beach on the east side of the island where long boats were drawn up on the grubby sands and kids were having an early morning shit at the water's edge. Goats, ducks and chickens roamed, waddled and strutted in search of pickings and fishermen squatted to mend their nets. I cut inland and proceeded through the hut part of town along the central avenue, which was elevated above the reed roofs, looking down into mud compounds where women dressed in *capelanas* and head scarves, bright moulded plastic sandals on their feet, swept up the debris of the previous day. Other women sat in the shade of their huts applying their ground bark face masks against the day's sun.

We caught a truck and crossed the causeway where boys were waiting by fishing lines trailing into the grey water. We had passed a signpost pointing towards the cemetery the day of my arrival with Mohammed Abibo Haji Cassano, but I wasn't at all sure how far it was from the island. We had stopped several times to let people climb on and off before Silvano called out and pointed to the signpost, printed in Portuguese and English. We shouted for the truck to stop and jumped out to march back up the road to where Silvano had seen the sign. It was pointing off to the right. We turned to the left, using a cunning piece of local knowledge with which Keith Shannon had furnished me. 'Walk in the opposite direction,' he had said, 'the signpost is always slipping on its pole.'

We struck off the tarmac on a sandy track and walked for twenty minutes with the sea just out of sight to our right, past *machambas* with small mandioca plants set back from the track and some colonial-style brick houses, most of which looked empty. Two young girls approached us from the opposite direction and we asked them if we were on the right track. One of them smiled and led us a hundred yards back the way she had come to where she could point out a low green metal fence.

'There is the cemetery,' she said.

It was a small area, perhaps forty metres square, hemmed in by the sturdy fencing, and overhung by a spreading mango tree which was dropping its green fruit in one corner. There were about eighty graves, set out in lines of knee-high head-stones in front of a central stone monument with a cross and the inscription 'Their names liveth for evermore'. The square was neatly maintained, the sand in which the headstones were set had been raked recently. Immediately in front of the first set of headstones, four small palms splayed their fronds like bursting fireworks caught in a freeze frame. Long, shiny black millipedes with bright orange legs slunk across the sand and huge yellow and red grasshoppers wandered aimlessly in their laborious way. Just behind the cemetery a woman was tilling her mandioca beneath a large cashew tree.

All the deceased had fallen at Lumbo in 1918 fighting a force of Germans retreating from German East Africa. Most had been attached to the King's African Rifles. Sergeant Major J. Malcolm of the Gordon Highlanders had fallen on 30 August, a quote from Byron on his headstone. Sapper Robert Edward Wallis, of the South African Engineers, 'In most proud and loving memory'. Sergeant S. J. Haywood of the Military Police Corps was 'Loved by all and really missed'. From their final resting place they looked out over the sparkling ocean, Ilha de Moçambique and the smaller Ilha de Goa sitting on the horizon in a sea full of fish.

11

TETE IS BONITA

Nothing seemed to be happening in Chimoio. It was a one horse town, and I think the horse was away for the weekend. There were people, quite a lot of them, but they were all congregated around the *chapa* stop, apparently eager to leave. I was waiting with them, for a lift to Tete, but it was early afternoon and I seemed to have missed all the connections.

There was no hint of a breeze, the heat was sauna-like and I was itching all over from an encounter with Mozambican micro-vermin the night before. The flies were out in force and showing a keen interest in the drips constantly forming on my brow. My shirt and trousers were clammy against my skin after several hours sitting wedged into a plastic seat cover. My entire body felt sticky and dirty – my hair, my fingernails, the small of my back, under my armpits and in my crotch. I didn't want to stay in Chimoio and I was going to have to.

I went in search of the town's hotel. The entrance was hidden up a covered concrete side alley which couldn't have looked less like a hotel foyer. The man behind the desk, which was enveloped in cage wire and resembled a sentry box, looked as if he were serving a stretch for child abuse. One eye was above the other, his lip was permanently curled over a set of crooked brown teeth and his blue denim shirt was minus its collar. He was not interested in admitting guests.

'Hi, do you have a room for tonight?' I asked.

'No,' came the reply.

'It's just for tonight.'

'No rooms.' He was looking at me as if I were a burnt match, or a piece of wallpaper, something which happened to be in his line of vision.

'Nothing at all?'

'Nothing.'

'You're full.'

'We're full.'

Other than the fact that the man behind the bars looked like a liar and a cheat, I had no reason to disbelieve him. My eyes wandered over the bare concrete walls all around me, there was nothing to confirm that this was a hotel. For a start, the electricity was on, which made it very unlikely. There had been no sign outside, and there were no clues inside: no board with room keys, no pot plant, no clock on the wall, just stains.

'This is a hotel?' I ventured.

'Yes.' He wasn't even looking at me now, I was that uninteresting.

'Is there another hotel nearby?'

'No.'

'Any other hotels in Chimoio?'

'No.'

He was a man of few words, and I felt like making him a man of few teeth. Perhaps that was why he was behind bars. Instead, I thought it might just be worth going for a bit of sympathy.

'I have been travelling all day. I'm very tired,' I told him, not really expecting a compassionate reaction. He looked at me as if to say 'so what?'

I squatted down against one of the walls and pulled some chewing gum from my pocket, unwrapped the stick and folded it into my mouth. My mind was about to start running through the options for spending the night rough in Chimoio.

'Are you alone?' came the voice from behind the bars.

'Yes.'

'We have a room for twenty thousand.'

He wanted the money up front, so I unfolded some bills

and gave him one of my best sneers as I fed them through the cage wire. He didn't react to my sneer, but pushed a key attached to a small piece of wood under the grill. I climbed the concrete stairs beside the cage.

On an open verandah an old man didn't look up from ironing a frayed sheet with a heavy implement filled with hot charcoal inside its open bottom. A small monkey tied to a rope on a post was playing with a used mango skin. I found my room and pushed the unlocked door open. Inside was a double bed made up with a sheet. Across the way was a bathroom, all cracked tiling, no taps on the sink and a single bucket sitting in a badly stained enamel bath. The bucket was empty.

Places to eat were thin on the ground in Chimoio, capital of Manica province. I found an elongated bar-cum-restaurant where the counter was at the opposite end to the entrance across the red concrete crazy-paving floor. There were white tiles on one wall and grey paint on the other. Pillars either side of the entrance and by the window were decorated with black-and-white mosaic pieces which formed stripes: thick black ones and thinner white ones.

I was the only customer.

The man behind the counter smiled widely as I approached him. Propped against the wall beside him on the bar was a blackboard the size of a school slate, with prices of drinks chalked on it. I ordered a *cerveja nacionale* and asked whether he had any food.

'We have rice. We have chicken,' he told me.

I said I'd like some of both and took my brown half-litre bottle without a label to one of the tables.

Two large speakers, mounted on opposite walls, were pumping African pop rhythms into the still air. The air was still because the four ceiling fans were not turning. I sank some of the refreshing beer and began to sweat again. A lion roared at me from a red circle on a black background on the table cloth. The lion had red eyes and a red tongue.

The place was dimpsy inside, but now that he had a customer the smiling bar tender switched on the three neon strip lights without covers. After a while, he brought me my chicken and rice.

Two men walked in, ordered beer, and sat down near the window. They couldn't see out of the window because it was covered by a thick drape of an indeterminate dark colour. They didn't talk to each other, just sat, letting the time go by. One of the men wore a grey suit with collar and lapels turned up as you might do if it were raining or cold. He had a thick beard on his gaunt face and his pink shirt matched his pink flip-flops. His friend was dressed in a black leather bomber jacket and a blue and white striped shirt with a white collar, like the ones city slickers wear.

Over the loudspeakers, Tropical Band, an Angolan group popular in Mozambique, were singing. The man in the grey suit drained his beer bottle, got up from his seat and left. His friend in the city slicker shirt carried his bottle over to my table as I was finishing my dinner and asked if he could join me. He sat down and introduced himself as Charles.

There was the usual sharp intake of breath and an exclamatory 'Epah!' when I told him I was from England. Charles was from Ilha de Moçambique, he told me, and he had three children and no job. Now that the war was over he thought that he might get some work on a farm somewhere. He was interested to know about England: 'Are there blacks there?' he asked.

'Yes,' I told him.

'Are there Mozambicans?'

'Yes, some, but not many.'

'Where is England?' he asked, furrowing his brow as if he were trying to remember, 'it's close to the USA, isn't it?'

'Not really,' I said, 'near France and Portugal.'

'Ah, yes,' he nodded knowingly, and took a swig from his beer bottle. 'It's cold there?' he asked.

'Yes,' I told him, 'especially in these months.'

'Is there hail and snow?'

I nodded.

'Epah! There's no hail, snow or even ice here – it's a normal climate. In Inglaterra I would die in one day.'

'You would get used to it,' I said.

We finished our beers, and Charles asked me if I would like to take a walk around the town. It was cool now in the evening, he said.

A bit of a wind had risen to turn the air over and a see-through plastic bag was rolling gently along the pavement as we emerged. The streets were more lively: people were milling around, sitting outside on the pavements talking. The dim glow from hurricane lamps lit kiosks run by Indian women who looked bored. We hit a couple of bars before arriving in the Sports Bar, a small establishment with no tables, just bar stools at a counter curved in the shape of an 'S'. There were large white tiles on the floor and blue patterned *azulejo* tiles around the walls. Everyone in the Sports Bar knew one another and I was introduced to them all. Most were Mozambicans, but there was one old Portuguese man who nursed a bottle of *cerveja nacionale* at one end of the counter. A bartender in a white shirt and black bow tie asked me what I wanted to drink. I ordered a beer and scanned the lines of well-stocked shelving behind him. My eyes picked out an unfamiliar bottle from the assortment of whisky, gin, beer and soft drinks. The label said it was Lágrima de Leao (Lion's Tear), aguadente de Manica. Charles asked the barman to pass the bottle and said he recommended it. We each had a shot poured out to chase the beers.

'Are there lions in Manica?' I asked Charles.

'No, they all ran away during the war,' he said. Then he smiled a cheeky grin and added, 'but there is another type of lion here.' His hands grasped his pectorals and he threw his head back to laugh heartily. He slapped me on the back and said: 'You can find them outside on the street.'

Lions were not the only large mammals to have suffered during the war. As we had passed the turning to Gorongosa national park earlier in the day, my mind had turned to the plight of Mozambique's elephant population. Renamo, whose headquarters was in Gorongosa, had been implicated in the mass slaughter of elephants. Ivory had allegedly been traded for arms with South Africa. At independence in 1975, Mozambique had around 65,000 elephants. Initial post-war estimates suggested that about 15,000 remained.

It wasn't particularly late, but I had to be at the *chapa* stop at four the following morning, so I told Charles I should be getting to my bed. He followed me out of the Sports Bar, and when we were on the street he asked me whether I wanted a woman to take back to the hotel. No thanks, I told him.

'Not expensive,' he said, 'only five thousand meticais.'

'No thanks, Charles,' I said, 'I'm not interested.'

He stopped a girl who was hanging around outside a building, beside some pillars which held up a balcony. Large areas of the plaster on the underside of the balcony had disappeared, and you could see through holes in the fabric in places. The girl, who had very short hair and a T-shirt which said 'Viva Saddam Hussein' across her small breasts, looked about fifteen years old.

'OK, she will go with you,' Charles told me after a short parley. I told him again that I wasn't interested and I shook my head at the girl and said, 'No thanks.' We walked on and I said goodbye to Charles outside the hotel.

I had shut my room door and was removing my shoes when there was a knock at the door. I opened it and the young girl stood in the doorway. I looked at her.

'That man wanted me, but I didn't like him,' she said gazing at me with the honesty of a child.

'I'm sorry,' I told her, 'but I don't want to do anything.' She didn't move, just looked slightly coy, and stared at my bare feet as if she hadn't seen a pair of feet like that before. 'Sorry,' I said again. The girl took her eyes off my feet and looked straight at me again. There may have been just the hint of a tear in her eye.

'Sorry,' I said for a third time, and then I tried to sound final, 'but no thanks. Goodbye.'

Still she didn't move. She looked around the room behind me, and then said in a barely audible voice, 'I'm hungry,' and tried to look waif-like, which she did very well.

In whatever time it takes for half a dozen thoughts to shoot through your mind, I stood looking at her standing awkwardly half inside my doorway, her feet playing with her flip-flops. If I gave her some money would this encourage her to solicit some more? If I didn't, would that do anything to stop her? Was she really short of cash, or was it just a ploy? If the girl really was hungry she would simply go back on to the streets and find someone else to sleep with. I dug into my pocket and pulled out a 1000 meticais note. I handed it to her and she took it, shrugged, turned, and walked away.

I shut the door and locked it. I'd had enough of Chimoio.

It was still dark the next morning as I walked with my bag over my shoulder the half mile to the *chapa* stop. There was a chill in the air and I stopped by a tree to yank the jumper out of my hold-all and pull it over my head. Shadowy figures were lying prostrate on the two benches outside the railway station which stood to one side of the area where the *chapas* stopped. A large goat, tied to a rusting oil drum full of refuse, was tugging at some titbit. Cockroaches scuttled across the cracked paving stones. Other bodies, wrapped in blankets, could be seen hunched along the station wall.

Trains were making train noises somewhere far off, although there had been no passenger services for many months, and cockerels started to crow as a rose-pink splash of dawn travelled towards a crescent moon in one corner of the sky over the station. A street sweeper shuffled by, wearing a bright blue coat and hood, pushing a small handcart with a broom sticking out. Gradually a steel-blue light tinged the scrawny clouds and rounded hills which became visible in the distance across the road.

A lorry and a minibus stood parked in front of the railway station building, and the passenger door of the lorry opened to let a man unfold and climb out. He stretched with his fists clenched and thrust up towards the moon, and patted his breast pockets. He pulled a packet of cigarettes from inside his jacket, selected a bent one, straightened it and struck a match which he cupped in his hands to light the cigarette. He looked around and I said good morning.

'Good morning,' he said back, exhaling a long plume of smoke from his lungs into the cool dawn air.

'Where are you going, Senhor?' I asked him.

'Beira,' he said. He stretched his arms again and walked around his vehicle checking its tyres.

People began to stir all around me as I sat on the raised pavement kicking my heels and wishing I were still in bed. The sliding door of the minibus was pushed open and a number of bodies lying across seats became visible. There was early morning stretching and a general pushing and shoving of bags inside as figures began rearranging themselves and emerging from the minibus to look around bleary eyed. A man almost fell out of the driver's seat on opening the door and when he had recovered his composure I asked him where he was headed. He was also going to Beira. Another half hour and several passing vehicles later, the morning had broken by the time an orange and tan combi, with the words 'Transportes Kamuba' stencilled on the side, pulled up and the driver said the magic word 'Tete' in response to my enquiry. I opened the passenger door, plonked my bag on the floor, and climbed in.

It took twenty minutes for passengers to wedge their assortment of bags, cardboard boxes and sacks into every available space inside the combi. The driver raked a comb through his hair in the cracked wing mirror, climbed into his seat, selected a cassette from the pile on the dashboard and pushed it into the player. He turned the key in the ignition, revved the engine and pulled away from the kerb to the sounds of the black South African singer Brenda Fassie. We drove a mile or so to the edge of town and turned off the asphalt along a track to a collection of round mud huts and corrugated iron lowdowns. A man dressed in a long orange vest which reached down to just above his calf-length brown socks emerged from one of the lowdowns which had white mandioca laid out to dry on the roof. In each hand the man carried a heavy plastic jerry can. The driver jumped out of his seat and disappeared into the lowdown, adding another set of footprints to the dirt which had been methodically swept in a pattern of sine curves. He emerged similarly laden with jerry cans, and the two men proceeded to fill the combi with petrol.

A small boy, his face shadowed by a wide-brimmed straw hat, ambled past us carrying a hoe over each shoulder, on his way to the *machamba*. He wore a brown T-shirt, baggy red trousers gaping at one knee, and a single dirty white plimsoll on one foot. The driver appeared at his cab door wiping his hands clean with a large banana leaf. 'Vamos,' he said.

Within twenty minutes, we had turned off the main highway of the Beira Corridor and were driving northwards, along the Planalto de Chimoio, parallel to the Zimbabwean border and along the length of Manica province. Manica has long been noted as a fertile region, and in early Portuguese times its frequent storms of thunder and lightning were put down to the quantities of metallic substances lurking beneath the lush tropical vegetation. Gold and copper have been mined and sifted from the province's rivers for centuries, while bauxite is a more recent quarry.

We passed frequent reminders of the war, which until just a couple of months before had made this route impassable to all but those with a death wish. The stumps of decapitated telegraph poles lined the road like broken centurions from a forgotten age, and the burnt-out remnants of trucks rusted quietly in the undergrowth. Just beyond Catandica, a defunct Shell filling station stood lonely and roofless and an armoured personnel carrier still had its rear wheels on the tarmac, its paint scorched and blistered by the fire that followed the ambush. A monkey slipped across the road fifty metres in front of us, jumped into a tree and looked on with a puzzled expression as we whizzed by. Villages were marked by the rush roofs of huts floating in a deep green sea of maize plants. At one place, small boys in rags threw stones at us, but elsewhere they just waved and screamed with delight.

As we slowed down for a military checkpoint coming into Changara, hundreds of white butterflies flew towards the combi like a storm of confetti. The green signpost at a roundabout said that Rodesia (sic) was 49 kilometres to the left, only 'Rodesia' had been scratched out. We took the right turn, which the signpost said would lead us to Tete in another 95 kilometres. It was just after one p.m. when we drove into town and I caught my first glimpse of the suspension bridge over the River Zambezi, which was as wide as the Thames at London.

Tete is the capital of the province of the same name. It is Mozambique's most north-westerly province, the stunted left-hand fork of the letter 'Y' which the country resembles on a map. It is bisected by the Zambezi, southern Africa's greatest river, which rises in north-western Zambia, nips into Angola, and forms the border between Zambia and Zimbabwe before flowing on down through Tete and central Mozambique to the Indian Ocean, a total distance of some 2700 kilometres. At its mouth, the Zambezi delivers an average 3600 cubic metres of water every second throughout the year, which is a lot of water.

The Zambezi was a *cause célèbre* for David Livingstone, who saw it as the highway into the interior, along which Christianity and commerce would bring 'civilisation' to the innermost reaches of southern Africa. Livingstone sailed up the river in 1858 in a seventy-five-foot steam launch, the *Ma Robert*, named after his wife whom the locals referred to as Ma (mother) of her eldest son. The *Ma Robert* was built with a newly invented steel plate only one-sixteenth of an inch thick which, Livingstone said ironically, had been 'patented but unfortunately never tried before'. It rapidly developed small holes and leaked like a sieve. The vessel was also fitted out with rather inefficient furnaces, and much time was wasted cutting wood to keep it stoked. Livingstone lamented that the journey as far as the village settlement of Tete could have been done with half the toil and expense in a canoe.

Tete was a small outpost in the ineffectual Portuguese empire in the mid-1800s, with about thirty European stone houses, the majority of them thatched, surrounded by a ten-foot-high wall. Most of the local inhabitants preferred to live outside the enclosure. The settlement was the headquarters of a battalion of nearly 300 men (less a few dozen detained in the cells) of whom just over a hundred were actually stationed in Tete. Most of the soldiers were so-called *degreda-dos*, men banished from or convicted of a crime in the more hospitable coastal ports.

Tete is now a busy town of around 50,000 inhabitants. Its roads were constantly thundering with huge articulated lorries, 'Caution 17 metres' signs on their tails, plying to and from Malawi, Zimbabwe and Zambia. They roared through the town as pick-ups and combis, all painted a dull orange colour and sporting an HCB logo on their doors, scuttled back and forth from the nearby hydroelectric dam at Cahora Bassa. Tete seemed a relatively prosperous place, not as run down as other Mozambican towns and cities. The streets were well-swept, electricity did not appear to be a problem, and water gushed from the taps for two hours in the morning, an hour at midday and for two and a half hours each evening. The electricity and water came courtesy of the dam at Cahora Bassa.

The residents of Tete were proud of their town. I was often asked the question, 'how do you like Tete compared to other cities?' and I was able to answer truthfully that I liked it very much. Mozambicans talked about towns in good basic terms. Towns were either large or small, clean or not clean, bonita (pretty) or not bonita. Chimoio was small and clean, Beira large and not clean. Tete was small, clean and bonita.

After I had settled into my room overlooking the suspension bridge across the Zambezi, and eaten a meal of goat and rice in the restaurant at the top of the five-storey hotel, I ventured out in search of Assado, the student I had met at Macúti in Beira. He had given me detailed instructions for finding his father's house, which was across the bridge in a part of town called Matundo, between a small church and a bar owned by Donna Joaquina.

The suspension bridge over the Zambezi is an important one as bridges go, since it makes a direct link possible between Malawi and Zimbabwe. It is only the second serious bridge to be constructed across the Zambezi in Mozambique. The first, a rail bridge at Sena some two hundred kilometres downstream, was completed in the 1930s by the Cleveland Bridge and Engineering Company of Darlington, England. At the time it was the longest bridge in the world, and would still be the longest rail bridge in Africa if Renamo hadn't blown it up in 1986.

There was a small toll booth at the opposite side of the bridge, and I asked a youth who stood outside it propping up the wall, looking cool in his dark glasses, if he could direct me. He wanted to know exactly where I was headed in Matundo and why; I told him and he smiled at me. He had been at school with Assado and would take me to his father's house.

We scrambled down the steep embankment and walked along the river bank. Joseph, as the youth in the dark glasses introduced himself, was an only child who lived with his elderly mother. His father had died when Joseph was eleven. He was now twenty-seven, and he worked in an office to keep himself and his mother in food, but times were hard: salaries were low and food was expensive.

'Life is down here, not like in Europe,' he said as we cut in away from the river bank, up a dried mud incline towards a dilapidated building with a wooden verandah overlooking the Zambezi.

'This is the Bar da Donna Joaquina. There is the church of

Matundo,' he pointed farther up the incline, but I didn't register the church until we were right on top of it, because I had been expecting a steeple and this church just looked like a brick house. We passed the church, which did have a small crucifix attached to the wall, and walked behind it.

'The house of Assado's father,' Joseph announced, as I caught sight of the blue Ford truck belonging to Assado's father that I had nearly grabbed a lift to Tete in.

Assado was not at home, and neither was his father. A small boy emerged when we called at the door and looked acutely embarrassed as I asked him where Assado was and when he was likely to return. The boy didn't know, so I scribbled a note and gave it to him. He looked very determined when he said he would give the note to Assado as soon as he got home.

Joseph and I returned the way we had come, and he was happy to tell me how Mozambique had changed during his lifetime. Although the going was tough, in some ways life was better than before.

'In the times of Samora [Machel, the country's first president] I would have been arrested and tortured for talking to a foreigner like this,' he said in his measured, easily understandable Portuguese. 'Samora was a poorly educated man, just four years at school. He was not a good man to run a country.'

Samora Machel *was* poorly educated, but this was largely because he was forced to spend most of his time at the missionary school cultivating cash crops for the church. Later he trained as a nurse, before becoming involved in the independence movement. Although he did run a tight-fisted regime in Mozambique until he was killed in an air crash in 1986 in South Africa (under circumstances which were never satisfactorily explained), he was also a charismatic leader. A top United Nations official who had been in Mozambique in the early 1980s told me once that Machel would often stop in the middle of a long speech and break into song, complete with actions, before continuing with his monologue. Then he would finish his speech with more songs, and everyone would join in.

But as Joseph pointed out, things were difficult for ordinary Mozambicans in those days. Internal movement within the country was restricted, and criticism of the government was countered with a stretch in the re-education camps. Joseph also had bitter memories of the legions of Russian advisers who turned up in Mozambique to help during the early years of the revolutionary process. 'There were many, many Russians here in Tete, but now they have all gone. And I can tell you something,' he said as we climbed back up the embankment to the suspension bridge, 'they were racists.'

We walked along the bridge towards the other bank, where my hotel was located. 'We had some Russian teachers at school,' Joseph went on, 'and they always refused to drink from the same cups as the Mozambican teachers because they said that Mozambicans were not as good as Russian people.'

A truck, carrying three men in civilian clothing around an anti-aircraft gun, trundled along the bridge towards us. I had seen the same vehicle driving around the streets several times that day. They seemed to be searching desperately for an aircraft to practise shooting at.

'But the real problem here in Mozambique, that foreigners don't understand,' Joseph continued, 'is tribalism. The president and all his men are from the south, they are of the Shangaan tribe. All provincial directors are from the south, and they don't like the north or northern people.'

We had reached the end of the bridge and Joseph was going in another direction from mine. 'I shall tell you a story,' he said, 'but it is not a story because it really happened. The wife of the provincial director of Tete went to Chimoio with her driver and they stayed in the government's house there. When she arrived she wanted some food, but when the food came she complained that she could not eat or drink because the plates and cups were not from the south, they were not proper. She said to the waiter, "Get me some real plates and cups", but the waiter was lost and didn't know what to do. He said, "This is all we have", and the wife of the provincial director left and later complained to the provincial director at Chimoio.'

Joseph smiled. 'Tribalism is the real problem in Mozambique,' he repeated, then he disappeared down the bank.

The restaurant at the top of the hotel served a grilled fish from the Zambezi for dinner, followed by one of the best 'puddims' I had eaten in Mozambique. Lightning forked, thunder rolled and huge raindrops began to fall vertically from the skies to smack the pavements far below as I drank my cup of instant coffee. Flora, the waitress, told me that there were many fish in the Zambezi, but also crocodiles, so it was not a good river for swimming in. She asked me what I was doing in Tete and I told her I was hoping to visit the dam at Cahora Bassa.

'Cahora Bassa, ah yes,' she said, 'it is bonita. There is much water there. Songo, the town near Cahora Bassa, is bonita. The mountains are bonita.'

12

THE FIRST BLACK MAN IN SONGO

I awoke the next morning to a bright and sunny day. There was that fresh snap in the air that comes after a rainstorm in the tropics, and strains of Afro-jazz were emanating from the *chapas* at the stop below my window. It felt good to be alive.

After breakfast I sat on the verandah outside the hotel entrance and watched the world go by. On the opposite side of the road, on the pavement outside a line of shops, youths hung around holding single packets of cigarettes for sale. A boy wearing a V-necked white T-shirt, which hung off one shoulder, walked up the road from the Zambezi carrying two fat fish on a string. People were ambling down the road towards the river where a girls' national basketball tournament was going on in a small stadium. The hotel was on a crossroads, and diagonally opposite, in front of a disused petrol station, three notice boards were stuck in the forecourt concrete. Passers-by stopped to read the fliers advertising films at the local cinemas. Two young women, strategically placed in a line of six children, all holding hands, stopped to read the advertisements for children's karate films and *Delta Force II*.

Behind the notice boards, two small boys played with old bicycle wheel hoops which came up to their chests, pushing them along with long sticks. Painted on the wall behind the boys a peeling slogan said, 'Always produce more and better'.

A group of men and women were sitting near me in the

hardwood chairs outside the hotel. Some read the national newspaper, *Noticias*, while others just sat. The copies of *Noticias* were the previous day's, which had just reached Tete. The women hailed friends and acquaintances with a loud hissing sound made with the tongue held to the roof of the mouth. Men used the same sound, or an exaggerated kissing noise, to the same effect. People would pass the time of day or stop to chew the fat for a while.

At around 9.30 Assado appeared, loping across the road in his relaxed gait. He was wearing blue plimsolls and a voluminous white short-sleeved shirt not tucked into his black denims. He climbed the verandah and held out his hand for me to shake. The hand was soft and his bones felt as if they were made of rubber.

'Welcome to Tete,' he said, smiling broadly, 'you made it. I am very pleased to see you again.'

He could not stay long, as he had to help his father who was working on the truck, but he had remembered my desire to visit the hydroelectric dam at Cahora Bassa, and told me that his cousin would come soon to help me. It was necessary to obtain special permits to visit, and this involved several rather complex bureaucratic procedures.

We chatted for a while and Assado told me he was looking for a new girlfriend, since his previous one here in Tete had found someone else while he was studying in Beira. 'I have been writing love songs,' Assado said, 'I want to find one girl who likes love songs too.' He told me he wanted to show me some of his songs and his poetry.

Assado's cousin turned up, an older man, perhaps in his late-thirties, whose name was Angelo. He looked rather shifty, like a small-time hustler. He had one boss eye which surveyed the scene over your shoulder while his good eye looked at you. This gave him the air of a slightly anxious individual, on the qui vive for someone who might catch up with him. He wanted to know why I was so keen to visit the dam. I told him that it was a key installation for the future of Mozambique, the most powerful hydroelectric scheme in

Africa, a powerhouse for future development. I was a geographer, this sort of thing interested me. Angelo nodded sagely, his one good eye looking at me with suspicion. Geographers were clearly an odd breed, to be treated with caution.

The dam also had a nagging, deep-rooted significance for me, I went on. I remembered writing about Cahora Bassa in a school 'A' level geography essay more than a decade before. At the time, in the late 1970s, I had said the same thing: Cahora Bassa was the hope for development in this southern African country, an exotic and far-flung entity coloured purple in my school atlas. But my textbook was elderly, and I had kept pestering my geography teacher, Mr Hall, for more recent information on the dam. He had not been able to answer my enquiry. Now here I was, to look for myself. Angelo was more satisfied with this explanation; this was obviously the real reason I wanted to visit the dam.

Getting permission was a very difficult exercise, he said. It required great skill. But he had that skill, and he was willing to help me. My time schedule was pressing, and we should start immediately. Assado left us and we walked up the road, away from the river, to where Hidroeléctrica de Cahora Bassa had an office. I immediately realised that without boss-eyed cousin Angelo to help me I wouldn't have had a hope of getting to the dam. The office was up two flights of open stairs behind a kiosk in a minor street. There were no plaques or signs either in the street below or on the door that Angelo led me to.

Angelo was a forthright character. There were two individuals waiting patiently at the small hole conveniently positioned at navel height in the door. He bade them good-day and pushed straight past to rap a knuckle on the tiny counter. A male face appeared at the hole and Angelo bent double to speak to the face. Angelo explained what he wanted. The face looked at me suspiciously, then back at Angelo. Our request was obviously outside his jurisdiction and could be dealt with only at the highest level, but the chief was currently out. We should come back next week. Angelo scoffed.

202

OK, tomorrow then, the face suggested. Angelo told him that we didn't have that much time. We would still have to wait, the face said. Angelo stood back and shrugged at me. He bummed a cigarette from one of the other guys who were waiting and checked out the balcony on which we stood from behind the hand cupping the flame of his match. I asked Angelo what he did for a living and he said that he had not had a job for ten years.

When he had finished his cigarette, Angelo bent down to speak into the hole in the door again and whispered some urgent-sounding instructions to the face. Then he turned to me and said, 'Let's go.' He led me back down the stairs and out into the sunlight on the street. 'We should go back there at three,' he said, 'I shall call for you at the hotel.' With that, he threw a quick glance up and down the street, hunched his shoulders, and walked quickly across the road and into an area of kiosks selling drinks and cigarettes.

On my way back towards the hotel, I noticed a small door in a line of shops, which said that it was the Tete Tourist Office. I had never seen such a thing before in Mozambique, so I took hold of the handle and pushed the door open. Inside was a small room with two desks in it. I couldn't actually see the desks, but I assumed they were there because they must have been underneath the two mountainous islands of folders and papers piled high in a sea of other folders and papers strew all around the room. Shelving which reached the ceiling was also laden with documents, so that you couldn't see the walls, but again I assumed they were there, although it could have been that the entire office was constructed from papers.

An anxious face peered from behind one of the mini-Kilimanjaros and said good morning.

I said good morning and asked whether this was the tourist office.

'Yes,' the woman with the anxious face said, looking relieved, 'how can I help you?'

I was momentarily nonplussed; what did I want to know

about tourist attractions or facilities in Tete? I couldn't really believe that there were any. But remembering my geographical training, I thought that a map might be a useful place to start, so I asked for that.

The woman looked perplexed. She turned her head back and forth to scrutinise the heaps of paper all around her. Slowly she shook her head. 'Sorry, we have no maps,' she said unconvincingly. There must have been maps somewhere in the mounds of paper, but it would have taken an archaeological excavation to find them.

'Perhaps upstairs,' she said helpfully, 'wait a moment.' She unearthed a bakelite telephone and dialled some numbers. She quietly asked if the respondent had a map of Tete. She nodded as she listened to the answer and replaced the receiver in its rest. She beamed at me and said, 'Yes, they have a map upstairs, go to the second floor please.'

She climbed from behind her desk and led me back through the door I had entered and down a side passage to some stairs. 'Second floor,' she repeated. I thanked her and climbed the staircase. A man stood on the landing of the second floor ready for me. 'You are the gentleman who wants a map,' he said, 'good morning, my name is Senhor Solinho.'

Senhor Solinho led me along some corridors with doors leading off them into offices, to a small room with two chairs and a table in it. There was nothing on the table and a poster advertising a Frelimo Congress on the wall. Otherwise the room was empty. Senhor Solinho disappeared and soon returned with a large rolled map covered in squashed flies. He unfurled it on the desk to reveal a street plan of the town, which judging by the street names and the fact that the suspension bridge was not marked, dated from Portuguese times. I studied the map with interest and recorded in my notebook the locations of a few buildings and parks. I asked Senhor Solinho whether he had copies of the map. He shook his head, no, this was the only one. I thanked him for his help and went on my way. I had no idea what this office was, I didn't think it could possibly have been further departments of the Tete Tourist Office.

Three o'clock came and went, followed by three-fifteen, and then three-thirty. Boss-eyed cousin Angelo did not appear. I wandered down towards the river and walked upstream along the bank. Some boys were having fun jumping into the water from a part of the bank which was built up high. They could run at full speed, leapfrog over a low wall and plunge into the brown water holding their knees up to their chests to make a bigger splash. The river was fairly fast moving and they were cocky and unperturbed when I asked them about crocodiles.

Assado reappeared that evening and said his cousin Angelo had gone down with a stomach bug, but would meet me the next day to tackle the Hidroeléctrica de Cahora Bassa office once again.

There was the same face at the low opening in the door at the office. He smiled this time and said that we should come inside. Inside the small office, which was air-conditioned, three men sat at desks looking busy. The chief stood up and shook my hand, gesturing for me to sit down on a plastic easy chair. Unlike petty officials in so many countries, he seemed friendly and interested in my request. Angelo did some explaining and the chief nodded wisely. It should not be a problem, he thought, but it might take a little time. Angelo turned to me and said that his uncle worked at Cahora Bassa, showing visitors around the dam and hydro-electric complex, and he would now ring him to see whether he would be there to receive me. The chief busied himself with a huge ledger while Angelo picked up the telephone receiver and dialled.

After a short conversation, Angelo replaced the receiver and said that his uncle was not there. The chief told us to return that afternoon to pick up his written authorisation, since he was too busy to do it now. He lit a cigarette, and put his feet on his desk.

We returned that afternoon, and had to wait only an hour before the authorisation was handed to us through the hole in the door. It was scribbled on a half page torn out of an exercise book. I thought that was it, and was happy that we had triumphed over the bureaucracy. But not a bit of it, this was only the first stage. We had obtained permission from the company which ran the dam, but next we had to get clearance from the local government administrator.

Angelo was looking characteristically shifty as we stood outside on the street once more, his mind obviously working on the angles. Usually such permission from local government, which also involved liaising with the police and the military who controlled the roadblocks in and out of the dam zone, took several days, he told me. But I was to meet him in one hour, at four o'clock.

At four o'clock Angelo turned up with Assado at his elbow. We passed a cigarette stall and Angelo asked whether I could buy him some. It was the least I could do. We trudged uptown, the sun was getting low, but was still sweltering. A modern low block of offices, the provincial administration, appeared around a bend in the road. My heart sank; the building looked as if it were swathed in red tape. Inside the office complex, we passed numerous rooms, most containing people who did not seem to be doing anything. A woman playing with an old mimeograph machine, her hands covered in smelly purple ink, directed us to the waiting area. Assado and I sat down and Angelo loped off. Two young men and an elderly woman sat with blank stares on their faces; they looked as if they had been waiting there for several weeks.

Suddenly, we were in an air-conditioned office, in front of a smart man wearing a well-cut grey jacket. His grey and white striped tie looked as if it had just been taken out of its wrapper and his light blue shirt ironed only minutes before. He was sitting behind an imposing desk twisting a large gold ring on his little finger. The usual black-and-white portrait of President Chissano looked down from the wall behind the desk.

Angelo was looking foxy again as he introduced me to the important-looking man, who displayed a couple of freshly pressed creases in his suit trousers when he stood up to shake my hand. He listened carefully to my explanation of why I wanted to visit Cahora Bassa, and said he would help me because I would tell people in England about Mozambique. Cahora Bassa was an important area which I should certainly visit. He picked up the telephone on his desk and made two calls. When he finally replaced the receiver, he told me he had smoothed everything out, and that he hoped I would have an interesting time at the dam. I thanked the man and we all trooped out of his office.

As we made our way past the waiting area, the woman and the two men still sat, motionless like shop-window dummies, waiting for something to happen. Angelo may have been unemployed for the last ten years, but he certainly had the local bureaucracy taped.

Early the following morning I checked out of the hotel and carried my bag downstairs to the foyer where I had arranged to meet Assado. He had offered to come with me to the dam. He had nothing much else to do with his vacation and it was some years since he had been there, he told me, but he had no money, so would it be possible . . .

We waited for half an hour beneath a huge black and white photograph of the Cahora Bassa dam under construction, which covered an entire wall of the hotel foyer, before cousin Angelo turned up. He was flustered, there was a *chapa* about to leave for Songo, the town near to Cahora Bassa, and he had arranged for the driver to keep us seats, but we should hurry. We dashed up the road and Angelo pulled a man out of our place to make way for us. Angelo wished me well and set off across the road, shoulders hunched grifter-like, smoking a cigarette, as the yellow Peugeot *chapa* set off.

It was a three-hour drive to Songo. We drove out of Tete,

back along the route I had come a couple of days previously, and turned off this road just beyond a police checkpoint beneath a baobab tree. The two policemen on duty were asleep in the shadow of the elephantine trunk. We passed herds of cattle as we slowly climbed into mountainous granite scenery. Somewhere off to our right were the Quebrabasa Rapids, the point where Livingstone was forced to give up his mission to follow the Zambezi in the *Ma Robert*. He took to his feet to survey the rapids, in search of a way past them in his steamer. In doing so he nearly had a mutiny on his hands. The going was very arduous, over huge black boulders and through dense thorn bushes, and his Makololo porters told him that they had thought that he had a heart, but now they realised he had none. That he was venturing where no living foot had trodden was a sure sign that he was mad. The porters tried to convince Livingstone's companion, a Doctor Kirk, not to go on, but Kirk did not speak the local dialect and Livingstone didn't enlighten him about the porters' attempts at dissuasion. Livingstone could not find a way through the raging white waters, which stretched for fifty miles and involved two almost vertical drops of 600 feet, and had to turn back.

At the foot of the final stretch of road which wound and twisted its way up to Songo we stopped at a military checkpoint with a barrier across the road. We proffered our letters of permission to enter the dam zone to an officer on duty inside a small building like an immigration post. He took passports and identity cards and painstakingly entered their details into a ledger before throwing them into a drawer below the counter. One young man in our *chapa* had not obtained the necessary pieces of paper, and he was refused entry. He sat down outside the building looking disconsolate, to wait for a lift back to Tete.

Songo was a non sequitur. It was perched high in the mountains and looked orderly and prosperous, unlike any other Mozambican settlement I had visited. The streets were well swept and without pot-holes, and blessed with numerous lamp-posts, all of which shone brightly each evening after the sun went down. Prim flower beds and luscious, well-groomed lawns bordered every roadway and sat neatly in front of the houses of the dam's maintenance crews. Water flowed all the time from every tap and there were never any power cuts. Songo was at a high altitude, so even the weather was better behaved. Although still hot, the air was heated in a tasteful and delicate way, markedly less searing than the rank and torrid humidor of Tete or many of the coastal towns. The evenings were beautifully fresh and scented with the smells of eucalyptus and tropical flowers. It was like entering a magical mountain kingdom.

Assado and I checked into the town's guesthouse, the Pousada dos Sete Montes. But although we were now within ten kilometres of the most powerful hydroelectric scheme in Africa, we were not there yet. We had a couple more tiers of bureaucracy to surmount. We had to get further permission, again in writing, from the district administrator. Then, we had to make contact with Assado's and Angelo's uncle, who took visitors to the complex. There wasn't the option of simply walking down into the valley ourselves, because there were more military checkpoints, and presenting oneself without a representative of Hidroeléctrica de Cahora Bassa would mean instant suspicion of being a saboteur.

Assado and I spent two days chivvying the local authorities and waiting for the cogs of Songo's bureaucracy to turn in our favour. The district administrator was clearly an eminent local dignitary who spent most of his working hours out of the office on urgent business, usually conducted over lunch. I passed the time swatting flies, scribbling in my notebook or watching the sun warm the grass on the manicured lawns. Assado whiled away the hours thinking about his woman trouble – the trouble being that he didn't have one. He wrote love songs to his imaginary sweetheart on scraps of paper which, when finished, he would sing to me in his gentle melodious tones.

'If you are poor, you don't have the chance to get a good

girl,' Assado said as we sat at the foot of the flagpole outside the district administrator's office one afternoon, waiting for the man to return from lunch and give us his written permission to visit the dam. Assado spoke English, which was a relief for me, since concentrating on Portuguese made me tired.

'All boys lie, and girls too, because life is difficult in Mozambique. I can say, "I am Assado, and my father is rich. He has one car, I have one brother in government and I study in university in Maputo." When I say this, girl she says, "OK, you are my boyfriend".' Assado sighed, and drew aimless patterns in the dirt with a stick.

'I take her to the house of my friend or my brother to see TV or car,' he pointed to the imaginary objects with his stick, 'and she likes this. If I have a recorder, girl she says, "Take me to your house, I want to listen to that music." But if I haven't these conditions, she leave.'

'But do you want a girl who is only interested in these things?' I asked Assado as I slapped my thigh and added another fly corpse to the row of five lined up on the concrete where we sat.

'No,' he said emphatically. 'In Beira my school very far from Macúti where I live, and my friends say, "Who you live with?" I say, "My brother." "What does he do?" they ask. "He is a soldier," I tell them, and they say, "OK." ' Assado waved his hand in a dismissive gesture.

'But they don't know, and I don't say, that my brother is very high-up soldier. He has video, good recorder, car, big house. I am looking for girl who like Assado, not my conditions.'

'You'll find her,' I said, trying to sound helpful, 'probably when you stop looking.' I took a swipe at another fly, and missed.

Assado sighed some more and poked at the ground with his stick.

'Do you have to do national service?' I asked him in an attempt to change the subject.

'Me no, because my brother protects me. Soldier service is big problem for all boys. Many people change age to avoid soldier service, but I have not that problem. My brother tells me, "You go to school." '

He smiled. 'I prefer to go to school,' he said. 'Once someone catched me for soldier service, but my brother take telephone and talked to one friend and protect me. "Who catch that boy there?" they ask. "Me," man say. "You don't know that boy is brother of high man?" "No, sorry Commandant." "Take that boy to his home," they say.'

The flies seemed to be getting worse, and my legs were sore from my attempts to dispatch them. I was beginning to wish I had worn my long trousers.

'But now, no such problems because war is over,' Assado said. 'Before, in time of Samora, they go to school one car, at ten a.m. when students all there, to catch boys. In these times very difficult, impossible to avoid. Marcelino dos Santos, when he was governor of Beira, said, "Whoever escapes conscription I will give him my daughter to marry." In these times very bad conditions, no pay, one hundred, two hundred soldiers die each day. No one likes to be soldier. But in future people will like – good money, good conditions.'

My line of deceased flies had reached eleven by the time the district administrator returned from his lunch, at 3.30 p.m.. He signed our document and we walked over to the telephone exchange to put a call through to Assado's uncle. Assado's uncle had gone home for the day.

We spent our evenings at Songo's restaurant, the Flower of Albufeira, where every night they served up a delicious beef soup followed by steak and chips with an egg on top. The staff at the Flower of Albufeira never seemed to be terribly bothered whether they had any customers or not, which was just as well became Assado and I were the only ones they entertained during our stay in Songo.

The restaurant had an old red curtain at the doorway which led you into a large space, mostly open, with tables at one side. Oversized and very bad oil paintings of Bob

211

Marley, Bruce Springsteen and Santana adorned the walls, and a few old Christmas decorations were still hanging from the light fittings. The place was run by a very relaxed large woman in her forties who had five children and as many rolls of fat around her middle. She had various minions to help her. Our food was brought to us by a young man with a round and honest, trying-hard-to-please face who said his name was Roger Tesora. Roger insisted on speaking to me in English, which involved a lot of charade-like sign language, and I thought he was a part-time hair dresser throughout the first evening. The following day he was able to use my dictionary to tell me that his name, Tesora, meant 'scissors' in English.

The food was cooked by the fat lady and her assistant, a tall, handsome young woman with long thin arms, a long nose and delicate bone structure. A precocious and extremely pretty eleven-year-old girl named Maria sat at our table every evening, gazing into my eyes with her huge brown ones, blinking with eyelashes half an inch long and smiling the sort of smile which in a few years' time would make the most placid of men chew walls and spit bricks in an effort to impress her. But they never would. Maria was as sharp as they come and immediately she discovered that I wasn't married she tried to fix me up with the young woman with delicate bone structure. The only time Maria lost her composure was when we turned the cassette player up one evening and I asked her to dance. She went completely coy and had to be pushed on to the dance floor by the fat lady and the woman with delicate bone structure. She made a lot of faces to the assembled audience as we danced holding hands, and rushed out of the restaurant laughing when we finished and I thanked her with an exaggerated bow.

The Flower of Albufeira restaurant was owned by the same man who ran the Pousada dos Sete Montes where Assado and I were staying. He was a grumpy individual who scowled a lot, particularly whenever we, his guests, asked for anything like a drink. The *pousada* had a restaurant part, but the grumpy owner refused to serve us any food because he had his family with him and was too busy being grumpy with them to pay any attention to us. He was separated from his wife, but she was at the *pousada* while we were there because they were getting ready for the wedding of one of their daughters. The father was a black Mozambican, the mother an Asiatic-looking woman from Ilha de Moçambique, and their daughter was an almond-eyed beauty who knew it and looked as if she had broken a few hearts on the way to her wedding day.

One afternoon, the mother explained to Assado and me why she had left her husband, as she did some ironing behind the bar in her curlers and we drank cans of Sprite in front of it. Her husband was mean, she told us. He owned this *pousada*, the only restaurant in Songo, and one of the shops. He made lots of money, but never spent any. He refused to pay for his children's education because he had very little education himself and did not see the necessity. His wife had tried to persuade him, because she thought education very important, but to no avail.

To be fair to the *pousada* owner, the education system he had suffered under had probably scarred him for life. The Portuguese colonial set-up had been characterised by staggeringly high failure rates (98.7 per cent in 1950, around the time Mr Grumpy would have been at school), and according to many accounts, high failure rates had been one of its unstated aims. A series of age restrictions made it virtually impossible for Africans to proceed upwards in the system, because by the time the student had learned enough Portuguese to pass one of the exams, he or she was too old for the next level of education. So while education was upheld as the only legitimate channel for evaluating a person's worth and enabling them to advance, the schools worked to make it impossible for the vast majority to succeed. Failure was calculated to increase the Africans' perception of their inadequacies for being the wrong colour, and to bolster the belief that all they could usefully do was work as forced labourers.

213

The grumpy *pousada* owner's son was also in residence, a youth in his early twenties who was studying electronics in Maputo. He told us that he didn't get on with his father, because he refused to help him with his fees and living expenses in Maputo. 'He has done very well, my father,' the son said, 'he was the first black man to arrive in Songo, in 1970. Before that, this was an island of whites only, but my father came and has established his businesses. Now he is a rich man, but he is too stupid to realise how he should spend his money.'

The effects of the Portuguese system on the Mozambican sense of self-worth will take a generation or two to work out.

Finally, on the last possible day for me, since I had to get back to Harare for my flight to London in two days' time, everything was arranged and Assado's uncle was due to pick us up for the trip to the dam. The appointed time of 3.30 p.m. came and went. Another guest at the *pousada*, an employee of DPCCN in Tete, told us that he too was going to the dam that afternoon and he was meeting the Hidroeléctrica de Cahora Bassa man at the district administrator's office.

We panicked. Was this the same trip? Should we go with the DPCCN man to the district administrator's office, or wait at the *pousada* and risk disappointment? We opted for the former course, and climbed into the back of the guy's pickup with his son to be driven the mile down the road. At the last minute, the *pousada* owner's son decided to come along too for the ride. We all met outside the district administrator's office, beneath the gently fluttering green, black, yellow and red flag of Mozambique, with its crossed symbols of a kalashnikov and a hoe on a yellow star. Assado's uncle arrived driving his own orange Hidroeléctrica de Cahora Bassa Toyota pick-up, and we were off.

The road wound down towards the dam through a hilly landscape infested with granite boulders and larger outcrops. Every available square metre of soil between the rocks was planted with a tall green maize plant. The sun was warm on my face and it was good to feel the wind blowing in my hair as we glided past gleaming metal pylons which marched across the hillsides. A thick pipe followed the road, bringing water up to Songo from the reservoir behind the dam. After fifteen minutes, we rounded a bend and caught our first glimpse of the neat horseshoe of concrete which ponds back the reservoir stretching for 250 kilometres, as far as the borders with Zambia and Zimbabwe.

The dam, which took six years to complete, is located in a deep gorge known in the local Matheema dialect as 'Cahora Bassa': 'the place where work is over'. Although the dam looked tiny in the awesome gorge, there was a profound sense of its strength. Steep tree-covered slopes plunged down to be lost in the still water behind the concrete parabola. From the inside of the curved structure, plumes of white spray gushed forth to create a permanent rainbow as they cascaded down into the frothing gorge, their work turning the turbines done, to continue their journey to the Indian Ocean.

Cahora Bassa was built in the early 1970s, before Mozambique's independence, with a number of political agendas in mind. Most of the electricity generated by the waters of the Zambezi runs through overhead transmission lines to South Africa, which, when the idea of the dam was first mooted by Salazar, was in dire need of new energy sources to power its growing industries. From Portugal's viewpoint, the huge reservoir was designed partly as a physical barrier to halt the incursions of Frelimo guerrillas from their bases in neighbouring Malawi and Zambia. The dam became a target for Frelimo, who saw it as a symbol of a new phase of foreign imperialism in their country, particularly since it was proposed to settle up to one million white farmers in the area. Frelimo raised the slogan, 'Cahora Bassa Delenda Est' – Cahora Bassa must be destroyed. But they didn't manage it, and now the state of Mozambique owns 18 per cent of the complex, while the remaining 82 per cent belongs to a Portuguese-led private consortium.

Huge dams like this were the concrete-and-steel realisations of a generation which believed technology could triumph over nature and solve the problems of humankind. But unlike many similar schemes in other parts of the tropics, Cahora Bassa has not suffered the setbacks experienced by its brothers in Egypt, Ghana, India and the Philippines. Few people had to be resettled in this remote region before the reservoir was flooded, the hundred-year projected lifetime of the dam has not been threatened by silt building up in the waters behind it, and there is still plenty of river flowing downstream of the structure for Mozambique's other users of the Zambezi to benefit.

We drove down the twisting hairpin bends to pass through another military checkpoint, where the soldier on duty made us wait while he made a call from his pillbox. Deep inside the gneiss mountains, it seemed as if we had been magically transported outside Mozambique to the generating rooms and control panels of a James Bond film set. It was spotlessly clean, and cool and airy after the heat of the day outside. Bare rock faces were visible behind the concrete internal skeleton of the main cathedral-like chamber. The orange heads of five turbines sat inside yellow circles, each the size of a basketball court, on the reverberating rubber-surfaced floor. Illuminated clocks and control panels with coloured lights surrounded us. The eerie hum of machinery filled the huge chamber. Inside the control room, perched aloft at one end of the main chamber, a matt-grey control panel covered the back wall. Its face was a mass of dials and knobs and switches which illuminated banks of coloured lights in reds and greens and dull whites.

The five turbines have a combined capacity to generate 2075 megawatts of electricity, Assado's uncle told us, among a deluge of statistics. The plant had been designed to be the power house of southern Africa, but just two of the five giant machines were turning, since other political necessities had got in the way of Cahora Bassa's future. I had to ask Assado's uncle to say it again when he told us that only 250 megawatts were required to keep the whole of Mozambique going. This was half the output from just one of the turbines. Yet most of the country continued to suffer blackouts and power cuts because most of the proposed transmission lines had never been built, and those that had had been obvious targets for Renamo. Their soldiers had continued to destroy pylons even after South Africa had began to supply Frelimo with new equipment and uniforms for government troops guarding the powerlines in 1988.

We stopped on our way back to Songo at the top of the gorge, to look down again on the dam, a European engineer's dream deep in Africa's heart of darkness. The cute little concrete structure, dwarfed in the rugged mountains, seemed to symbolise the whole European experience in Mozambique. Cahora Bassa and Songo were islands of high-tech prosperity in a country where most people still live in mud huts.

The dam should still become the central powerhouse to drive the political changes in southern Africa towards greater prosperity. The engineers were already talking about implementing phase two of the project, to build another power plant, Assado's uncle had explained. It remains to be seen whether they can transform Cahora Bassa from its white-elephant status of the past eighteen years. Mozambique's people are far from lacking in resourcefulness and vitality, and now that the war was over I felt they had a good chance of putting their country back together again.

The one *chapa* which ran between Songo and Tete, which was owned by the district administrator, left town each morning at 5 a.m., and Assado and I were positioned on the roadside in front of the Pousada dos Sete Montes at 4.30. The flies had risen before us and were waiting.

All being well, I figured we should hit Tete by 7.30, in time for me to jump on another vehicle headed for the Zimbabwean border. Assado assured me that there were frequent

217

chapa departures in the mornings, but if these failed to materialise, I should be able to hitch a lift in one of the trucks which plied between Malawi and Zimbabwe. I had already given up on the idea of returning towards Chimoio, to leave Mozambique and enter Zimbabwe via the Beira Corridor, as my Mozambican visa stated that I was required to do. It was Friday morning, and I had a flight booked from Harare to London the following evening. If I were arrested trying to exit the country through the wrong border post it would be a good enough excuse for missing the university tutorials I was scheduled to give the following Monday.

People started to pass us on their way to work in the fields as 5 a.m. came and went. Each time I heard the roar of a motor engine in the distance I stood up in anticipation, only to be disappointed. Eventually, every vehicle in Songo, except the one we were waiting for, drove past us. I took my mounting frustration out on the fly population, as Assado sang me some of his latest love songs, written with his new pen on a pad of airmail paper, both of which I had presented him with. He seemed unperturbed, but I was worried about missing a connection in Tete. And even if I did manage to hitch a lift to the Zimbabwean border, I had no idea how I was going to get from there to Harare.

But what could I do? Nothing, except swat more flies. I had almost resigned myself to spending another day in Songo, with the strong possibility of missing my Saturday flight from Harare, when the *chapa* sped along the road towards us at 7.30. We arrived in Tete at ten o'clock. There followed a frantic hour touring the *chapa* stands and the defunct bus station in a vain search for a lift towards the border. Everything had gone. One helpful man told me condescendingly that I should get up earlier.

The heat was sweltering and my shoulder bag got progressively heavier as we trudged around town checking out the options. We passed the airline office and I ducked inside feeling for the emergency hundred-dollar bill secreted inside the fabric of my belt. But there were no flights to anywhere of use to me.

We made our way down to an area by the river where trucks stopped to refuel en route. After several semi-permanent breakdowns and a couple of possible lifts to Malawi, a small man dressed in overalls which were more oil stains than material said that he was going all the way to Harare. I almost hugged him. I beamed at Assado and held out my hand to say goodbye.

'On Sunday,' the man in the overalls added.

I felt nearly beaten, and Assado was looking worried. It was past midday. We stopped to take stock of the situation. I asked him whether he knew of anyone who had a car who would drive me to the border for a hundred bucks. He thought for a short while and then shook his head. I was about to start asking anyone hanging around a vehicle in the street, when Assado said that perhaps we could try for a lift by the suspension bridge. All the lorries from Malawi had to cross it, and if we flagged them down there, maybe I would be lucky.

We traipsed down towards the Zambezi and stopped beside a couple of guys selling soft drinks from white polystyrene containers and some others clutching candlesticks, oddly enough. Behind them, on a patch of waste ground on the river bank, three men were pinning a sheep to the ground while a forth cut its throat, and bright red blood started to pour from the ragged gash in its neck as it struggled. I asked one of the men whether trucks from Malawi stopped here.

'Yes,' he said.

Sure enough, a truck with a long trailer pulled up and was mobbed by the soft drinks and candlestick sellers. Beside the driver, the cab was full with a young woman and three children. I shouted to the driver to ask where he was headed.

'Zimbabwe,' he called.

'Any room for me?' I asked.

He shrugged, gestured at the small family beside him, and shook his head.

219

The driver purchased two candlesticks, ground his engine into gear, and roared slowly away. Several other trucks stopped, some with empty trailers and people on them, but none was heading in my direction. Then a long empty lorry pulled up, with a sticker on the cab door that said it was a *Wheels of Africa* vehicle. It was driven by a man wearing a blue and red T-shirt and he was alone in his cab.

'Where are you going, Senhor?' I called to him over the heads of the tradesmen.

'Beira,' he called back.

I did a quick mental calculation; perhaps I should ride with him to the turn-off for the border where I could hitch another lift.

The driver called to me in English, 'Where are you headed?'

'Zimbabwe,' I said.

'I have to refuel at Nyamapanda, that is across the border in Zimbabwe.'

'Will you take me there?' I asked.

'Sure,' he said.

I grabbed my bag and went around the lorry to the other side of the cab. I felt sad as I said farewell to Assado and climbed up into the passenger seat. The driver was buying some mangoes and brushing off the candlestick sellers.

'Thanks,' I said to the driver.

'Not a problem,' he replied, placing his mangoes carefully on the dashboard. 'My name is J. S. Banda. The J. S. stands for John Scott.'

I introduced myself and asked how long it would take to get to the border. John Scott Banda revved the engine and eased the gear stick forward. 'Around three hours, maybe three-and-a-half. I'm empty, so its faster. With a full load it takes five.'

He let in the clutch and we pulled away from the soft drinks and candlestick sellers. I leaned out of the window to wave a final goodbye to Assado, but he had turned to walk back up the road towards the suspension bridge.

BIBLIOGRAPHY

Africa Watch, *Conspicuous Destruction: War, Famine and the Reform Process in Mozambique*. Human Rights Watch, New York (1992).

Alpers, E. A., *Ivory and Slaves in East Central Africa*. University of California Press, Los Angeles (1975).

Axelson, E., *Portugal and the Scramble for Africa 1875–1891*. Witwatersrand University Press, Johannesburg (1967).

Barraclough, J., 'Slavery revisited'. *Oxfam News*, summer (1991): 9.

Bowen, M. L., 'Beyond reform: adjustment and political power in contemporary Mozambique'. *Journal of Modern African Studies*, 30: 255–79 (1992).

Direccao Nacional de Estatistica, *Anuario Estatistico 1991*. Comissao Nacional do Plano, Maputo (1992).

Egerö, B., *Mozambique: A Dream Undone*. Nordiska Afrikainstitutet, Uppsala (1990).

Finnegan, W., *A Complicated War, the Harrowing of Mozambique*. University of California Press, Los Angeles (1992).

Gordon-Brown, A., *The Yearbook and Guide to East Africa*. Sampson, Low, Marston & Co. Ltd., London (1950).

Hanlon, J., *Mozambique: The Revolution Under Fire*. Zed Books, London (1984).

— *Mozambique: Who Calls the Shots?* J Currey, London, & Indiana University Press, Bloomington & Indianapolis (1991).

Hermele, K., 'Land Struggles and Social Differentiation in Southern Mozambique'. Scandinavian Institute of African Studies, Uppsala, Research Report No 82 (1988).

Human Rights Watch, *Conspicuous Destruction. War, Famine & the Reform Process in Mozambique*. Africa Watch Report, Human Rights Watch, New York (1992).

Isaacman, A., 'Madzi-Mangha, Mhondoro and the use of oral tra-

221

ditions – a chapter in Barue religious and political history'. *Journal of African History*, 14: 395–409 (1973).

– 'Social banditry in Zimbabwe and Mozambique'. *Journal of Southern African Studies*, 4: 1–30 (1977).

Isaacman, A. & Isaacman, B., *Mozambique: from Colonialism to Revolution*. Westview Press, Boulder, Colorado (1983).

Junod, H. A., *The Life of a South African Tribe*. MacMillan, London (2nd Edition) (1927).

Livingstone, D. C., *Missionary Travels and Researches in South Africa*. J. Murray, London (1857).

– *The Zambezi and its Tributaries*. J. Murray, London (1865).

– *Last Journals*. Ed. Waller, H., J. Murray, London (1874).

Marshall, J., 'Structural adjustment and social policy in Mozambique'. *Review of African Political Economy*, 47: 28–43 (1990).

Mozambiquefile, 193. Mozambique News Agency (August 1992).

Munslow, B., *Mozambique: the Revolution and its Origins*. Longman, London (1983).

Nilsson, A., *Unmasking the Bandits: the true face of the M.N.R.* European Campaign Against South African Aggression on Mozambique and Angola, London (1990).

O'Neill, H. E., 'Journey from Mozambique to Lakes Shirwa and Amaramba'. *Proceedings of the Royal Geographical Society*, 6: 632–46 & 713–41 (1884).

– 'Some remarks upon Nakala (Fernãlo Veloso Bay) and other ports on the northern Mozambique coast'. *Proceedings of the Royal Geographical Society*, 7: 373–7 (1885).

Rita-Ferreira, A., 'Moçambique post-25 de Abril: causes do êxodo da população de origem europeia e asiática'. In, *Moçambique: Cultura e Història de um Pais*. Instituto de Anthropologia, Universidade de Coimbra, Coimbra (1988).

Salt, H., *A Voyage to Abyssinia . . . in the years 1809 and 1810; in which are included an account of the Portuguese settlements on the east coast of Africa, visited in the course of the voyage. . . .* London (1814).

Saul, J. S. (ed.), *A Difficult Road: the Transition to Socialism in Mozambique*. Monthly Review Press, New York (1985).

Stevenson-Hamilton, J., 'Notes on a journey in Portuguese East Africa from Ibo to Lake Nyasa'. *Geographical Journal*, 34: 514–29 (1909).

UN Economic Commission for Africa & UN Inter-Agency Task

Force, Africa Recovery Programme, *South African Destabilisation: The Economic Cost of Frontline Resistance to Apartheid*. UNECA, Addis Ababa (1989).

UN Development Programme, *Mozambique Development Co-Operation Report 1990*. UNDP, Maputo (1992).

Vail, L., 'Mozambique's chartered companies: the rule of the feeble'. *Journal of African History*, 17: 389–416 (1976).

Vincent, J., 'The Namuli Mountains, Portuguese East Africa'. *Geographical Journal*, 81: 317,323 (1933).

Vines, A., *Renamo Terrorism in Mozambique*. Centre for Southern African Studies, University of York, in association with J Currey, London, & Indiana University Press, Bloomington & Indianapolis (1991).

Wilson, K. B., 'Cults of violence and counter-violence in Mozambique'. *Journal of Southern African Studies*, 18: 527–82 (1992).

World Bank, *Mozambique Food Security Study*. Washington, DC (1990).

– *Mozambique Population, Health and Nutrition Sector Report*. Washington, DC (1990).

INDEX

popular support 125; South African control of 4; targets 120–121; violence 5, 125

Rhodesia 4, 5, 29, 31, 32, 33, 156

Rome Peace Accord 6, 99, 150, 152; negotiations for 44–45

Rovuma River 70

Rowland, 'Tiny' 46

Royal Geographical Society 179

Russians 38, 40, 69, 157, 164–165, 198

São Tomé and Principe 9

Salazar 31, 215

Salt, Henry 180–181

Samantanje 129

Scala café 166–170

Shangaan 198

Shetani 70–71

slavery 28, 29, 41, 94, 176–177

slogans, political 17, 33–34, 56, 119, 215

Smith, Ian 156

Sofala 28, 72, 121

Songo 199, 207, 208–209, 214, 217, 218

South Africa 4, 9, 10, 23, 29, 31, 32, 49, 50, 52, 57, 59, 83, 94, 190, 192, 197, 215, 217

spirits 70–71, 127

strip-tease 35

structural adjustment programme 44, 49, 89–93

Swahili 172, 177

Tanzania 54, 67, 70, 71

Tete 1, 25, 30, 194–195, 198, 200–201, 203–207

Tetrodotoxin 131–132

tomatoes 145

transit camp 126–127

tribalism 67–68, 198–199

turtles 180–181

Ujamaa 70–71

Unilateral Declaration of Independence (UDI) 4, 43

United Nations Development Programme (UNDP) 13, 72

United Nations Disaster Relief Organization (UNDRO) 86–87

vaccination 128, 133, 138; campaign 58

Vicente, Gil 17–18

witchdoctors, suppliers 26–27; *see also curandeiros*

World Bank 4, 44, 49, 60, 78, 89–93

World Vision International 78

Xai-Xai 18–20, 46

Xipamanine 21, 22–27

Yao 176

Zambezi River 4, 37, 61, 194–195, 208, 215, 216, 219; bridges over 196

Zambézia 30, 89, 103, 109, 128, 129

Zambia 156, 176, 194, 195, 215

Zimbabwe 1, 4, 7, 156, 161, 195, 219, 220

zombie cucumber (*Datura stramonium*) 131, 132

ZoZo's 35–36

All Orion/Phoenix titles are available at your local bookshop or from the following address:

Littlehampton Book Services
Cash Sales Department L
14 Eldon Way, Lineside Industrial Estate
Littlehampton
West Sussex BN17 7HE
telephone 0903 721596, *facsimile* 0903 730914

Payment can either be made by credit card (Visa and Mastercard accepted) or by sending a cheque or postal order made payable to *Littlehampton Book Services.*
DO NOT SEND CASH OR CURRENCY.

Please add the following to cover postage and packing

UK and BFPO:
£1.50 for the first book, and 50P for each additional book to a maximum of £3.50

Overseas and Eire:
£2.50 for the first book plus £1.00 for the second book and 50p for each additional book ordered

----

BLOCK CAPITALS PLEASE

name of cardholder ....   *delivery address*
                     ....   *(if different from cardholder)*
address of cardholder ....
....
....
....
       postcode ....   *postcode* ....

☐ I enclose my remittance for £............................

☐ please debit my Mastercard/Visa (delete as appropriate)

card number ☐☐☐☐☐☐☐☐☐☐☐☐☐☐☐☐☐

expiry date ☐☐☐☐

signature ....

prices and availability are subject to change without notice